Bound by Spells

Book two in the Bound Series

Stormy Smith

Cover design by Zach Higginson of Caedus Designs
Editing by Monica Black of Word Nerd Editing
Formatted by Allyson Gottlieb of Athena Interior Book Design

For more information about this book and the author, visit
www.stormysmith.com

To my parents, for telling the world their baby wrote a book, and always believing I could do anything.

Chapter 1
Aidan

I woke up naked—again. The dry leaves and small twigs crunched and snapped as I lifted my head and looked around the dark forest floor. Exhaling in an exasperated huff, I dropped my head back to the dirt. I had been running for hours. She walked away, got in Micah's SUV, and didn't look back. So, I ran. It wasn't the first time I had shifted without seeing it coming, but the change erupted from me like a volcano. It was violent and painful. Bones broke and reshaped in seconds, muscles stretched, tore, and reknit before I could let out the scream of agony that came out as a howl. I couldn't pinpoint the moment it happened. I lost myself in the change and no longer had human thoughts. The last memory I had was her stick-straight back and methodical paces toward the car as she whispered goodbye. She didn't want to, but she left me anyway.

I closed my eyes as the weight of the truth pulled me deeper into the damp ground. She didn't even look back. Thinking about the pain she'd caused brought the animal inside of me out again. I heard the howl echo in my head, but I didn't want to shift again so soon. I slowly inhaled, letting my breath fill my lungs, expand my ribs, and push into my back. The air released through my mouth and nose as I tried to calm the fire pulsing in my mind. The sensations always started at my core. A deep thrum vibrating every cell in my body, making me look down at my skin to ensure nothing was bursting through as my insides popped and shoved against each other. Even now, hours later, when I had no idea where she was or what she was doing, Amelia filled my head and the vision of her violet eyes was like pouring salt on the open wound she left in my heart.

She made a choice. Now you make a choice, I scolded myself, frustrated with the emotion I didn't want or need, and the vulnerability only she made me feel. I shoved up from the ground, brushing myself off as I tried to come to terms with being completely naked. No one had been around to explain what had been happening to me these last few months and I had hoped not to wake up miles from my car, my clothes ripped to shreds. But it had happened before, so at least today wasn't a shock, just a nuisance.

I turned in a circle, unsure of which way to go. Then, something in my head clicked and I knew exactly where my car was. I still had no idea where all of the subtle instincts and knowledge came from, but I couldn't complain about getting lost ever again. It was the middle of the night and odds were, I wouldn't run into anyone, but just to be safe, I stayed back from the tree line and tried to keep my thoughts calm. Calm meant my eyes stayed their normal gray and not the blue glowing orbs that stared back at me in the mirror when this *thing* took over. After my first shift, my eyes stayed electric blue for a week. Every time I'd look in the mirror, I felt like a freak. I couldn't leave the house without sunglasses. I stopped going to class. I could feel and sense so much more. It was overwhelming and exhausting.

As I moved quickly and quietly through the trees, I remembered what it was like just months ago when I would have left a trail for anyone to follow. Now, my feet barely moved the foliage and even the best trackers would have problems knowing where I'd been. The frustration was I *wanted* to be found. The heaviness of solitude was a yoke around my neck, weighing down my body and mind. My parents had been dead for so long, I had only the memory of the emotion I felt when remembering them. It was a fleeting ache of knowing I had once been loved and wanted. Since then, I had bounced from foster home to foster home, only to constantly be told I wasn't a fit for my current family.

Then, I found Amelia. Through our first month of class, I sat back and observed the quiet girl who moved with the same weighted motions I did. She understood loneliness. It was clear in the way she would brighten at an instructor's question, but dim as she refused to allow herself to answer. The way she moved with awkward grace, always bumping into things, but never people. I had overheard her and Bethany talking, and I knew she would be at that party. It was why

I'd gone. But I felt like a creeper. I had been hiding out, berating myself for being there, when she came flying down the stairs.

I watched Amelia leap from the bottom stair of the deck like she could fly—all of the awkwardness gone and her movements fluid and beautiful. She pushed her way into the oncoming tide. She was lit up in the moonlight as her head dropped back and from my angle, I could see her smile. I was an intruder on the moment, but her smile broke something open inside of me. She was content and I was jealous. I wanted to know her secrets. I wanted to know how she found that place. She was my beginning and my end. Because now that she's gone, I'm some kind of magical freak and I'm alone—again.

Dawn was breaking through the trees as I finally got to my car. It was parked right where Micah had told me to put it. It was hard to reconcile the fact that just hours ago I had been kissing Amelia in these very same trees. As I dug in the trunk for my workout bag and spare clothes, my anger rose again. The realization of Micah being some kind of prince, engaged to my girl, had me yanking on my mesh shorts and t-shirt with violent motions. As my shirt came over my head and I pulled the hem down, I both felt and heard the rip of fabric. Looking down, I jumped. My right hand had partially shifted into a paw with claws that shouldn't be there poking through the blue weave.

I untangled myself and sat on the bumper of my old Honda, breathing and staring until the fur melted away to skin and the razor-sharp nails became fingers. This time, I hadn't even felt the change coming on. Usually, I had at least the forewarning of building sensations—the "too big for my own skin" feeling, telling me I would soon stand on four legs instead of two. This time, though, there was nothing, which was even scarier than the change itself. I had become something. I wasn't sure whether it was Amelia who had changed me, or if this was the difference all of my foster parents had always felt in me. I was an animal and I needed help before the wrong people realized it. I didn't know who those people were, but I could hear what Amelia hadn't said earlier tonight. There was so much more to the story and no one was safe—least of all, her.

I needed help. It didn't matter whether I wanted it or not. She told me to go to Cole, but I wasn't ready for that. I couldn't look at him without seeing her. I couldn't walk inside his gym, past the training room where I'd held myself back from kissing her so I wouldn't scare her away. Tossing my bag back in the car, I slammed the trunk down with a little more force than necessary. There were so many thoughts in my head but most of all, I worried about Amelia. She still didn't know who she was. I had tried to give her space to find herself, to see that the two of us together were more than we could ever be alone, but too much had happened too quickly. Now, I just prayed she was safe.

It was still early morning, but I couldn't go home. I was too amped up from everything that had happened last night. Since I was always starving after shifting and a night of doing who knows what, I stopped at a local spot for a monster-sized breakfast burrito. I tossed my flip-flops back into the car and walked toward the beach, scarfing down the burrito in record time. I watched as the waves came in and the surfers navigating them. There were hordes of surfers, most just sitting on their boards, bouncing up and down as the water beat against the shore.

I dropped to the sand, losing myself in the sound of the waves and the seagulls searching for their own breakfast. The world stood still in those few minutes and my mind was quiet. I felt like myself. Aidan the man. Not Aidan the beast.

Looking on while one surfer rode a wave, stretching across the horizon, I was shocked to see platinum blond hair standing out like a beacon down the beach from me. I pushed up from the sand and slowly walked toward her. Bethany sat in much the same way I had just been, her knees drawn up and her arms wrapped around them as she stared out into the water. Her hair whipped around in the breeze and I couldn't see her face. As I closed in on her, I saw the familiar motion of wiping away tears.

"Bethany? Are you okay?" I looked down at her as she contained her wild hair and looked up at me with red-rimmed eyes. She wasn't wearing any make-up. I'd never seen her look so vulnerable.

I shouldn't have been surprised when she responded with her normal sarcasm. "You know, I can't imagine why anything would be wrong,

Aidan. My best friend was kidnapped right out from under my nose, I was held hostage by a psychopathic Queen on a power trip after I had been kidnapped by animal witches, or AniMages, or whatever they're called, my boyfriend turned out to be a two-timing douche with magic powers, and I'm nothing but a human who gets used as bait and leverage. Can I do anything to help any of them? Nope. Sure can't. So, it's been a fine week. How about you?" she ended, a completely fake smile on her face as she stared daggers up at me. I couldn't help but laugh.

"Well," I said as I dropped into the sand beside her, "I don't know if I can beat that, but I'll counter with the fact that my girlfriend is engaged to a prince of some kind of magical people I didn't know existed until last week, who also happens to be a guy I thought I was friends with. She had a chance to run away with me and didn't take it, choosing him over me and pretty much eviscerating my heart in the process. *And* I woke up not long ago suddenly able to turn into a wolf. My eyes light up like blue headlights and I lose entire chunks of time. I wake up naked every time it happens and have no idea where I am. How'd I do?"

She actually snorted. Which then turned into a chuckle. Which became all out belly laughter. I couldn't stop myself from joining her. What we had just laid out sounded completely insane—completely and utterly insane. And yet, we were living it. There were parts of her story I hadn't heard, and I was sure she didn't know the full truth about me yet, but it didn't matter. I bumped my shoulder into hers as we settled down.

She turned to me. "She told me you were a part of the supernatural club, but a wolf? And you wake up naked?" Her eyebrows rose and she gave me an incredulous look. I could only shake my head and laugh again.

We both turned to stare back out to the sea. As quickly as the laughter had come, it was gone. There was total silence between us as we sat there. The true weight of our words, of the realities sitting in front of us, stole any happiness I'd had like a plug being pulled from a drain. She was gone. Amelia was gone.

And then, Bethany hit me. She punched me in the shoulder with more force than I'd expected from a girl so small. I rubbed the spot and turned to her. She was grinning. "What's gotten into you?" I asked.

"Here's the thing about me, sweetie," she said with a wry smile and a matter-of-fact tone, "I don't just sit around. A girl needs a good wallow every now and again, but then you dust yourself off and get back on the horse. It's time for us to saddle up."

Chapter 2
Amelia

I stayed true to the promise I had made myself. Once Micah drove us away, I hadn't shed another tear. But as his SUV took me farther from Aidan, the madness within me spread, burrowing into every crevice and threatening to push me over the edge. I heard her voice, but couldn't make out the words. It was all emotion and sound and color, but nothing I could understand. It was a feral agony and it consumed me.

I didn't understand what made today different, but with every mile we drove, it got worse. I was in no physical danger. There were no threats. Still, my small violet light was reduced to a tiny flame as the dark blot of power the Keeper magic represented took over. After Uncle Derreck had explained my power came from five female Elders, I had taken to personifying my Keeper as a girl instead of just a thing. And right now, she was pushing me past anything we'd experienced to date. My head throbbed, sweat built on my forehead, and it sounded like a horde of bees had taken up space between my ears. My blood raced in my veins and the violet smoke I'd grown to love turned on me, swirling around my fingers and building in my palms, even when I willed it back down. She raged in my mind, wailing and screaming in a multitude of tones and pitches, making me want to bash my head against the glass of the window just to let it out and make it stop. Micah kept glancing my way, never fully turning to look at me, but watching me as the situation grew worse. Finally, he stopped the car and turned to me.

"Amelia," he said softly, reaching a hand in my direction. My head snapped toward him and I could only stare, panicked, at his outstretched hand.

"Don't touch me," I gritted out through clenched teeth. I hoped he could see the fear. I was teetering on the edge of losing myself to her and even with everything we'd been through, I didn't want to hurt him.

He slowly retracted his hand and nodded. "Okay, I won't touch you. But Amelia, you have to control this. Or, at least, just make it back to Esmerelda's. The room will quiet the pain." He threw the car into drive and punched the gas as he continued to watch me out of the corner of his eye.

The room. I sighed audibly. For the first time, I was looking forward to the enchanted bedroom quelling my power. I could feel my mother's bracelet in my pocket, but there was no way I was putting it back on. I knew nothing about the bracelet or what it may have been meant to do. The only sure thing was it had given me my power back, and right now, all I wanted was for that power to go away. If only Micah understood this wasn't pain. Pain I could shove into a little box and file away in the back of my mind. This was agony. This was the very fabric of my soul being shredded into jagged pieces, slicing and splitting me open, then dropping to the ground beside my broken heart.

My head fell back against the seat and I fought her with everything I had. I had lost Aidan, I couldn't lose myself.

I sat in the center of the giant, four-post bed, staring at the wall. Finally, she was quiet. The room had done what it was supposed to do and the fighting had stopped. But, now, I was left alone. Alone with my thoughts. My memories. My regrets. I heard him, his words plain as day in my mind though they had been barely a whisper between us. *Pick me, Amelia. Please be the one who finally picks me.*

The weight on my chest intensified as my lungs refused to give me the air I needed to keep going. All I could think about was the pain I had caused us both, for reasons I couldn't even explain to Aidan, reasons I couldn't even truly explain to myself. What had I done? And why?

I dropped back onto the bed, forcing my thoughts away from his smoky eyes and the feel of his arms around me. Instead, I thought about the last few weeks. I rewound through all of my conversations with Cole, Uncle Derreck, and

Elias. I needed clarity. I needed facts. I had to separate myself from my emotion. But the more I thought about all the reasons I needed to be here, needed to fulfill the obligations my mother and the prophecy had laid out for me, the more I wanted to run. I questioned every decision I had made and couldn't find the answers to help me justify the ache in my soul. The Keeper was quiet, but my heart was not.

The idea of walking away from my first real relationship—from the first person to ever pursue me, spend time getting to know me, and truly fight for me—broke through the walls I'd been trying to build. The ones that were supposed to make me strong and give me purpose. As I rolled to my side and pulled my knees to my chest, I slammed my eyes closed and repeated that I was doing the right thing, over and over. No part of me believed it, but there was no turning back now.

I woke up to a commotion in the hallway. The voices were loud, but muffled through the door. I scrambled out of the bed to press my ear to the old, thick wood. I could hear a woman whose voice sounded familiar, but the damn door was blocking too much of the sound. She was yelling, arguing with someone. Their voices grew louder, meaning they were moving closer.

I backed away from the door, worried Queen Julia was finally coming. Concerned over not having my power for protection, I dove into the pile of clothes from last night and ripped my bracelet from the hoodie pocket, clutching it in my hands as I stood. In the same moment, the door started to open and I heard, "I am so sorry, Aunt Ryannon. I didn't expect to see you here and these Hunters have never met you. They don't understand who you are."

Micah pushed through the door and the last person I expected to see followed him in. My mouth dropped open as Rynna strode into the room in full regalia. A long, fitted gown, her hair curled and styled in a beautiful up-do, and jewels sparkling from her neck and ears.

"Rynna?" I whispered. Micah gave me a knowing smile, only baffling me further. I didn't have a chance to ask another question before she ran across the room and pulled me into a hug. I stood still, confusion muddling my thoughts as words I didn't hear and couldn't fully understand spilled from her mouth.

Finally, Rynna pulled away and shook my shoulders. "Amelia Bradbury. Look at me." Her sharp tone, the one I'd heard every time I'd been in trouble over the years, pulled me back to the present. My eyes finally connected to hers and I saw so many things. Apologies. Regrets. Relief.

"Listen to me, dear." She cupped my cheek in her palm. "I know none of this makes sense, but we don't have much time. I had to dress the part and Julia can't know I'm here, so I can't stay long. Mikail, can you please give us a minute?" She gave Micah a cool look, making it clear it wasn't a request he should turn down.

His royal upbringing took over as he responded, "Yes, Aunt. Of course. I'll be just outside." He dipped his head and quietly left.

Rynna pulled me toward the bed and we sat. She grasped my hand and part of me wanted to pull away while the other wanted to bury my head in her lap and beg her to fix it all, as I had when I was a child. But, she couldn't fix it then and I doubted she could fix it now.

"Amelia, you aren't safe here. There's only so much I can do for you right now, so I'm here to explain what you must remember once she takes you away. You must listen. Are you listening?

I nodded, still stunned Rynna was sitting in my enchanted bedroom. Rynna, who was actually Ryannon, the Queen's sister.

"Mikail spoke the truth. I am his aunt and the Queen's sister. But, many years ago, I made a choice to walk away from this family and this life and I've never looked back, outside of my communication with Mikail. Especially not after what happened to your mother. I had a responsibility to you, your brother, and your father. It was my family who did these unspeakable things and I had to help in any way I could. Our life, our relationship…none of it was a lie. I love you, Amelia. I love your brother. And even though your father wouldn't allow me to explain everything I wanted to you, I tried my best to help and protect you. It is exactly what I'm doing now. Do you have your mother's cuff?"

I gripped it tighter in my fist as I recoiled a little, instantly on alert. I heard her words, but I had no idea if Rynna was still someone I could trust.

"It's very important you keep it hidden from the Queen," Rynna continued, not acknowledging my reaction. "She can never know you have it— ever. Do you understand?"

My brain was slowly coming back to life and questions finally rose to the surface. "Why? I mean, I already know it brought my power back even though I'm in this enchanted room, but what else can it do? What if I don't want the power anymore? I can't control it, Ryn. It controls me."

Rynna's lips pursed, her frustration becoming visible. "That cuff is your lifeline, Amelia. Your mother had it specially commissioned and it is the one thing allowing you to maintain control over your Keeper power until you find your mate. It will permit you to use what you have for good. It will give you the opportunity to work with the Keeper, to break down the walls, and work as one for short periods of time. It will be draining, but if you keep working at it slowly, you'll continue to gain control. If you don't wear it, there is a chance you could lose yourself."

Those words had me on my feet. "Lose myself? Lose myself how?"

"Calm down, Amelia," she said, looking back over her shoulder at the door. "Please. Calm down. I know this is scary and it wasn't supposed to be like this, but I'm trying to help you. Can I see it, please?" she asked.

Still leery, I coaxed the cuff from my pocket and held it out on my flattened palm. Her word choice made sense. I had been calling it a bracelet, but the ends didn't connect and the flat metal was wider than most bracelets. Rynna reached for it, her hand extended, but looked up at me for confirmation before she took it. I nodded stiffly as she simply flipped it over and pointed to one of the many symbols etched in the silver.

"These are your mother's initials. LRB. Liana Rose Bradbury. This was her addition to the cuff. A piece of your mother lives inside this cuff. It will give you what you need, and should give you comfort." Rynna spoke quietly as she placed the cuff back in my palm. "She knew something was going to happen the day you were born. She took me aside and told me a day would come when I would be the only one who could reach you and I would need to make sure you had, and understood, the power in the cuff. She wanted to make certain you knew you weren't alone—that she hadn't left you."

I stared down at the beautiful calligraphy making up the only remaining piece of my mother. Loops and swirling lines drawn by her. Power given by her to me.

Rynna continued as I stared. "The Queen will take you away tomorrow, to her home in Washington State. She refuses to go back to the castle in Syria unless she absolutely has to. I don't know what she expects from you, or what she'll do to you, but she will ensure you are guarded day and night by Hunters. Use the cuff. Use it to control your emotions and reign in the Keeper. And do everything you can to learn the truth of what's happened and how we can stop it. There must be more to this than simply her need for power. I know my sister, and no matter what people want to think, she's more controlled than this. We just haven't been able to find the true source. While you do, we will be trying to find a way to organize those who are left. We can't allow her to have you, Amelia. It's too dangerous. For you and our future. But, if you're going to be there, we need you to use the time wisely and bring us more information."

I took a step back and continued until I hit the wall, allowing it to hold me up as I worked through her last statements. "So, you knew? You knew I would have to do this—end up in the middle of all this?" My heart raced as my mind flew through the events of the past few months and my conversations with Rynna. "You told me I didn't have to 'be part of the Immortal soap opera.' You told me I could choose my own path. Why did you say those things? Why tell me that story about my mother?" The question I didn't ask was why she allowed me to believe I could have Aidan.

For the first time in as long as I could remember, Rynna would not meet my eyes. She stared down at her clasped hands resting in her lap and answered quietly, "It wasn't fair of me. I wanted more for you. I wanted you to run from this and have the life you wanted. The one I wanted for you. I wanted you as far from this as possible. I shouldn't have. It was selfish. I know exactly what you mean to our people and how much we all need you, but you were just a young girl and this was all so much. I didn't think it would happen so fast. I thought we would have time to prepare you and you would have time to find some happiness."

A soft knock on the door, likely from Micah, signaled our time was over. Rynna approached me cautiously. She held out her arms, asking, "May I?" I nodded, emotion filling me as her words settled into my mind like rocks weighing me down in the water. There was a good chance I could drown, but in this moment, Rynna was part of my life raft. She had handed me knowledge and power and asked for nothing but patience in return. For now, I had to overlook the rest. At this point, who hadn't only given me part of the story in the name of protecting me?

Rynna pulled me into her embrace and whispered, "I love you, Amelia. Your father loves you. Your uncle and brother love you. We will not allow this to happen. Just stay strong. Be smart. Know we are coming for you. And trust Mikail, he is an ally to you." She pulled back and pressed a kiss to my cheek. "Okay?"

I gave her a small nod. "Okay."

"You are your mother's daughter. And you are so much stronger than you think." She squeezed my hands one last time, an indecipherable look haunting her eyes as she turned away from me and left the room without looking back.

I thought Micah might come back inside, but he didn't. I stood, rooted to my spot, staring at the closed door, realizing my future and the future of so many others was in my hands.

Chapter 3
Aidan

"Didn't we just start wallowing?" I asked, sullen.

"Yep. And now we're done," she countered. "We're going to do something about all this. I may be the only lowly human in this debacle, but I've got my ways. We need to find Cole. We need to make a plan. We have to get Amelia out of there."

I instantly stood up, sand falling everywhere as I turned to Bethany. "No. Oh, hell no. I'm not going to Cole. I can't." I tried to cover my emotion with indifference. "And she made a choice, Bethany. She *chose* Micah. Don't you get it? She could have left with me. He couldn't have taken me. Not then. Not with her fighting with me. He wouldn't have stood a chance. We could have run and been fine. But she picked him."

While I had been speaking, Bethany had stood, crossed her arms, and assumed what I called the "chick stance"—one of her hips was cocked to the side and she actually looked annoyed, and impatient. Like she wanted me to shut up already.

"What the hell is that look for? Where do you get off looking at me like I'm the idiot here?" My hands clenched and unclenched on their own accord as my anger spiked. It had been getting harder to keep the beast at bay once my emotions took over. I was shocked as she took a step toward me and shoved both hands into my chest, sending me back a few steps and fumbling in the sand.

"Oh, no you don't, Aidan Montgomery. Don't think you can stand there all macho, tough guy with the weird blue eyes and scare the little southern girl. I've dealt with jerks my whole life. Guys with worse tempers and scarier intentions than you've even dreamed, so you can take all your huffing and puffing and shove it.

"And while you're at it, you can just get the hell over yourself. You don't even have half the story. Where do you get off judging Ame's choices when you don't know what's at stake—what it would have cost her to decide to go with you? Do you think, given everything you do actually know, it would have been as simple as just running off to live her happily ever after with you? Have you even been paying attention?"

Bethany stood less than a foot in front of me, posturing better than most guys I'd fought growing up. She didn't show an ounce of fear, even though I knew my eyes shone brightly and had taken on the look of an animal—slanted with a large black pupil in the center. I could tell it had happened by the way the landscape had changed, the colors brighter and the smells crisper. I wanted to ask her what she meant about other guys, but I was focused on her main point—all the things I didn't know.

I sighed, taking a small step back and relaxing my rigid stance. I put both hands up in surrender. "Okay, Bethany. I give. Educate me."

She nodded, managing to look down on me from six inches below. "That's right. But before I say anything, you're buying me breakfast." She turned on her heel and walked away, not even waiting to see whether I would follow.

Women. I could only roll my eyes and jog a few steps to catch back up.

While I had been okay with a breakfast burrito on the beach, I wouldn't say no to more food. I was always hungry these days. The difference was Bethany needing a meal in a real restaurant, with real silverware. So, looking as scrubby as could be, the two of us sat down at a corner table on the patio and ordered breakfast from a server who scowled down at us, likely questioning whether we were homeless. I pulled my wallet out of my back pocket and set it on the table, giving the kid a look. He shrugged and disappeared with our order.

"Alright. Spill it. What else didn't she tell me?" I rubbed my hands over my face, suddenly exhausted. I would have almost preferred the anger to come back. At least I knew what to do with it. This feeling of vulnerability, of wondering what Amelia had sacrificed for me, or others…I didn't want that. I could give things up. Other people weren't supposed to.

Bethany sipped her orange juice, sat back in her chair, and looked around, confirming they hadn't sat anyone close to us. "Buckle up, because this is going to be a ride," she started. "I guess I should start at the beginning, the day Amelia was born. I'm going to tell you the real story first, but know that Amelia didn't learn the truth of most of this until the last few weeks. Her whole life has been one lie after another. The fact that she didn't lose it completely is a testament to how strong our girl really is."

I could only nod. Amelia was strong. She didn't think so. She didn't see it. But I saw it. Bethany saw it. I was glad Amelia at least had Bethany, someone who obviously cared about her, through it all.

"Her mother was murdered by Queen Julia's Hunters, which I understand to be some magical ninja-like matrix-looking badass guys who are basically Julia's henchmen. There had been a prophecy made years ago by an Elder—that's what Ame is, like a super-charged Mage—and the Hunter believed Amelia was the subject of the prophecy. So he forced Amelia's dad to betroth her to the Prince. Amelia's dad went a little crazy and tried to stay away from her. Her whole life was supposed to be about being this amazing Elder, but no one would help her actually become one. Instead, her dad kept her away from everyone and punished her when she used her power. That's how she met us. She finally couldn't take it anymore and moved here. She never knew she was part of a prophecy or special outside of being an Elder."

Wrapping my head around a Queen, Mages, and Hunters—it was like she was speaking a foreign language. But, like me, Amelia had lived a life on the outside. No one got too close and no one made her feel anything aside from inadequate. I wished she were here, telling me this story herself, so I could pull her into my arms and show her there was someone who cared about her, not any of the other crap.

Bethany continued. "But Cole had been searching for answers. He couldn't understand his dad's behavior either, so he left and travelled everywhere, trying to find other Mages or Elders who could tell him what was happening. He found answers, but not the ones he had hoped for. He was the one to realize Amelia was the last living female Elder, which made her valuable to the Queen because she had something no one else had. And then her Uncle Derreck filled in even more of the blanks. I never met him—he didn't bother to show up for my rescue—but he explained Ame is not only an Elder, but a Keeper. She has all this power from other Elders inside her, which confirmed her as the subject of the prophecy. But it got hard for Amelia. The power was more than she could handle. Things started getting out of control and she'd lose herself inside the Keeper power."

Bethany took a break as the server delivered our food, but I was no longer hungry. I thought back to the night at the theater, when the red-haired woman attacked us. Amelia had commanded the wind, tossing benches and trees hundreds of feet. I was sure I saw the Keeper power Bethany was talking about that night. Amelia was too close to enjoying her attack on the woman. She had barely heard me as I tried to pull her away—looking at me like she'd never seen me before. That was the first night I had fully shifted. Something had happened during the night, taking the building energy inside me and letting it loose like a bullet blasting from a gun. It had taken everything in me to get Amelia somewhere safe before I could run. The change had happened every night that week. One second, I would be sitting on my couch, exhausted, trying to figure out how to call her and what to say, and the next, waves of pulling, stretching pain would rip through me. I thought I was dying the first time it happened. Human thoughts stopped and I remembered nothing until I woke up again. Thankfully, my ground floor apartment had a patio door and after the first night when I shredded the screen, I was easily able to get in and out.

I was trying to connect the dots when I realized Bethany had dropped something big in the last story. I looked up at her as she used her fork and knife to delicately cut into her omelet, using every bit of manners I was never taught. "B, why did you need to be rescued?" It probably should have felt odd for me to call her B, since I had only heard Amelia do it, but it felt right and she didn't balk at it.

She shrugged, as if it were just a run of the mill question. "Well, that's another fun one. Apparently, this redheaded bitch was looking for some leverage over Amelia and I was it. I spent a few days hanging out with some folks you probably should get to know. You have their weird blue eyes, so I would guess you're like them, based on what I understand about how this all works."

"You met the redheaded chick, too? The one who attacked Amelia and me? She took you? What do you mean, they are like me?" The questions came out rapid fire. I couldn't compute the information fast enough.

Bethany put her silverware down and pulled her napkin from her lap, wiping her mouth. "Well, I'm glad I'm not the only one this has been a little overwhelming for. Let me finish Amelia's story and it might answer more of your questions. And eat. Don't waste food, especially bacon."

She was right. Growing up in houses crammed with kids being fed from a state budget, by parents who wanted the money more than the kids, I had learned not to waste what was in front of me. I picked up the bacon and started eating, though it had no taste at all.

"When Cole took Ame to meet her uncle, Melinda—the red-haired lady—and her goons took the opportunity to grab me from the parking lot at work. They weren't really that bad, but I didn't know anything about all of this magic business, so it was a bit disconcerting to watch a person suddenly become a wolf, or an owl, or a panther. They taunted, scared, and used me to get to Amelia." She stopped for a second, a scowl taking over and her eyes narrowing. "They burnt my damn hair, but otherwise I was fine." I wanted to laugh, but it was clearly not a laughing matter.

"They convinced Amelia she had to come get me alone, and she did. She talked a lot with their head guy, Elias, who was nice enough. He let me go immediately and didn't do anything to hurt Amelia, though he did get inside her head somehow. He just told her there were more lies and she couldn't go to the Queen. She had to talk to him more and help his people. He said they were the ones who had been hunted and killed by the Queen. And then he told her about Micah being the Prince."

Her last words were quiet. I felt for her. I had gotten smacked in the face with the same information not long after she had. I opened my mouth to say something, though I'm not sure what since nothing reassuring was coming to mind, when Bethany lifted her eyes. They were hard, angry.

"I tried to help Amelia after she ran into you on the beach. She said she had a plan. But her plan ended up getting us both taken again. We were kidnapped and held in separate rooms. Once her father and brother came, we were all put back together and the Queen managed to scare Amelia into agreeing to the betrothal and moving up the timeline. I tried to stop her, but I had seen enough to understand Micah is a coward and his mother is insane. The Queen would have come back for me. For you. For Amelia's family. There was no other option and Ame knew it. This was how that chapter needed to end. But now we need to start a new one. We have to get her out, Aidan. They will use her. They will *hurt* her. I don't understand who I met or what happened to my boyfriend, but the guy I saw in there wasn't him. And that woman is terrifying." Bethany looked away and I could almost see the memories floating past her eyes. I was instantly even angrier that I hadn't been there, for her or Amelia.

How had Amelia taken all of this on herself? Why hadn't she trusted me? Were there really others like me? Could someone help me control what was happening?

I stood up, my knees crashing into the tabletop as I went, knocking everything over. I looked down at Bethany, determined for answers.

"We're going to find Cole and this Elias guy. And we're going to find her. I swear to you, B, I'm going to find her."

She stood, smiling her first genuine smile since I'd found her on the beach. "Then let's get to it."

Chapter 4
Amelia

I was stuck in my own head all night, my thoughts spinning and swirling until the enchantment of the room finally cleared them. Now, I was focused on the words Rynna had left me with.

I love you, Amelia. Your father loves you. Your uncle and your brother love you. We will not allow this to happen. Just stay strong. Be smart. Know we are coming for you. And trust Mikail, he is an ally to you.

They were coming for me. I just had to figure out how to keep it together and find the information they needed. It gave me a purpose and something to focus on. Aidan flitted through my mind, but I shoved him out. Every time he appeared in my head, it made my heart hurt, like I was walking away all over again. By making this choice, I could only hope to keep the Queen from ever knowing he was an AniMage, protecting him from becoming her next target. When Micah slipped quietly into my room that morning, I was ready for him and ready to leave. I had made it this far, I could do this—I had to do this.

The flight was the first test of my cuff. It took some time to work myself up to even putting it on but as I sat with it in my hands and thought about what Rynna had said, I could almost see the story play out in my head. My pregnant mother going to the best enchanters of her time and using their hatred against the Queen to help her create a piece to keep me safe. I had to trust her. There was no one I truly trusted anymore, not even Micah, even after all he'd done for me these last few days, but I had to trust her. She put this inside me and I had to believe she had taken precautions. I was her daughter, after all. So, I tucked the cuff high on my forearm, clasped the two ends together tightly, and pulled my long sleeves down to hide it, thankful for the cooler weather we were heading toward. When I wore the cuff once before, nothing felt different until I had asked it for my power back. So, as I walked with Micah and Baleon toward our gate, I muttered to myself, asking the Keeper to stay quiet and calm during the flight.

I'm not sure what I had been expecting, but flying coach with Micah and Baleon hadn't been it. Apparently, his mother flew in a private jet. I was more than happy to sit in a back row seat to avoid spending hours with her. Micah wouldn't tell me how he had gotten her to agree to the plan, but I was actually worried about him. Lines of exhaustion were etched deep in his face and hints of bluish purple sat beneath his eyes. Not for the first time, I wondered how he was protecting me. He tried to sound like his normal pretentious self, but something was missing.

I was shocked to find Baleon didn't speak unless Micah directly addressed him. While it had been amusing to watch him coax the human TSA agents into letting him through without using the metal detectors, and the "What the hell is wrong with that guy?" looks from the other passengers had me smirking, I didn't want to spend the whole flight sitting next to a mute. I tried to engage him in conversation once we were in our seats, but he stared ahead, not acknowledging I was mere centimeters from him. Micah actually chuckled. A sound I hadn't realized I missed. Laughter seemed like a foreign concept.

"He won't speak to you, Amelia. Bale has been with me since I was born and he is my sworn protector. He is not here for conversation and especially not with you," Micah explained. I turned to look at Bale, as Micah had called him, and studied his features. Not as tall as Rhi, but still a large, looming man who was easily six-foot-four. His head was shaved and he wore the silver collar around his neck, as all Hunters did. He also wore the same long, black trench coat, making him look like he'd walked straight off the Matrix set. His skin was like milk chocolate, and I saw hints of tribal-looking tattoos peeking out below the cuffs of his jacket and on his neck. He looked a little older, but it was all in his eyes. His eyes had seen things.

I leaned forward, making my study of Baleon obvious. He stared directly into the back of the seat in front of him while I stared at him. The longer I looked into his eyes, the more I felt like I was falling off a cliff. There were things there I didn't want to see; I could feel it in the bottom of my stomach and in the reaction from the Keeper in the back of my mind. She went on high alert and the responsive protection she always provided flooded my veins in an instant. I looked away quickly, trying to rein her back, but not before I saw his eyes dart toward me, questioning. Wondering if he could somehow feel what I did, I silently pled for her to go back to her corner and sat back, fixing my eyes on the seat in front of me. I smiled a little to myself, realizing I wasn't the only one who wasn't so great at doing what I was told.

From the Olympia airport, Bale drove us out of the city and toward the coast. As we drove through the Olympic Mountains, I couldn't pull my face away from the car window. I thought Northern California was beautiful, but I'd never seen trees so green. Green was all you could see until you got to the snow-capped mountains standing out against the horizon. Micah allowed me to take it all in for the majority of the drive. When we started winding our way into thicker groves of trees, he finally spoke.

"We will reach Cresthaven soon," he said. "I've lived here most of my life. When my mother first set out on her mission to cleanse the bloodlines and put Immortals into their proper place in the world, our races scattered across the globe. She hated everything associated with the castle and decided she would conduct royal business from here. Cresthaven was once intended to be a summer home, but now it's just home." Micah stared out the window as he spoke, never looking at me.

As we rounded the final corner and the house came into view, I gasped. It was humongous. And gorgeous.

"A summer home? *This is your summer home?*" I asked, gaping at the massive structure in front of me. It was a classical European villa. With two floors, hundreds of windows, and columns spaced along the front, I could only imagine what the inside would look like. We drove up the huge stone circle drive leading to the front door. As our car approached, Rhi, along with a swarm of Hunters, came out to meet us, forming two lines perpendicular to the front door. Once they were settled, with their feet spread wide and their hands clasped in front of them, Julia stepped out. She stood on the front stoop, looking expectantly at the car, irritation blatant on her face.

Outside of the little incident with Bale on the plane, my Keeper had sat quietly in the back of my mind, allowing me to travel in peace. Now she was screaming, trying to break free from whatever constraints the cuff put her under. Somehow, it kept her contained. While I could hear her, her cries were muffled and the power I expected didn't ricochet through me. Her anxiety, however, became my own. My power started to rise, meeting the increased pace of my heartbeat and the fear taking hold. I started tapping my foot on the floorboard as I sat stick-straight in the seat, my hands clenched in my lap.

Micah, who I knew both saw and felt the change in me, took charge. "Bale, can you give us just a second? Please tell my mother I'm having a private moment with my fiancée."

Micah's words were quiet, his eyes never leaving mine. He snaked a hand between us, uncurling my clenched fingers and twining them with his. Baleon spoke for the first time. "Yes, Prince Mikail." His voice surprised me, soft with hard edges. Baleon was the quiet guy in the corner. The last one you wanted to get up.

As soon as the door clicked shut, Micah grabbed my other hand and turned me fully toward him. "Amelia," he said cautiously, "you have to breathe with me. You have to control this. She can't see you like this on the first day.

This is what she wants. She wants to know how to unnerve you, how to force a reaction like you had at Esmerelda's. She needs to know the extent of your power and control. This is all a game, Amelia. It's always a game to her and you can't let her win."

As Micah spoke, his grip on my hands tightened almost painfully. The sensation was sharp as my fingers smashed together, but something about the discomfort brought me back to myself. In that instant, I was able to see my fear for what it is was. Even without the Keeper, I had to remember I did have my own power. But, I shouldn't need to use it. She was the one who needed me. I took a deep breath and slowly let it out, feeling my heartbeat return to normal.

"Are you okay, Amelia? Are you ready for this?" Micah asked. It suddenly occurred to me we were still holding hands. I yanked mine out of his, wiping them on my jeans.

"Yes. I'm fine. Thank you. I'll be fine. I heard you. I won't let her win." I couldn't look at him as the awkwardness set in. I'd been sitting there *holding his hands.*

"You do understand, Amelia, we are betrothed? Engaged?" His words were sharp, his expression pinched. "If you have any hopes of making it through this, you are going to have to play the part. You cannot look at me with such...disdain in front of my mother."

What first felt like a betrayal of Aidan was now guilt over offending Micah. "I didn't. I mean...Micah—"

He raised a hand and closed his eyes. A brief second later, when they opened, his empathy had returned. "It's fine, Amelia. I understand. I'm not him and I never intend to be. My only intention is to try not to make this harder than it has to be, so you are going to have to trust me. Okay?"

Rynna's words were in my mind again. *And trust Mikail, he is an ally to you.*

"Okay. I do trust you, Micah. I'm just scared." It was hard to force both a lie and the truth from my lips.

"As you should be," he muttered as he opened the door and pulled me out of the car.

Micah took my hand as we walked around the side of the car where I faced Queen Julia for the first time since the night I agreed to move up the timeline. She had no idea I saw Aidan and walked away from my first shot at happiness—my first shot at love. She didn't know I had my mother's cuff and a way to control the power she saw at Esmerelda's. Most importantly, she didn't know Rynna and the others were coming for me. As Julia sneered down at me, I focused on the fact that I was doing what I had to do and it wouldn't be for long. Like Micah had said, I just had to play the game.

I connected my eyes to hers and gave her my most convincing smile. "Good afternoon, your highness. It's lovely to see you again."

Micah squeezed my hand and looked down at me, perplexed. I gave him a tiny shrug before I looked back at his mother. Julia looked surprised by my pleasant tone, shocked even. She recovered quickly, though.

"It's nice to finally have you where you belong, dear. Away from your crazy father, mistrusting brother, and all of those bothersome humans," she said, clearly trying to get a rise out of me. I refused to take the bait.

"What exactly is it you want with me, your highness? What is it you think I can do for you?" No reason to waste time.

Julia laughed, her throaty cackle sending a shiver up my spine. "What do I think you can do for me? More than I can even start to explain, Amelia. To start, though, I want you to marry my son. I want you to consummate your marriage and I want it to happen soon."

Her words had me reeling backwards. Physically, I stumbled, but Micah caught me before I fell. I wanted to shove him away from me, but he whispered, "The game, Amelia," into my ear and I gritted my teeth as I allowed him to steady me.

I looked up at Julia, her sense of victory emanating from every pore. I wanted to blast her with everything I had. To yank off the cuff, call on the wind to send the Hunters scattering, and pin her to the wall in the way she had done to me. I wanted to watch her smile disappear as she fought to breathe, just as I had done.

Clearly, the Keeper still had some impact, even from her locked room inside me.

Instead, I allowed a slow smile to develop. I squeezed Micah's hand and took a step toward the Queen, bringing him along. I pushed my power through me, sending a slow wave of energy from my core outward, allowing it build.

"You can force this betrothal. You can force a marriage. But you cannot force me to consummate anything." Pressure built at the base of my skull and I saw the reaction from the Hunters in my peripheral vision, confirming my eyes were shining in the Elder violet no one had seen in years. My eyes never left Julia's as I continued. "I am not enslaved to you like these Hunters, or an AniMage who fears for their life. You need me. We both know it. Which means you do not have all the power here."

Micah pulled me into his chest just as she exploded. Red fire shot from her palm, missing me by a hair. "That," she said evenly, "was intentional. I will not miss a second time."

Adrenaline coursed through me and I took a half step forward, while Micah tried to pull me back to him. "Be careful, your highness. If there are so many things you need me for, you're going to want me working with you, not against you. And it is my choice to make."

"So this is how it is going to go, is it, dear? I shouldn't be surprised. You're more like your mother than I thought possible." Julia turned to Micah. "You had best figure out how to control this one, son. If you don't, I will."

She turned and walked back into the house, the lines of Hunters falling in behind her.

Chapter 5
Aidan

"You have no idea where Cole lives, do you?" Bethany asked as she tried to maintain a straight face, but her tone and arched eyebrow gave her away.

I looked around, the adrenaline from my declaration and our departure demanding action. The problem was, she was right. "I've actually only seen him at the gym," I confessed. *Busted.*

She laughed. It was a welcome melody amidst all of the insanity and emotion surrounding me the last few weeks. It was like an exhale. I had been inhaling for so long, pulling it all in, straining my lungs and holding the air for fear I might not have another breath to take. But the normalcy of a girl laughing, with her hands on her hips and her eyes shining, it was all the air exiting in one huff, leaving me empty in all the best ways. I smiled back at her and it felt good. Not in the romantic, secretive way it had been with Amelia, but good to know there was someone who got it. Bethany understood the overwhelming madness and was ready to fight with me. Right now, all I needed was someone on my side.

"Come on. Let's check the gym first and then we can walk to his house. I know where he lives and it isn't far." Bethany shook her head as she led me down the sidewalk. I picked up my pace a bit to catch up and then slowed so my leisurely strides ate up two of her quick steps.

As soon as we came up to the gym, I could tell Cole wasn't there. The kids who were usually beating the bags inside were standing outside with their hands cupped around their eyes, looking in the windows, trying to figure out what was going on.

I tapped Joey on the shoulder. "Hey. What's up?"

He looked back at me, recognizing my voice. "Oh. Hey, Aidan. We came to train but everything is locked up. It's been like this for a few days. Mr. Cole never leaves everything locked up. He would at least hand the keys off to Trey."

Trey was nineteen and probably the most responsible kid in the neighborhood. He'd been coming to the gym since Cole opened it and was a mentor to a lot of the younger kids, who otherwise would have been hoodlums. He stood near the corner of the building, and once he caught my eye, gestured me over with a quick flick of his chin toward the back alley.

I gave Bethany a look and she started chatting up the boys. They were all around thirteen, and the attention of an older, pretty girl had them distracted in seconds. She caught my eye and gave me a look telling me to get on with it already, so I jogged around the corner.

"What's up, man?" I gave Trey the customary handshake, half-hug and stepped back.

Trey was a little squirmy. He paced back and forth just a few steps at a time before I finally reached a hand out and stopped him. With my palm on his chest, Trey looked up at me, his fear apparent. "Hey," I said. "Dude, you can tell me. Where's Cole? What do you know?"

"You're not going to believe me. No one will ever believe me. Aidan, these *people* have been coming around." Trey stopped, looking left and then right again. I couldn't help but notice the way he'd said "people," like he wasn't sure whether it was the right word. Immediately, I was on alert.

"Cole hasn't been around much and I've been pretty much taking care of the shop," he continued. "But these guys...they've been coming in almost every day and asking about him. They came five days straight last week. And then Cole finally showed back up. I tried to tell him, but he acted like it was no big deal."

Trey's eyes grew round, his pupils dilating and the color draining from his face. I softened my tone and took a step back. "Hey, man. It's okay. Just tell me what happened."

He nodded, the motions jerky. "I know. I know. They came back last night, after Cole was gone, and they yelled at me, wanting to know where he lived. I didn't want to tell them. I tried not to, Aidan, you have to believe me. But they...no way, you won't believe me." Trey turned and started quickly walking away, his strides close to running and his hands shaking. I ran after him, matching his stride. As we got to the end of the alley, I stopped him, wrapping my hand around his bicep and turning him to me.

"Trey," I warned, "if something happened, I have to know what. I can't help Cole without the facts. I don't give two shits whether you think I'll believe you. There is more going on here than you'll ever understand, so you just need to be out with it. Now." Those last words came out more like a growl. I stayed calm and kept my voice level, but I did not let him look away, making it clear this was not a negotiation.

He must have gathered as much because he immediately started talking. And crying. "Oh, man," he said, collapsing against the wall behind him. "Man, they just wouldn't stop coming at me. I tried to kick them out, but one of the guys grabbed me and when he put his face close to mine, he..." Trey looked around again and his voice dropped to barely a whisper, "he wasn't human, man. His eyes looked like a cat's and they were blue—like, blue on fire. They hadn't been blue before. And he growled at me. Growled. Like...like an animal, man. I had to tell him. I didn't have a choice. You know?"

It was a sucker punch to the gut. He could have been describing me over the last week. Right now, it was clear Cole was in more danger than Trey.

I crouched down next to him. "Trey. Hey, man, look at me." When Trey's eyes met mine, they were filled with unshed tears. Guilt and fear radiated from him. "It's not your fault, Trey. You did what you had to do. And Cole can take care of himself. I'm going to go now and check on him. It's going to be fine, alright?" Trey just kept staring at me, not acknowledging a word.

I held out a hand and nodded to him, encouraging him to take it. He finally did and I pulled him to standing. Still holding his grip, I looked Trey dead in the eyes and said, "Understand this, Trey. I'll deal with Cole, but there's a group of kids out there who need you. I know Cole trusted you with the extra set of keys, even though you don't use them, but you need to now. Let the kids in. Open the gym. You saw what's out there right now and these kids don't need any part of that. Okay?"

I watched as the change I needed came over Trey. He stood taller, his eyes sharpening as he cleared his throat and gripped my hand in return. "Yeah, man. I've got this. Don't worry. You just gotta make sure Cole's alright."

I nodded once more and we turned back toward the front of the building. It was all I could do to maintain a steady pace when everything inside me was screaming we needed to get to Cole—fast.

It took a few minutes to disengage Bethany from the kids. She smiled and laughed as they tried to play tough and one up each other. It was the positive attention they needed, but we needed to get out of there. Finally, I cut Joey off mid-sentence, telling him we had to go. I grabbed Bethany by the arm and started to walk away, but I should have known better. She let me get about three steps before she stopped, hauled off, and punched me in the shoulder.

"What the hell is wrong with you?" she hissed as I let go of her arm to rub my own. Damn if someone didn't teach that girl exactly how to deliver a right cross. I turned to look behind me, making sure the boys weren't watching. They were too busy jumping up and down while Trey unlocked the front doors. He turned and gave me a tentative smile. He would take care of the gym, I had no doubt.

"Calm down, princess," I started.

Bethany cut right in. "Don't call me that. Cole calls me that and I hate it," she said, sounding insolent and more childish than normal.

I quirked a brow but decided to let it go. More than likely, it wasn't in my best interests to ask questions.

"According to Trey, a group of guys have been coming around looking for Cole," I explained. "Guys, um, like me. After he resurfaced, but wasn't actually at the gym, one of them roughed up Trey and gave themselves away. Eyes changing, growling...pretty much everything but the fur." We were already walking fast in the direction I assumed Cole's place was, but Bethany picked up the pace even further.

"Dammit. Just...DAMMIT ALL TO FREAKING HELL!" she yelled, clenching her fists as she charged forward. I don't think she was talking to me necessarily, but she kept talking all the same. "I've had it. Had. It. If Elias and his damn monkeys touched Cole, I'm going to skin every single one of their disgusting hides and let my daddy hang them on his cabin wall. Elias told us they would control themselves, that he would control them." She huffed, our speed and her outburst catching up to her.

We turned a corner and I started to ask more about Elias when Bethany gasped. I followed her line of sight and looked up at an apartment with nothing but windows facing the water. Every light was on and we could see the room inside was destroyed. We both took off running at the same time.

"Which unit?" I yelled over my shoulder.

"203," she yelled back.

Normally, I would have tried to slow to her pace but this wasn't about Bethany, this was about Amelia's brother. I had her by thirty yards as I pushed my way into the building, sprinted up the steps, shoved the unlocked door open mid-stride, and burst into the room, ready to battle.

The adrenaline had unleashed the beast and I was instantly more aware of everything. My skin felt too tight and the lights in the room had me squinting against their brightness. I could smell everything. Sweat. Fur. *Blood.* And something...off. There was a smell I recognized, but couldn't name, and it sat heavy in my nose. I prowled through the room, a low growl escaping every now and then as I fought off the change but tried to embrace the senses it gave me. The main living area was wrecked.

I was pushing through broken dishes, upended lamps, and overturned furniture when Bethany finally made it into the apartment. "It's clear. No one's here," I called. I didn't search out the blood, not wanting to worry her since we wouldn't know whose it was. She didn't respond and I turned to find her standing in the center of the entryway, staring. Her head moved all the way left and then right. I took a few steps toward her when she suddenly jumped.

"Oh my god! Charlie. CHARLIE! CHARLIE!" Bethany started screaming out the name and it took a moment for me to remember who Charlie was. The dog. The giant Great Dane who had been with Amelia on the beach. The one who had known what I was before I even really knew what I was, and well before Amelia did. Bethany tore through the apartment, wrenching open doors and screaming his name, but he was nowhere to be found.

"No. No. No. He has to be here. He would have never let someone take Cole. And no one would take him, either. He has to be here. Amelia will kill me if anything happens to him," Bethany muttered as she reopened the same four doors she'd already looked inside. Then I heard it. A deep *woof* so faint, there was no way she was hearing it.

"Wait! Listen!" I commanded. I stood still. So still, I thought my heart stopped beating. Bethany stopped moving as well. There it was again. I could hear him. Bethany looked around, hopelessly. "Outside! He has to be outside!" Before I could move, Bethany was tearing down the staircase, screaming Charlie's name again.

I took the steps down two at a time behind her and we ran back around the building to the beach. The baying got louder and I could smell him. I scanned the lower level and finally found what I was looking for. Under Cole's apartment building was some type of storage area barricaded by a huge wooden door. I could hear Charlie scratching and howling from behind it. I took off around Bethany and dove for the door. It was padlocked. Without a second thought, I grabbed the padlock and pulled it from the old wood. The rusty latch didn't give without a fight, but beast strength was on my side. I stepped back just in time. The door flew open and out came a very irate Great Dane.

Charlie dove out from the storage area, taking off for the apartment. There was nothing we could do but follow. I couldn't even keep up with how fast his four huge legs moved him. When Bethany and I finally pushed back inside, we found Charlie whimpering and sitting next to the blood I'd smelled. Looking at Charlie, there was no question it was Cole's.

Chapter 6
Amelia

I stood, staring at the closed door smugly, until Micah whipped me around, his face just centimeters from mine.

"Are you absolutely insane? Do you understand what you have done? You could have just played along. You could have at least given her time to get to know you. You did not have to force this already. Damn it, Amelia."

Micah continued to berate me, his perfect English and proper accent becoming increasingly annoying. Finally, I yanked my hand from his and stepped back, crossing my arms over my chest. "Did you hear her? Consummate our marriage? What in the hell is she talking about?"

Guilt and frustration came from Micah in equal measures as he dragged a hand through his hair. "We are betrothed, Amelia. What exactly did you think she expected?" He rolled his eyes, his shoulders dropping as his body deflated of anger and settled into frustration. "And you could have at least afforded her the respect of being my mother—of being the Queen. Would that have been so terrible?"

I narrowed my eyes, questioning how he could possibly be an ally when he was clearly delusional. We stood in stalemate for another moment, until he finally exhaled loudly, yanked his hair back into a low ponytail, and held out his hand. I looked down, wrinkling my nose.

Clenching his jaw, Micah's eyes narrowed as he snatched my hand up again and pulled me to him, whispering, "Now, more than ever, *fiancée*, you're going to have to play the part. Because I am the only protection you have. So, you will stay by me at all times and I will try to keep you from getting yourself killed. Understood?" What had been frustration melted into a silent plea as his eyes softened.

He wasn't just angry; there was a hint of fear that unnerved me more than it should have. I still didn't understand, but I slowly nodded anyway, uncomfortable with the expression Micah wore. He closed his eyes for a brief moment, nodded, and led me into the house. As we crossed the threshold, his whole demeanor changed. To help me acclimate or as part of the show, I wasn't certain. I had a hard time hearing him, though. All I could think was how beautiful this house of terrors was.

I turned my head from side to side, trying to take in the entryway filled with marble so polished, I could see my reflection, huge pieces of art depicting people I had to assume were royals, and a ceiling so high, I almost fell over trying to look to the top. I forced myself to look past the Hunters, who were everywhere. There were male and female Hunters and it occurred to me not all of them were dressed like those who served Julia in her guard. Black trench coats on the men were replaced with a servant uniform on the women.

"Are there anything but Hunters here? Who works here?" Micah had been pointing and explaining something, but I wasn't listening to at all. He frowned at my interruption.

"No, there aren't. My mother has ultimate control of the Hunters via the collars they wear, so they are the only ones she surrounds herself with." His face held a look of disgust he couldn't mask, but as another Hunter strode through the entryway, holding a covered tray, Micah quickly grabbed my elbow and turned me toward a painting.

"Watch what you say here, Amelia. They are always listening." His words were barely audible and I had to bite my tongue from telling him he sounded just like my father. Then again, my father had been right, and likely so was Micah.

Still gripping my elbow, Micah turned me toward one of the long corridors jetting off from the entryway. As we entered the hallway, Baleon appeared behind us. I hadn't heard his footsteps and jumped a little as his shadow fell over me.

Like the entryway, the hallway was all marble floors and high ceilings. The light fixtures emitting a soft glow were medieval-looking sconces spaced every five or six feet. Micah spoke quickly, his head whipping between me and the things he was pointing out. He smiled as he explained the architecture and decor to me. He pointed out pieces along the corridors that came from the Fertile Crescent—items sculpted by his ancestors or painted by famous Mages from our history books. I was particularly drawn to the paintings and struggled to keep up as Micah kept walking, wanting to study each one to see what our homeland actually looked like.

Baleon followed just behind us, but each hallway we passed held another Hunter. As I looked back at the Hunters, they all stared me directly in the eyes. Their orange eyes swirled, looking far too much like a close-up of the sun as it spat solar flares into the universe. Their eyes would narrow as our gazes met and I could see the animosity coming from them. They made it perfectly clear they'd rather have me buried out back than walking their halls.

I was lost in my own thoughts as Micah finally slowed and stopped in front of a room. He didn't speak for a moment and I was afraid of what would come next.

"We aren't sharing a room!" The words were out before I could stop them and both of my hands flew to my mouth. I looked around to make sure no one else had heard my outburst.

Micah actually chuckled, a low reverberation reminding me far too much of Aidan and the sound he would make as he laughed. "No, Amelia. We will not be sharing a room. We are betrothed, not married—much to my mother's dismay. This is your room and mine is directly across the hall. I paused because I was in the midst of making a decision."

Micah turned away from me to face Baleon. "Bale, from now until the wedding, I am assigning you to protect Amelia. You will protect her with the same vows you swore to protect me. Understood?"

Baleon did not look thrilled. "Yes, Prince Mikail. As you wish." Bale took up the position next to my door, never even acknowledging his new charge standing right in front of him.

"You're joking, right? I mean, Micah, we both know I was right. Your mother needs me. She wants something from me she can't get if I'm—"

Before I could finish, Micah shoved me into my room and kicked the door shut.

"Will you stop?" he whisper-yelled. "Listen very carefully to me, Amelia." He pointed his finger at me and waited until I nodded, looking up into his eyes.

"Every single person in this home works for my mother. Trust no one, no one but me and Baleon. He is my man, of that I am certain. And you misunderstand your position. Yes, you have something my mother wants, but she is playing a game I don't even understand yet. Yes, there's the prophecy, but she doesn't seem anywhere near as concerned with it as she is with this wedding. It's all she's talked about. It's the reason we flew alone. She wants us to spend time together. She wants you to…" He trailed off and looked past me.

"She wants me to fall in love with you? Are you joking?" Instantly, I knew I'd hurt his feelings and the laughter in my voice fell away to silence.

"Yes, that's what she wants. And while I understand I'm not Aidan, we also have something bigger to deal with here. We have priorities. People's lives are at stake, Amelia. And I don't want or need you to love me, I just need you to stay alive and help me. Which means you have to stop pissing her off."

I thought he was going to stop, but Micah stood back and crossed his arms over his chest, a cold look transforming his features. "You don't understand what my mother has been through or how her mind works. I do. Believe me when I say you are not safe. You are not protected. You are a prisoner and I am your only lifeline. So, you stay by me. You listen to me. And you keep your damn mouth shut. Do you understand?"

For this moment, I had to disregard his patronizing tone and focus on the dots slowly connecting in my head. "Is that why you become someone else in front of her? Why you wear this mask of fear and intimidation around her and no one else? Because I don't get you, Micah. One minute, you're ordering me around, sneaking me out into the night, and the next, you're cowering in your chair, acting like she just might turn you into a toad." I stood a little taller, feeling good about finally calling him out on all his crap.

He simply shook his head and rolled his eyes. "You aren't listening to me. You have to play her game. You cannot underestimate what she'll do or the lengths she'll go. She doesn't bother with me because she thinks I'm not worthy of bothering with. She doesn't know the extent of my knowledge or power, because while I am the spitting image of my father, I am nothing like him." Micah paused, his brows drawn together and expression pained. "She never hesitates to remind me I am nothing at all like my courageous, charming, and powerful father."

He turned from me, the stiffness of frustration making it seem as if he were growing taller while he tried to control his emotions. I could feel it all and knew better than to push for more answers right now, but his father had something to do with all of this. Instead of asking for elaboration, I decided to give us additional common ground to stand on.

"It's strange how similar our childhoods seem to be. I would catch my father looking at me like he was seeing a ghost. Like it pained him to even turn his head in my direction. Rynna told me how much I looked like my mother and instead of bringing me closer to him, it only pushed him away." I started to pace the room, anxious energy filling me as Micah's words rolled around in my head.

I stopped and turned back to Micah. "Do you truly believe you can protect me?" The words were hushed. I didn't want to actually say them and I wasn't sure I wanted to know the answer.

"If I can't protect you here, Amelia, no one can."

It wasn't until the door closed behind him that I thought to ask why he was so intent on protecting me in the first place.

Thankfully, Micah and I were the only ones present for dinner the first night. When I asked where his mother was, he shrugged. "She does what she wants. She could have jetted off to some council meeting or she could be sitting in her room, plotting our demise." His attempt at a joke fell flat as my mouth dropped in shock.

"Hey, hey, joking." His hands rose in surrender. "I was merely joking. Baleon, can you please find out whether mother will be joining us?" Baleon nodded and disappeared, coming back minutes later to break the strained silence.

"Your mother was called away, Prince Mikail. The Eastern territories are reporting possible sightings and she wanted to confirm for herself."

Micah nodded but gave himself away as he chewed his bottom lip.

"What does that mean? What sightings?" I asked.

"AniMages. It means they are reporting sightings of AniMages and if they aren't being careful, it could mean even more are in the area. It's been years since they've allowed themselves to be seen and my mother thought she had all but wiped them out. Now, they are becoming more blatant and allowing the other races to know they've outsmarted her. My mother will have none of that."

Micah started pushing his food around on his plate. All I could do was wonder whether these were the "others" Rynna mentioned.

"I'm not hungry either," I announced, acknowledging sitting here was the last place either of us wanted to be right now. "I'll just go to bed. It's been a long day."

He looked relieved. "Very good, Baleon will escort you. I have some things to attend to. I'll see you in the morning, Amelia. With my mother gone, there's time for us to work on your preparation."

I wanted to ask for what, but I didn't think I could take the answer, so I nodded and followed Baleon from the dining room. Finally, I was alone in my giant suite of rooms. I knew Bale was on the other side of my door, but I wasn't entirely certain whether he was keeping other people out or me in.

Right now, I was so exhausted, I didn't care. I stepped into the shower, hoping to rinse some of the journey and madness of the day away, but as soon as I was under the warm spray, emotions started building. The realities of where I was and what the Queen wanted. That I wasn't safe and had no idea whether Rynna would actually be able to get to me. And I had no clue what had happened to my brother, my father, or Bethany once they left Esmerelda's. Or Aidan when I walked away. The questions surrounding him were the worst. I had left him alone, like so many other people in his life, and worse, I left him to manage a power he knew nothing about. I didn't entirely know what he was either, but I could have helped.

I had to stop the building ache in my chest, so I pushed him out of my mind and looked down at the cuff clasped around my forearm instead. How exactly was this cuff supposed to help me communicate with my Keeper power? It was another question without an answer.

Once dry and dressed, I sat back into the pillows, closed my eyes, and wrapped my left hand around the cuff. The metal grew warm under my fingertips as I muttered to myself, "What do I do?" over and over again. It had worked when I wanted my power to come back, so why not give it a shot?

I suddenly found myself in the confines of my own mind, standing in front of a door—the door. The one that opened into the room the cuff kept the Keeper bound to. I could feel her, pacing in frustration. I could feel the emotion bleeding around the doorframe. Rage. Envy. Anger. It was as if an animal were prowling the room instead of the woman I personified her as in my mind.

I stood there, waiting for something to happen, but nothing did. My curiosity got the better of me, so I cautiously reached out and cracked the door open just an inch. Instantly, she was there, overwhelming the sliver of space and making me feel claustrophobic, caught within the swirl of emotions she radiated. Instinct took over and without understanding why, I further pulled the door open and shoved my arm between it and the frame. The silver cuff glowed white as it made contact with her form.

The dark void that had always represented the Keeper power sprang apart, color bursting throughout the room. I had to shield my eyes at first, but eventually could make out different figures—not people, more like the auras of what used to be people. I had to assume they were the Elders who made up the Keeper power because they were all a varying shade of violet. One was surrounded in an electric blue haze, one with red, one with green bolts of light bursting through it, and another was filled with what looked like an orange electricity storm. They stayed back from me, but I could feel the relief they projected at being apart from each other. I wanted to speak, to take a step toward them, but I was suddenly drained. I struggled to hold my arm out, the weight of it becoming too much. As I let it drop back at my side, the five figures smashed together in a chorus of shrieking howls, piercing my ears and giving me the jolt of strength I needed to step backward and shove the door closed.

I was back on the bed, laboring to breathe, completely exhausted from the minute-long ordeal. I reminded myself that Rynna had told me it would take time as I fell back against the pillows and instantly fell asleep.

What felt like seconds later, I was awake, but not really. I was dreaming, back in the forest that had haunted my dreams these past few months, the fog sweeping through and feeling alone. I was at least still on two legs, which was different than the last time I'd been here after I brought Bethany home from the AniMages. Oh, how long ago that seemed. It was hard to believe it had only been weeks since I truly started to understand who I was and what was inside me. I was lost in my own head as I pushed through the trees. I wasn't scared—I had been here so many times before. The trees surrounding me had become friends. Their leaves slid through my fingers as I wandered around, grazing my fingers along the rough trunks.

I felt safe here. For the first time in weeks, I truly felt safe. As I turned to head in a new direction, the brush rustled and I could feel the vibration of something coming toward me. Every hair on the back of my neck stood up. For the first time, I wasn't alone—someone or something was here with me.

I looked around, trying to decide whether I could run and which way made the most sense. I searched inside myself and found only my small violet flame. The Keeper was nowhere to be found and I was unsure of how much power I held without her. I went to take my first running step when it burst through the trees.

I was flat on my back, gasping for the breath that had been knocked out of me. Two paws dug into my chest and a snarling lip curled around pointed teeth. I still wasn't breathing as my eyes traveled up and connected to brilliant sapphires I would know anywhere. Recognition flitted through his eyes and the growling simmered to a low whine as Aidan stepped off and away from me.

His movements were slow and calculated as he moved backward, never taking his eyes from mine. I struggled to shove myself up while maintaining our connection. I had no idea what to say. 'I'm sorry' surely wouldn't cut it. It wouldn't even begin to tell the right story—the one he deserved to hear that I couldn't give him that night.

"Aidan? Can you hear me?" I asked, still breathless as I tried to regain my composure. His ears pricked up and he seemed to nod, his head tilting up and then down, ever so slightly. "Okay, so you understand me? Lift your left paw if you understand me," I responded.

He cocked his head to the right and simply stared. Had he had an eyebrow to lift, I was sure he would have.

"Alright then, fine," I huffed. "So you understand me. Got it. Is it dumb to ask if you can talk?" I took a few steps toward him and he recoiled a bit, so I stopped. We stared at each other and I held out my hand. He came forward one painfully slow step at a time and ducked his head underneath it, forcing my fingers to tangle in his thick fur coat the color of his hair—rich soil. It was deep and dark and it took everything I had not to collapse on the ground and wrap myself around him.

Aidan let out another low whine and I crouched beside him so we were eye level. It was still weird, looking into the eyes of a wolf, but I saw him in there. I felt it in the way he tucked his head over my shoulder and pulled me into him. The way he nibbled into my hair, inhaling in small snorts. I exhaled into him as I gave in to my urges, wrapping my arms as far around his massive body as they would go. "I've missed you so much, Aidan," I whispered into his fur. I was thankful this was a dream and I would wake up soon, because it felt like my heart was breaking all over again.

Chapter 7
Aidan

I pulled up to Bethany's apartment—Amelia's apartment—and just sat in the car. The idea of walking into the space that had been Amelia's was daunting. I took a deep breath and mentally berated myself yet again. If I were going to get her back, I was going to have to do a lot worse than walk into her old living room. Everything Bethany and I had talked about was shuffling around my brain. The facts, the magic, the evil she was up against…it all banged against the confines of my mind in rapid succession. There were pieces of the puzzle I was missing and it pissed me off. I shouldn't have needed help to get to her, but I couldn't put it all together and just get to the bottom of it.

I slammed my palms against the steering wheel. It felt good to hit something. Last night, I had shifted again without being able to stop it. I had been out all night, but even running hadn't burnt off the energy the way I needed to. I hadn't been to the gym in weeks and nothing sounded better than a heavy bag right now. I needed to beat the hell out of something—anything. My hyper-hearing picked up Charlie's thunderous *woofs* and I looked up to find him in the window of the apartment, barking nonstop, his eyes on me. I couldn't break my gaze from his as he carried on. It was then that I realized he was *talking* to me. I couldn't understand him, but that dog had something to say. I shook my head a little, trying to understand where those random thoughts came from.

You're losing it, Montgomery. Get in there and deal with this.

I slammed the car door as I got out, feeling good about the rattle of the steel as it connected with the rest of the frame. I pushed my way into the building, up the stairs, and to Bethany's door. The door I whispered my love for Amelia into. I rapped on it with my knuckles and moved inside, not waiting for Bethany to answer. I walked in to find her yanking on Charlie's collar, trying to contain him, while he pulled toward me, simply dragging her along for the ride. His barks were deep and vibrated with his obvious need to communicate something. She was swearing at him as she stumbled over her feet and then finally let him go with a, "God damn dog. I don't know why I thought you were so great." She only acknowledged me with a gruff, "coffee," as she walked into the kitchen. It wasn't a question. She wasn't offering. Apparently, everyone has their vices.

I stooped down to get eye-level with Charlie. He stood in front of me, his huge ears pointing toward the ceiling as he continued to bark, though softer now.

"Dude, Charlie, what's your deal? What exactly is the problem?" I asked him.

Charlie cocked his black and white spotted head at me and something in his eyes made me snap my head back. He understood me. Some part of me realized he heard my words and knew exactly what I was saying.

"Charlie?" I asked as I leaned back in. "You obviously need to tell me something, so tell me."

I could have sworn I saw a smile shine through that dog's eyes as he lifted one massive paw and set it on my thigh, just above my knee but below where my shorts stopped.

In a split second, I found myself watching a gruesome scene through Charlie's eyes. At first, the flashes were hard to keep up with. As if he could sense my confusion, Charlie started the scene over, more slowly. This time, it started with Cole coming through the front door, Charlie— and me—following behind. I could hear Cole talking, apparently to Charlie, as he bemoaned how long he'd been gone and how he hadn't been able to do anything to help Amelia. He cursed her stupidity and impetuousness, slamming cupboards doors as he continued to curse his father and Derreck, neither of which were responding to him. As he leaned against the kitchen counter, running his hands over his face and smacking himself lightly on the cheeks, as if trying to wake himself up and get his head in the game, there was a knock at the door.

Charlie sat quietly, which Cole took as a good sign. "Who is it?" he called out as he crossed the room. The infamous Uncle Derreck that Bethany told me about responded. Cole wrenched open the door and immediately peppered Derreck with questions. The guy looked like hell and didn't answer a single one of them. He walked in and dropped onto the couch.

"I either need tea or a drink, Cole. Let's start there," Derreck said, his expression pained as he pinched the bridge of his nose.

Cole silently threw his hands in the air and then put a teakettle on. A few silent minutes later, he shoved a steaming mug in his uncle's face.

"Where in the hell have you been? Do you know what's been happening? I could have used your help. They have her." Cole's face was red, his voice wavering.

Derreck's gaze flicked up, his tone sharp. "Of course I know what's happened. What do you think I've been doing? I've been trying to find help. Trying to figure out what to do. Didn't they find you?"

"Who?" Cole asked, pacing. "The guys who were harassing the kids at my gym? I just got home. I've been out looking for you. Looking for Rynna. My dad. Anybody to help me." Charlie fell in step with him and it felt good to walk. I felt

Charlie's anxiety as if it were my own. He didn't want to be far from Cole.

"Daniel should have found you. He's an AniMage. He's part of Elias's pack. They were supposed to take you to him so he could explain things and you could work together. Damn it." Derreck and Cole stared at each other, so many unspoken words shuttling between them.

"Where were you, really? The night they had Amelia's best friend, when you were supposed to be helping us, where were you?" Cole questioned.

"I was there. With Elias," Derreck answered, his voice steady as his jaw muscles clenched. "I tried to get to him before she did. To stop whatever it was he was trying to do. But honestly, he didn't want anything but her time. And what he told her she needed to know. She needs to understand the truth of what's happening, Cole. She needed to hear him, see it, and believe in this rebellion. So I stood back in the trees and watched. She did great. She was strong and controlled, and I was proud of her."

Cole's instant reaction to Derreck's words shocked me. Charlie immediately started to growl, a low vibration deep in his throat as he bared his teeth at Derreck.

"You knew about everything this whole time, didn't you? Get out. Now. Just get out." His words were measured, cold. Cole's eyes were burning green coals as he stared his uncle down.

Derreck looked first shocked, then accepting. He stood and as he turned to go, he said, "You're going to need to understand, too, Cole. This is bigger than her. It's bigger than anything you've given up. She has to do this. She has to fight with us. Every Immortal has a stake in this."

"The only thing my sister has to do now is survive, and while you were all plotting your rebellion, no one bothered to teach her how. So you and your buddy, Elias, better pray she's okay up there. Because when I find her—and I will—I'm going to get her out and you're going to do more than fly into a wall when she sees you again. Now, get out."

Cole never turned toward Derreck. He didn't move until the door clicked shut. Then he walked to the windows and dropped his head against the glass. Charlie stepped up beside him and with a small whimper, ducked his head under Cole's palm. Cole wrapped Charlie's head in his hand, pulling him into his leg.

"I'm sorry, Amelia. I'm sorry for failing you. I'm so sorry." His words floated down in a soft whisper, his voice thick.

I thought the memory would fade and Charlie would let me out. Instead, the moment disappeared and a new one took its place. This time, it was confusing. The images flashed in my mind and I could barely make one out before the next was there and gone. Charlie's agitation was growing and he was having a hard time showing me what he wanted to. The images started to repeat themselves.

The door crashing open. Swarms of men in long leather jackets with dark skin and white hair. Cole screaming at Charlie to hide. Cole blasting green bursts of lightning from his palms as he fought. Charlie going after them and being immobilized. I heard a voice say, "Lock the Sentinel away, where he can't cause us any problems." What was a Sentinel? Clearly, Charlie was more than simply man's best friend.

The leather jackets laughed as Cole tried to fight, the largest of them walking straight up to Cole as he shot blasts. The man absorbed them without a flinch, until he reached out a hand and, without touching Cole, lifted him off the ground and pinned him against the glass windows. Cole's head whipped left and then right, bruises formed and his cheek split open. Blood dripped steadily from his cheek to the glass, pooling onto the floor where I'd found it in the apartment. Charlie's barking was so loud in his own head, I couldn't hear the words of the man. The last thing I caught was, "The Queen requests your presence, Mage." Cole tried to spit the blood from his busted lip at the man and he simply laughed. He shot one bolt of orange and Cole slid down the glass to the ground, unconscious.

As Charlie finally removed his paw from my leg and the flashes stopped, I fell back into the front door and onto the floor. Bethany was crouched in front of me in an instant, snapping her fingers in my face and clapping, shaking my shoulders. I could hear her, but the words were miles away. I could see her mouth moving, but whatever Charlie had done to me had sapped my energy and left my brain in a fog.

I looked over at him, sitting perfectly still and straight, his eyes never leaving mine. He cocked his head again and I heard him in my head, saying, "So, what are you gonna do about it?" I dropped my head back, actually satisfied to hear the *thunk* of it landing against the hollow paneling of the door. Bethany's words were becoming more high-pitched and I simply held up a hand.

"Elias. You have to take me to Elias," I said. I barely got the last word out before everything caught up with me and I, too, lost consciousness.

I woke up still on the floor, a blanket covering me, and Charlie stretched out beside me. His length wasn't far from my own and there was something comforting about his quiet snorts. I opened my eyes to see Bethany, now dressed and apparently properly caffeinated, tapping her foot repeatedly as she stared over at me from her chair.

"You mind telling me what the hell that was all about? I've only seen that happen once and it was when Elias did it to Amelia, but she didn't lose it afterward. Well, I guess she did, but not like you did." Bethany's tone was clipped, but laced with worry.

I struggled to sit up, disrupting Charlie as I shoved myself back against the wall, massaging my stiff neck with one hand while I scratched his head with the other. "I don't get it, Bethany. I don't know what's happening either. Every day, it seems like I can do more than the day before. Apparently, today's accomplishment was having a dog show me his memories."

I filled her on what I saw of Cole, both with Derreck and the men. She paled.

"The men who took him, you said they wore long leather jackets and had white hair? They had orange magic?" She cowered a little in her seat, the vision clearly making her uncomfortable.

"Yes. Why? Who are those guys? Obviously they work for the Queen."

Bethany slowly nodded. "They do. They are Hunters and they're evil, Aidan. They kill and they torture and they are the reason for all of this. They are the ones who took Amelia and me. They are the ones who killed her mother and betrothed her to...him. I think they find joy in other people's pain."

She still couldn't say Micah's name. She hadn't said it since we'd met up on the beach. It had to suck to know everything you believed had been a lie. At least I knew Amelia wanted me. She loved me. Or...I hoped she did. She'd never said it, though. Those thoughts were immediately replaced by cold fear, snaking its way down my spine and then igniting into anger. The beast roared for the first time in a while as I jumped to my feet and Charlie did the same.

"We've got to go. You said you could find Elias. Their uncle said they needed to find him. We need to find him. If he's planning something, then he has to know where she is and how to get her and Cole out. They've got to be together. And we have to make them help us."

Bethany looked a little wary. "B, don't do this to me now," I said. "We've got to stick together on this. She needs us." I walked over and held out a hand. She looked up at me and I watched as the strength took over. Her eyes narrowed and she nodded.

"She's damn lucky we love her," she said dryly. I laughed a little. "Lead the way, pri...B."

She arched an eyebrow as I caught my mistake again. Me and my propensity for calling girls nicknames. "After you, Bethany," I corrected with a grin. With one look, I was both put in my place and thanked for not asking questions she hadn't wanted to answer about where her fear really stemmed from.

I whistled and Charlie lumbered to my side as we left the apartment.

Chapter 8
Amelia

I paced my room for the fifth time. I hadn't had a cell phone since they had taken me at Esmerelda's and I had no way of finding Micah. I had been awake for hours, yet he hadn't come for me. He hadn't specifically told me I had to wait for him, but he had been with me constantly and pretty clear about his expectations. Frustrated, I yanked open the door and came face to face with Baleon.

"I'm hungry. And I want out of here." I stood, looking up at him as I crossed my arms, trying to project my most domineering self. He didn't even blink.

"You will not leave the room without Prince Mikail," he said, staring directly above me.

I huffed and decided I would do what I wanted. I took a step to go around him and his arm whipped out faster than I could fathom, causing me to run into what felt like a two by four.

"You *will not* leave the room without Prince Mikail," he said again, a growl behind the words, stopping me from a second attempt. This time, he lowered his gaze, his eyes burning brightly. The lustrous end of a firecracker right before it goes off.

"Fine," I responded, raising my chin when I wanted to cower. "But you need to find him. Now. I'm starving and I refuse to be treated like a prisoner. I'm his fiancée. Making me your soon-to-be boss."

One of Bale's eyebrows lifted in an uncharacteristic response to my threat. He quickly covered it up as he shoved me back into the room and pulled the door closed. I heard him order one of the others to find Micah and I laughed a little.

Amelia, 1; Bale, 0, I thought to myself.

It didn't take long for Micah to show up, and he looked inordinately pleased as he gestured me out into the hall.

"What's gotten into you?" I grumbled, eyeing him, wondering whether good for him meant good for me.

"Well, I have a surprise for you today, Amelia," he said, his eyes alight with mischief. His enthusiasm forced a smile from me.

"Yeah? Did your mom take a dive off the nearest cliff?" I couldn't help it. Sarcasm was my best offense and he had left it wide open. I was surprised to hear Micah chuckle as he shook his head.

"Well, in a manner of speaking, she did. I was informed this morning the situation in the East is larger than she expected and she will be gone for the rest of the week." He rolled his eyes as he continued, in more of a mumble, "All the better for us to bond, she said."

I chose to ignore that last part. A betrothal was one thing; this whole consummation business was something else. "What does that mean? Have they found the—" I didn't get to finish my sentence before Micah started speaking loudly over me, glaring at me intently as he did.

"It means we can do some uninterrupted work together and I can show you around. This home is one of my favorite places in the world and I've never really been able to show it to anyone."

I mentally smacked myself in the forehead. Of course. We were in the middle of the hallway and there were Hunters everywhere. I let my questions lie and jumped into his line of conversation.

"No one? Didn't you have friends growing up? Aren't there other royal people you hung out with? Did they keep you away from everyone, too?" It disturbed me to think he had been as isolated as I was and I was genuinely shocked to see the sadness Micah didn't bother to hide. He looked knowingly at me, all of his normal charm was gone and it was plain to see we weren't so different after all.

He clasped his hands behind him as we strolled along a hall. As we turned the next corner, he grabbed my arm and quickly drew me into a room, closing the door. "There are stories I owe you. Explanations you need. But this isn't the time nor the place for them." Micah's words were quick and hushed. He kept glancing over my shoulder at the door. "They are watching—always watching. They will report our every word to my mother. For both of our sakes, give me time and I'll find a way for us to talk openly. Just try to keep your more in-depth questions to yourself. Do you understand?"

His breath was warm on my face as I nodded. A hundred questions raced through my mind and I pushed all of them back but one.

"But why? Can you just tell me why you're helping me?" My own words were an exhale into his ear as I tried to be as quiet as I could. Micah's lips were at my ear as footsteps moved toward us. The loud, thudding footfalls could only be the Hunters.

"Blood does not trump madness. She must be stopped, and you are the key."

I didn't even have time to register his full meaning before he snapped his fingers, the drapes opened, and he started loudly describing the library and the hundreds of years' worth of knowledge stored there. The door banged open and an unknown Hunter looked disappointed to find us five feet from each other with Micah droning on about the ancient tomes of our people. Micah didn't spare him a glance as I smiled widely and winked at him. His lips pressed into a tight slash against his light brown skin and he strode from the room, leaving the door wide open.

I turned back to Micah, my smile real this time. "Hundreds of years' worth of knowledge, huh?"

His grin was all I needed to know I was right where I needed to be.

I started to walk the perimeter of the room, stopping in my tracks as I rounded a bookcase. My feet were rooted to the ground as I stared, my head swiveling back and forth. What I had thought to be a small room was only the entryway to a massive gymnasium-sized cavern. Three floors with rolling ladders and thousands of books. Micah sauntered past me and stood in the atrium of the room.

He spread his arms wide, and said, "Amelia, meet my friends. Welcome to my playground."

"Where did all of this come from?" I exhaled the question from a gaping mouth, my eyes wide. I couldn't even begin to estimate how many thousands of books were here. Micah's smile softened as he looked around fondly.

"Everywhere. Every royal family added to it and Tragar, the royal historian, maintains it. He's not here right now, he's out tracking down more volumes, but he'll be back soon and I can't wait to introduce you to him. He's hundreds of years old and a walking encyclopedia. He spends all of his time piecing together a history no one can agree on."

I couldn't miss the insinuation buried in Micah's tone as we stood across the room, knowing we were sharing a secret. Rynna had told me to find out everything I could and Micah had planted me exactly where I needed to be in order to make that happen.

I walked around the edges of the room, running my fingers along the bindings of the books. I was shocked to feel the Keeper flare in response. Certain books sent waves of energy through the pads of my fingers and brought an onslaught of noise and emotion from her. I had been afraid to try to approach her again, since I had barely been able to handle our last interaction, but I knew I couldn't keep wasting time. I dragged my fingers along another set of ten books and only one sent a jolt through me. I fingered the book and just as I was about to pull it from its place, Micah interrupted me.

"You have two options. We can start the arduous task of haphazardly trying to find books that will tell us something helpful, or we can wait for Tragar and start working on your training. Which would you prefer?"

Which did I prefer? I was being drawn toward the books and the information I knew I needed, but an underlying fear of what I could actually do without my Keeper had been nagging at me since I'd put the cuff on.

"Let's train first. I...uh, need to brush up on some things." I hadn't told Micah about the cuff and I hadn't decided whether I wanted to. Rynna said he was an ally, and he had certainly been acting like one, but I still felt like the only person I could depend on right now was myself.

Micah gestured to a few couches and we both sat while Bale stood guard at the door. Micah explained as long as the other Hunters knew he was with us, we wouldn't be bothered.

"How honest can I be here?" I asked.

"Well, out loud, we should probably still be careful. But we do have another way." Micah tapped his temple and I instantly felt like an idiot.

"Is it still there? I know I, uh, shut that down at one point." I wasn't necessarily sorry or ashamed of how we had fought after I found out Micah was actually Prince Mikail, but it was another instance where I had acted without considering what would come of it.

"Connections are never really gone. But, because you are the one who closed the door, you also have to be the one to reopen it. Shall we start there?" Micah leaned back on his couch and closed his eyes, clearly waiting for me to begin. By his relaxed posture, I knew he was defenseless right now. He had completely opened himself up to me, allowing me inside his head. I was surprised he would allow himself to be so vulnerable.

I took a long inhale, holding the air in my lungs for a second before letting it out in one continuous, slow breath. I closed my eyes and focused on the small violet flame deep within me. *Bigger. Bigger. Bigger.* I muttered the words until what had been a small candle flame was a kindling fire inside me. Warmth spread through me, fire simmering in every crevice. I opened my eyes but didn't allow them to focus. I saw a blurry Micah, still reclined on the couch, but now surrounded in a red haze. I pushed my fire out toward him, smoke tinged with lightning. It floated across the feet between us but flared in bright bursts, especially as it got closer to him. Micah had to feel me coming. His own power reached toward me, pulsing red. The two poked and prodded at each other, smoke swirling as they circled. Finally, as they had the first time, red and violet spun around and around, until they were braided together. At last, I both saw and felt the snap of electricity when they merged.

Still reclined, but looking quite smug, I heard Micah.

And here we are again, Amelia.

I rolled my eyes. *If you want to stay this way, perhaps we can use this to tell each other more truths and less lies, yeah?*

Oh, you pain me. You know I was only trying to help while we were in Brighton. I had to know where you stood to understand what we were up against.

And where exactly do we stand, huh, Micah? Because while I appreciate the library and not being a prisoner in my room every minute of every day, your mother is going to come home eventually and we both know she wants more from me than just a wedding.

He sighed and pulled himself up. Putting his elbows on his knees, he steepled his fingers and pressed into his forehead.

You ask as if it is a simple question with a simple answer. My mother is nothing if not entirely unpredictable. So, the only thing I can definitively tell you is you have a few days of reprieve and in that time, you need to work fast and learn fast. The library is at our disposal and there's a lot to learn here, but getting you ready to handle my mother and her Hunters is just as important.

"Okay," I said aloud, closing down our connection. I needed the mental space to reconcile the fear and determination swimming within my system like minnows and sharks in the same stretch of water. "I want to start." I stood up. "But I just need a minute, okay?"

I walked away from him without waiting for an answer. I couldn't leave the library, but I could find a quiet corner to collect my thoughts. I forced strong, sure steps that conflicted with the gut-wrenching realization that even his help would only go so far. I would have to handle the Queen on my own and there was no way to even guess what she had in store for me. For the hundredth time, I wished my mother had lived.

She could have prepared me for this. As it was, I walked into a minefield wearing clown shoes.

Chapter 9
Aidan

"Do you have any idea where we are actually going?" It was my turn to ask. We had been scouring the woods for a few hours, looking for some particular clearing Bethany was "just certain" she remembered how to get to. In response to my irritated question, she let a low branch fly back and almost smack me in the face. Thankfully, my reflexes were better than she likely assumed and I caught it before any permanent damage occurred. I glanced down at Charlie and muttered how lucky he was to be lower to the ground.

"I was sure this was the way we came. We came over a hill and then there was a scratched up tree and we went right. Or did we go left?" She turned in a circle, looking genuinely perplexed.

"Well," I stated dryly, "left and right are complete opposites, so it kind of makes a difference. We've come to this same tree three times now. Think, Bethany. Which way did you go?"

The breeze shifted and in my first inhale, I knew exactly which way we should go. "This way," I hollered over my shoulder, finally happy to be getting somewhere. I took off through the trees with Charlie on my heels. Bethany wasn't quite as quick.

"Aidan! Aidan, wait for me. Human, remember? No super-fast floaty running skills over here. Still tripping over the bushes and crap. WAIT UP!"

I heard Bethany's words, but I was on the trail. I made my movements more deliberate and sloppy so she could easily follow me, but I kept pushing forward. It wasn't fifty more feet before Charlie and I came out in a clearing—the clearing. I was sure of it.

The area was a stark contrast to the smells assaulting my senses. The scent of shampoo and body soap, of dirty denim and sweat. Wet fur, mud-caked paws, and excrement. Charlie let out a low growl and stuck close to my side. As my gaze swept across the trees again, I saw an owl sitting back in the leaves. Its eyes never left me as I took in the scene and followed me as I sidestepped to the right and left. I cocked my head and it did the same.

Finally, Bethany came crashing into the clearing unceremoniously, swearing as she yanked twigs from her ponytail and brushed her hands down her jeans. "What in the name of—"

I held a hand up and continued my silent exchange with the owl.

Bethany connected the dots and fell silent. "Stay," I quietly commanded Charlie.

I took a few steps forward and the owl hopped out farther on the branch. Feeling a bit ridiculous, I said, "We're here to see Elias. We're friends of Amelia's. He knows Bethany. We need to talk to him, please."

I added the pleasantry, thinking it couldn't hurt to be respectful in my demands. In response, the owl gave me a quick *hoot* and opened his giant wings. In two strokes, he was out of sight and into the forest.

"So, now what?" Bethany asked.

"I guess now, we wait."

The wait wasn't long, maybe half an hour. He announced his presence loudly as he made his way into the clearing and the once-empty branches behind him filled with bright blue eyes of all shapes and sizes. I commanded Charlie to stay with Bethany, no matter what, and received an indignant *woof* in response. I asked her to let me handle the meeting and received an eye roll in confirmation.

The owl swept back into the area, gliding on the breeze in a lazy circle above our heads, until he finally took up residence once again on the original branch. As he landed, I was sure he winked at me.

I pulled my eyes from the owl and focused on the man coming toward me. He was tall—built but lanky. He didn't scare me, but he also wasn't a guy I was intentionally looking to piss off. He was the only one in the bunch with normal eyes, likely by design. Pressure built in my chest. I was uncomfortable with all of the power around me, with the animals I expected walked on two feet for part of their days, like I did. I didn't feel like we weren't safe, but I surely wasn't at ease.

I stepped out to meet the man and extended my hand. He confirmed my suspicion and introduced himself. "I'm Elias. How can I help you?" He grasped my hand firmly, but without threat. Not willing to show an ounce of fear, I met his eyes and barely caught the quick widening and enlargement of his pupils as we shook and let go. Just as quickly as I saw it, it was gone. I couldn't help but wonder whether I had truly seen anything at all.

I went to speak when Bethany stepped up beside me. "Hey, old buddy, what's shaking?" Her giant southern smile was out in full force, but the confidence she exuded lacked a little of its normal spunk. I was happy at least to see Charlie locked at her side. It meant one of them actually listened to me.

Elias gave her an amused smile and tipped his head. "Welcome back, Bethany. Have you missed us?"

"You know, I can't say the wet dog smell and lack of social skills really did it for me. We've got bigger issues, though. You want to get to it?" She turned to me and I could only shake my head at her horrendous show of fake nonchalance.

"I'm Aidan. I was…am…might be…Amelia's boyfriend. But she's gone. She's with Micah—Prince Mikail—and the Queen. And we know you said you wanted to fight. And that you would help her. And now her brother is gone, too. And I know her Uncle has been here. We need your help. I have to get her out of there." The words coming out weren't the ones I'd been rehearsing in my head, but they were the truth.

Elias took a moment to answer. "You seem to know a lot for someone I've never seen or heard of before. How is it you've come to all of this information, Amelia's maybe boyfriend?"

Bethany piped up again. "Well, of course I filled him in on our last little rendezvous. As much fun as that was, you were the first person I thought of once we realized Cole was gone. We know your guys were after him, too. Just not the way the Hunters were—"

"Can you just be quiet?" I cut in, glaring at Bethany. She recoiled a little and snapped her mouth shut with a *humph*.

Elias chuckled. "Lively one, isn't she?"

"You have no idea," I responded dryly, feeling better about the fact that so far, he wasn't some kind of power-hungry douche.

"Still here. Still standing right here," she threw out in a sing-song voice. We both turned and once she took in the similar glares, Bethany stomped over to an overturned log. "I'll just be right here," she muttered.

There were more logs in the middle of the clearing and Elias gestured for me to sit. I waved a hand toward Bethany and she and Charlie joined our circle. This time, with minimal dramatic stomping.

"She's right. I really only know what I've been told." I left out being told part of the story by the dog sitting next to us. "But I know Amelia is in danger, and I suspect her brother is, too. I know you didn't want her with the Queen either, and you want to fight. So, I'm asking if you'll fight with us. Will you help us get them out?"

Elias rubbed a hand over his stubbled chin. "I think there's more to this than you're telling me, friend."

Alarms blared inside me at the same time Charlie let off a string of deafening *woofs*. I jumped up from the log and grabbed Bethany from her perch next to me. In just a few seconds, I had us on the other side of the clearing.

Elias stood slowly and turned, his hands out. "Now, now…no need for that. We're all friends here, aren't we?" With a small motion of his hand, the eyes filling the trees stepped into the light. Bethany and I watched as each and every one of the twenty-odd animals shifted right in front of us. Wolves, panthers, eagles, chipmunks, foxes, deer…they all changed so fast, I couldn't keep up with what they all had started as and then who they were moments later. Each one stayed crouched, naked as I always was. The last to shift was the owl. One moment, he was perched on the branch, and the next, a naked young boy with bright red hair was swinging back and forth, a huge grin on his face.

The red-haired woman came through the trees, fully clothed, and started tossing stacks of clothes out to them all. Bethany piped up beside me, "Still on a leash, are we, Melinda?" This time her grin was real and Elias erupted in laughter.

"I do love how you have a sense of humor, even though you are a human. Aidan, whether you realize it or not—because I don't think you have—you have already given yourself away."

Elias crossed his arms and leaned back on his heels.

My eyes. I turned to look down at Bethany and she shrugged, nodding. "Okay, so you know something about me now, too. It doesn't matter."

"Oh, but that's where you're wrong, my friend. I do know something about you, but it's more than you think. You are Aidan Montgomery, son of Zendrick and Kayla Montgomery."

I was stupefied. No one had spoken my parents' names since the day they died. There was no funeral because there was no family to organize the details and I was only two. From then on, my case workers and foster families never referred to them by name. When your parents die, people get weird about mentioning them—acting like they were never here to begin with.

"How do you know them?" I sputtered out the words and felt the world shift a little under my feet. Elias blurred and refocused in front of me as my head tried to keep up with my erratic heartbeat and the beast inside roaring in defensive frustration. A jolt of something blitzed through my veins and at once, I was right again. I tried not to outwardly show my confusion as Elias watched me closer than I would have liked.

"Why don't you two come with me and we can have a more cordial conversation? This way." Elias turned and led us through the group of people to a narrow trail winding out of sight.

Following him was obviously a better plan than staying with all of the AniMages, so I placed Bethany in front of me, sensing her desire to stay far away from Melinda and her friends. Charlie followed behind me, making me feel marginally safer. Eyes followed us as we walked through the group and I couldn't help but wonder if this was all some kind of set-up.

"No set-up. It sounds like we just need some time to chat in a safer place. But I will say, your arrival couldn't have been timed better." Elias's deep voice boomed out from ahead of us and I looked down at Bethany, wondering how he had known.

She shrugged as she eyed him. "He did that to Ame, too. Be careful what you think around this guy."

"Thanks for the heads up, blondie," I muttered.

Chapter 10
Amelia

I wiped the moisture from the bathroom mirror and stared at myself. I was exhausted from the hours I'd spent with Micah over the last few days. We had yet to dig into the library in the way I wanted. So focused on working on my power, he immediately forced me back to the couches and had me work on levitating stacks of books, shooting them across the room, and directing energy blasts he would intercept and break apart. All things I would have been able to do easily when my Keeper was free, but with her power bound by the cuff, I was forced to work with just my own and it felt like relearning how to ride a bike. It wasn't that the capabilities weren't there, she just amplified them so much when I had her on my side. Micah was frustrated and didn't understand how I'd lost so much ground. I was frustrated and couldn't decide when, or even if, I should tell him about the cuff. Even Baleon looked down on me as he walked me to my room, as if to tell me I needed to try harder, like I didn't already know.

I sighed as I acknowledged the bags under my eyes. My night was only beginning and I needed a lift. I concentrated, staring at my own eyes as I watched the hazel disappear into iridescent purple. I watched the bags fade and my skin brighten. Energy zipped along my spine and through my blood, a current of strength and focus. It did more than any caramel latte ever could have, though I would have killed for a syrupy-sweet sip right now. I closed my eyes and gave my head a few quick shakes. When I opened them again, I nodded into the mirror and held back my smile as I confirmed my once-wet hair was now dry and straight. Nobody needed heat damage, that's what Bethany would have said, and she would have loved the idea of never needing a flatiron again.

My smile faltered. I missed my best friend fiercely. I imagined the conversation around my tricks, hearing her in my mind. *"Oh girl, you have no idea how good you've got it! It took me years to perfect this."* She'd wave her hands around and act all put out, but she'd be lying. Bethany only ever wanted people to be happy, in whatever form happiness took. And she knew I was miserable at pulling myself together most days.

I pulled on clothes and ground my teeth together at the emotion I hadn't expected. My heart ached. Thinking of Bethany led me to thinking of Aidan and I couldn't. I wouldn't cry for them, or for me, and I couldn't do anything for them from here, aside from keeping the Queen happy enough to stay away from them. I gripped the thick quilt covering my bed with both hands, fabric straining and bunching between my fingers as I tried to get my mind back in the right place. I had to focus on me. I had to focus on this. *You are the key.* That's what Micah had said. I had yet to figure out to what, and how exactly to unlock myself, but I would try again tonight.

I relaxed my fingers, closed my eyes, and brought one hand up and around the cuff. This time, I didn't even have to say anything. As soon as my hand closed around the metal, I was standing in front of the door again. I put my hand out and simply flattened it against the wood, feeling heat and her. She prowled the room, a cacophony of sounds coming through the door and the fear she created landed directly in my gut—a ball of anxiety I couldn't shake. I could feel the anger, pain, and frustration she had as she paced. I jumped backward as she attacked the door from the inside. She beat on it, assaulting my ears with wordless wailing. Her pain hurt me, too. I wanted to understand why she was so upset. Was it just being locked in there? It couldn't be. Her actions reminded me of a crazy person in an asylum. There were no real explanations because she couldn't form the words. But in her own mind, the truth was buried, I just had to find it. I had to know why sometimes we could work together, while other times she overtook me like a wild animal. If I were going to survive, I needed her on my side. I needed her to let me control us.

I reached out hesitantly, grasping the handle. I stepped closer to the door and tried to block out the wailing rattling my nerves. I had only moved six inches, yet she sounded decibels louder. Before I could lose my nerve, I yanked the door open wider than I had before and shoved my arm inside. Instantly, the silver cuff illuminated a brilliant white and the blackness of the room filled with color. Relief washed over me as the painful emotions faded and something else invaded the air. Relief? Happiness? Whatever it was, it was intoxicating. Before I knew what I was doing, I stepped fully into the room, my arms spread wide as the colors surrounded me and a siren's song sounded in my ears.

I stood between five energy fields. Five individual sets of color and light. As they had before, four burned violet, but with other magic clearly embedded within them. Mage magic was represented by green and red, each individually swirling in violet light. The electric blue I had to force myself to associate with Elias and not Aidan—the AniMages. The orange could only belong to Hunters. And then there was the fifth. I hadn't seen this one last time. It was stark white and sparkled like hundreds of white Christmas tree lights twinkling at once. It was set back, away from the others, whisking quickly around the room. I reached out to touch it, but it moved away before I could fully extend my hand. I turned in a circle and ran my fingers through the energy of the other four, one at a time. Familiar spikes of power drew me back to being in Derreck's cabin. The same energy bursts had filled me then, but in such a dark way. Now I felt right—righteous even. If you asked me, I would have told you I could take Julia right then and there, but even my power-drunk brain knew it was a lie.

I allowed my hands to meld into their bright light, and with each one, there was a surge of something else. The violet and orange mix brought strength. I wanted to knock down walls and take on anyone who pushed me. Into the violet and blue, I heard and smelled everything in the room. The soap from my shower, the detergent in my clothes, the footfalls of Baleon as he paced the hallway outside my door. The violet and green brought on something different entirely. Baleon's emotions assaulted me. His discomfort at being assigned to me, his struggle over his beliefs, the fact that he didn't want to believe I was who everyone thought I was, but to him, it was so obviously the truth. I had to force my hand away and into the violet and red. There, I simply felt powerful. Like I had every magical trait at my disposal. I wished I wasn't stuck in this room, wished I could be out in the open to try them out. There was so much power in this tiny little room, buried deep in the recesses of my mind. Within each of these ethereal beings was more power than any one person should ever have. And they were all inside of me, just waiting to be called upon. Waiting for me to figure out how to use them.

I forced my hands to my sides and finally spoke. "We have to work together. You have to stay hidden and I have to wear the cuff. But I need you. It's going to get bad, I know it is. I can't risk letting you out completely, and honestly, I'm afraid of what will happen. But I need to know you're going to help me. Can you somehow tell me you'll help me and not make me crazy, like before?"

I was looking around, but I had no idea what I was looking at. These weren't people. They might have been the spirits of the Elders my mother had gone to, or some part of the essence of their power, but I wasn't sure. All I knew was they were locked inside me and I needed them. I saw how serious Micah had been and the situation with Julia at Esmerelda's had shown me enough.

If push came to shove, my power alone wasn't going to be enough.

I waited only seconds longer before they answered me in the only way they probably could. All of the colors, and especially the brilliant white light, grew brighter and brighter, until I had to cover my eyes. I could feel the heat, like I was standing too close to a bonfire and it was threatening to pull me into its dancing flames.

"Okay! Okay, I believe you!" I had to laugh. There was nothing but light and laughter in the air. I needed to leave but I was worried about what would happen if I walked away again. Would they merge back together like before? As quickly as the thought appeared, the purple and green-tinged light was inches from me. It collapsed down into a smaller and smaller ball, until it was the size of a basketball hovering right in front of my right hand. As I slowly lifted my arm parallel to the ground, it followed it up, staying level with my outstretched fingers. I inched forward and my fingertips grazed the ball of energy. It snapped and sounded like twigs crackling in a fire. It hurt, but not really. Without allowing myself another thought, I shoved my arm through the ball, all the way to my elbow, fully immersing the cuff. In one thunderous boom, the ball burst into a million individual particles, showering the room. I shielded my eyes from the bright light and was awestruck to find it snap back together just as fast. It stayed a small ball, hovering in front of me.

"What just happened? Will you stay this way now?" I didn't expect an answer, but the orb quickly illuminated, dimmed, and then settled in the back of the room. The violet and blue energy pulled together and came to me in the same way. I repeated the act of pushing my cuff through each one until the white energy was all that remained, but it didn't come to me. It hovered at the top of the room, refusing to come down. I cajoled and begged, but exhaustion was quickly taking hold again. Finally, I could barely hold my eyes open and frustration got the better of me.

"Fine!" I yelled. "You just stay up there and don't let me help you. But I'm going to need you and you can't mess this up!" It was maddening to know I was yelling at charged air. But the white ball reacted and then slid even further from me. With a harrumph, I backed out of the room and slowly closed the door. I looked through the crack right before I shut it and everything looked just as

I had left it. As I pushed the door firmly closed, I waited for the wailing and emotion to rise again, but felt nothing. It was quiet. Quiet was what I needed. Sleep was what I needed. I opened my eyes to find myself in my bed and only left them open long enough to pull the cord on the lamp and let sleep take over.

Aidan. He was there again, waiting for me in the woods. I found myself in the same place we had been last time and he was just across the clearing. I stood quietly, simply allowing myself to watch him. A part of me knew he had to know I was there, but he hadn't shown it. He continued to clean himself, taking slow licks across one paw and then rubbing it over his head. As a wolf, his movements were deliberate and sure, just like when he was human. The fur on the top of his head stood up in the same way his human hair had. I ached for human Aidan. I wanted him to hold me, to whisper in my ear...to make me laugh. I wanted a brief escape but my mind refused to give him to me in that way, so I took a step toward the only Aidan I was allowed.

As soon as my foot collided with the earth and the dry leaves crunched under me, Aidan's head lifted. I saw it in his eyes. He had been waiting for me to make the first move. His eyes never wavered from mine—a spotlight through the clearest blue ocean. If I did nothing but look in his eyes, I could pretend I was walking toward Aidan the man. My mind's tricks were everything I needed and everything I couldn't take, all at once.

As I stopped in front of him, unsure of what to do, I was suddenly nervous and unable to make eye contact. I fidgeted and a shyness I hadn't felt since his initial pursuit took over. As I waged an internal war over what to do, Aidan did what he did best—taking control of the decision for me. He had always known what I needed before I did. He got up and circled me. He stopped when he was facing me and sat down. Even sitting, his head was close to chest level. His tail swished back and forth behind him and his eyes were full of patience. He let out a low yelp and it was all the encouragement I needed to drop to the ground and wrap my arms around him. My body was positioned between his front paws and he nuzzled into my hair as I struggled to maintain control of my raging emotions. I held on to him, as if he were my life raft in the sea of uncertainty and fear I now lived in.

After a few minutes, I pulled back, feeling silly and uncertain. I was close to crying and cuddling with a giant wolf. A wolf my mind created to take the place of my used-to-be-human boyfriend. I was completely losing it.

Aidan must have felt my withdrawal. He let out a series of short yips and I looked up, seeing his frustration. The wolf wanted to talk to me as much as I wanted the real Aidan to talk to. Since I was there and we were both clearly looking for something, I just started talking. The words fell from my mouth like leaves from a tree in autumn, one after the other in a quiet rush to the ground. I had so many things I was never able to say to him and I was saying them now.

"I never wanted to walk away from you, Aidan, and though it seemed like I had a choice, I never truly did. Since I was old enough to understand, I've known a destiny had been set for me and it wasn't fair of me to involve you in any of it. You just wouldn't let me let you go."

He snorted, and it was too close to the sarcastic sounds he would have made in human form. I had to laugh.

"You gave me something I'd never had. You gave me hope. You made me believe I was more than the words from some old woman, more than the power inside me everyone seems to want. You made me believe that someone could choose me for who I was, not what I was." He whined a soft, low sound that brought tears to my eyes and forced me to take our conversation in a different direction. There was so much he didn't know about me and being honest with him felt good.

Every so often, I glanced up to find him looking me directly in the eyes. Aidan listened raptly as I explained who I really was and the story of my life. I started at the beginning, with what I knew about my people and my parents. And when it came time to explain the night my mother died, he came to me, not allowing me to relive the memory alone. He lay down and pawed at me until I lay with him. He stretched out and I put my head on his chest, near his head. I could hear his heartbeat and I breathed him in. I stopped talking and just savored each inhale, trying to memorize the feeling. I wanted to pull him inside of me and keep him there for whenever I felt alone. I turned on my side and splayed one hand into the fur of his chest. He almost purred in response, a throaty sound reminding me of the way his voice would deepen before he kissed me.

I told him stories about Baleon and Micah and he would sometimes snort or growl, which told me he knew what I was saying. Finally, I just lay there with my eyes closed, letting the feel of our magic together become the only thing I knew. I could see my violet smoke, wispy and wafting, encircling his blue fire. They pushed into each other, becoming a color I couldn't name but knew was just as special as what we had.

I sighed as I both thanked and cursed my mind for giving me this gift. I worked hard to only show Micah the strong side of me. To take everything in stride. But I was terrified and had no idea what I was doing. I stayed in the fetal position, relishing in the feel of him around me for as long as my mind would allow. When I woke up, curled around a pillow, I could still smell citrus and woods. I swallowed down the tears I wouldn't allow and forced myself to sit up. It was a new day and another day closer to when the Queen would come home. I had work to do.

Chapter 11
Aidan

The caves weren't so bad. Or so I kept telling myself. They were dark and smelled like dirt and wet fur. They were small and cramped. But, they were a product of volcanic activity and helped hide the AniMages from the Queen and her Hunters, so it wasn't like I could complain. Bethany, Charlie, and I had been kept together, as we were the only ones who didn't really belong. Elias put us closer to the entrance, since Bethany didn't have the benefit of nocturnal vision like the rest of us.

I had given up trying to sleep hours ago, as my too-long legs jutted off the end of a twin mattress. Bethany was just across the small space they called our room and Charlie sat sentry between us, tall and stiff. His only movements were to turn his head left or right, looking at Bethany or me when we would jostle on our beds. I hadn't forgotten the Hunter referring to him as a Sentinel, but it didn't seem like something anyone else had guessed or understood, so for now, I was holding that question for another time.

I was frustrated. We had come to find Elias. To get his help, to go find Cole and Amelia and get them out of wherever the hell the psycho Queen had taken them. Bethany had continued to educate me on the Queen and I still couldn't wrap my mind around the stories. Or being one of the people the Queen hated. With my blue eyes and my shifting form, I was lumped in with them, and we were numero uno on her shit list. I had so many questions for Elias, yet he managed to answer none of them.

We had walked for a while, following Elias down the trail until we came to another clearing. Campfires were set up and AniMages were stationed around them in small groups. Some were shifted, some human, but they looked at us like we were the ones to be feared. Wide eyes and hushed whispers followed Bethany, Charlie, and me around the area. All except Dillon. He was perfectly content to talk Bethany's ear off. He talked about how cool it was to be an owl and how much Elias trusted him to scout the area. He puffed up his little man chest and declared, "I only have to get a little bigger before I can fight. But don't you worry, Miss Bethany, I can protect you." She nodded graciously and we both fought to hold back our smiles as our eyes connected. B assured Little Man he was all she needed and you'd have thought she handed him the moon.

I tried to take in as much of the scene as possible, without making it obvious I was scouting. I counted twenty-three AniMages, including Elias and Dillon, and noted Dillon as the only child I'd seen. Were the other kids hidden deeper in the caves behind us? The opening to the cave was no bigger than a doorway and surrounded by shrubbery. It was a pitch black hole and didn't feel terribly inviting. Bethany stood close to me, her fingers gripping Charlie's collar as she, too, scanned the crowd. She'd been here before and wasn't overly thrilled to be back. It wasn't until Elias gestured us to a small fire pit with food roasting on a spit that her stomach growled, breaking the strained silence. Elias laughed and I heard chuckles coming from around the other fires. I relaxed a little and led the way to the pit.

Elias piled plates high with roasted meat and canned vegetables, even tossing Charlie a bone to gnaw on. Though, every time I opened my mouth to ask a question, he'd start another story. I knew he was reading my mind and I was losing patience with being respectful. We were wasting time. But his people surrounded us and I couldn't guarantee Bethany's safety. I wasn't sure I could stop myself from shifting and I still had no memory when it came to what happened while I was changed. I was more afraid of the unknown than I was frustrated with Elias. And my power was reacting to all of the AniMages around me. Each of them was a distinct energy and it was driving my beast crazy.

I kept trying to push him down and keep my abilities to myself, but whatever was inside me was going full-bore, ping-ponging in my veins, pushing against my skin, and threatening to come out. Pressure built in my head and power gathered in my hands. A light blue mist enveloped my palms and I clenched my fists so tight, I could feel my short nails embedding themselves in my palms. I hadn't blown anything up since that day on the beach with Amelia and I thought that part of my change was over.

"Will you keep denying it, Aidan?" Elias asked. He was picking the meat from a chicken bone and looking up at me like a teacher asking a question when they already knew how you would answer.

"Denying what?" I answered, challenging him. Giving him exactly what he assumed he'd get.

"What you are. Why do you disregard what you feel? Why do you not allow it to fully merge into you? All you have to do is accept it. It really is that simple." Elias spoke softly but clearly. Bethany slid a little closer to me on the log and a guttural growl started deep in Charlie's throat. I turned to find us surrounded by every person…animal…AniMage. Men stood with their arms crossed, or holding the hands of their women. Some had shifted and approached in their native forms of big cats, wolves, or bears. I was instantly calculating how quickly I could grab Bethany and get the hell out of there when Dillon broke through the circle and ran to Bethany. He postured in front of the crowd, his small hands clenched in fists as he stood beside us and leaned toward Elias.

"Mr. Elias, sir, what is happening? Why is everyone doing this?" Dillon put more force than necessary behind his small voice. It broke and a few laughs came from the group, only fueling him more.

"These are our guests. We have rules." He looked around frantically, his tiny arms locked at his sides. "We don't treat guests like prisoners unless they really are prisoners and we are tricking them. Are they prisoners, Mr. Elias? Are we tricking them?"

I was impressed. Dillon wasn't backing down an inch. He stuck his chin out and refused to look away from Elias. I raised an eyebrow, remaining silent as Elias and I stayed locked on each other.

Elias chuckled and shook his head, breaking away to look down at Little Man in front of him. "No, Dillon. These are not prisoners and yes, they are our guests. Everyone has gathered around because they want to see whether Mr. Aidan is who we think he is. Do you know who we think he is, Dillon?"

Dillon grinned as he nodded so fast, he looked like a bobble-head. "I sure do. We think Mr. Aidan is the one. He is our King and her companion. He is the one who will set her free. He will help her stop the Queen so we don't have to hide anymore."

"And how do we know for sure, Dillon?" Elias kept up his game, suppressing a smile.

"Because we can all feel it. If Mr. Aidan told us to do something, we would have to obey. We would only feel that way if he were our King." Dillon turned to me, pride and hope shining in his eyes. I could only stare—my mouth open and mind blank. Bethany gasped and Charlie let out a thunderous string of barks. Cheering erupted from every angle and Elias could barely be heard over the sound.

"You, Aidan Montgomery, are the key to the prophecy. You are your father's son. You are our King and you are meant to lead us to victory."

KING? The word rang loudly in my mind and my reaction was completely out of my control.

The beast roared to life inside me, responding to the overwhelming onslaught of power, emotion, and shock. I had only seconds to leap from my seat and take off running. As I pushed off one foot, I heard the ripping of seams and a fur-covered paw was the next thing that landed.

I had no idea where I was when I woke up. I was flat on my back and it was pitch black. My body ached and all I heard were Dillion's words. His high-pitched pre-pubescent voice telling everyone I was a King. Something about a prophecy. That I would free *her*. *Her* had to be Amelia.

"Are you going to lie there all night? I'm really tired and want to go home." The voice from my head was suddenly in my ears. I squinted and barely made out the small, half-naked body sitting a few feet from me on a low branch.

"Don't you have parents? Shouldn't you be in bed or something, kid?" I pushed myself up to sitting and had to duck as something flew at my head. Gym shorts.

"I'm not a kid. And no, I don't have parents anymore. They died. Just put those on and come on." He huffed as he dug behind a tree and pulled out a shirt for himself. "We're close enough to walk. Mr. Elias said I should give you food and show you where to sleep. Come on."

Dillon didn't wait another second before tromping through the brush. I struggled against my pounding head as I yanked on the shorts and ran after him.

When he finally pointed to my "room," I was exhausted. I'd eaten a few protein bars he tossed my way and was dead on my feet. Bethany and Charlie were pacing the small space and she looked like she couldn't decide whether she wanted to punch me or hug me when I stumbled in.

"Where in the ever-loving-hell have you been? As if it isn't bad enough that I watched you *poof*," she snapped her fingers, "yourself right into a damn animal, then you go and leave me with the dog and all these…these…people!" She was trying not to yell and it was clear her southern manners wouldn't let her call them what she wanted to. But I was too tired to do this right now.

"Gotta sleep. Sorry. Will try not to do it again. Just…gotta sleep." I might have actually been sleeping before I climbed into bed and the last words were out. It didn't last long, though.

Just a few short hours later, I found myself covered with a blanket, wide awake. I tossed and turned a few times before giving up.

"Stay," I quietly commanded Charlie as I got out of bed. He eyed me and stood up. I considered grabbing his paw to see whether I could control our exchange from my end, but I wasn't ready for another adventure in a dog's mind. "I'll be fine. Just stay with her." He exhaled in a huff and sat back down, begrudgingly.

I went back out to the clearing and sat by a dwindling fire. I heard a few *hoots* and looked up to see two large owls with bright blue eyes circling above me, likely lookouts. Throwing some smaller logs on, I stared into the dancing flames and let my mind wander. Amelia filled my thoughts. I was worried about her. I had no idea what she was up against. I only had vague notions of what the Queen was like from stories I'd heard. Some Bethany had told me, but others were just there. I was certain the Queen wasn't someone I wanted Amelia left with for long. And then came the question, who was I? And how did Elias know my parents' names so quickly? So easily?

"You are the spitting image of your father."

I jumped, so lost in my thoughts I hadn't heard him approach. I chastised myself for letting my guard down.

"Don't. Don't worry about it. It's been a big day." Elias spoke quietly as he came around me and sat across the fire. "You have questions. I know you do. I just didn't want to answer them for the group. Go ahead." He waved a hand at me as he sat back.

"Are you going to stay out of my head? If you know how to get in, you should know how to stay the hell out." Anger I hadn't really expected coated my words. Threats I didn't want to make stiffened my posture.

He held up both hands. "That's fair. I typically only use my gifts when necessary. I needed to know your intentions and I've gathered what I need, so I will indeed stay out of your head. And we'll need to talk later about how you learn to feel and defend such threats."

I nodded slowly and relaxed back onto the log. "My parents. How do you know them?"

A sad smile haunted his face. "I have known your parents since I was a child. Zendrick was my best friend and Kayla was the only woman he ever loved—from about four years old," he said, chuckling as he shook his head. "I had no idea they had even had you. They must have ran as soon as they found out. Your father was one of Julia's top targets and he would have done anything to protect your mother, and clearly, you."

"Why? I know she hates AniMages, but why was my father a target?" There were so many pieces of the puzzle missing.

Elias looked away from me, staring into the dark. "Your father led the AniMages and was part of the royal council. The Elders consulted with the King, Julia's father, and it was his job to put their words to action. The Elders were something we all believed in. They saw the future, they helped us assimilate as more humans entered our lands over the years...they even blessed our children. Julia never saw them that way, though. From her teen years until she was finally Queen, she believed the Elders should work for her and not the other way around." He stopped and slowly shook his head back and forth.

"The night before the Queen's birthday celebration and coronation, your father found out there was a plot to overthrow the royal family by one of the Hunters. The perpetrator's name was

Cane and he was a charmer, also belonging to a prominent family. He knew how to ensure everyone loved him, but he was a snake. You father confronted him and Cane went crazy." Elias's lips were pinched in tight line, his jaw locked. The cords of his neck stood out like ropes around a barrel.

"Cane was a very skilled and highly ranked Hunter. What your father did wasn't easy, but he was a fighter himself. Cane was young and cocky. He forgot the basic rule of fighting." Elias paused, a pleased look coming over him. "You're not out of the fight unless you're dead. And your father wasn't dead. When the fight was over, your father was found standing over Cane's body. Cane's brother was the one to find your father, and he took that information right to the Queen.

"Almost overnight, the Queen changed. She didn't just believe things should be different, she was hell-bent on making it happen. She became vengeful and hated the AniMages. The Queen convinced both the Hunters and Mages that AniMages should be eradicated. She told them our magic and our blood was polluting the Immortal gene pool. But then she surprised everyone when she went after the Elders, instead.

She tortured AniMages, and sometimes even Mages, trying to find anyone with Elder blood running in their veins.

"Some of us believed she and Cane had a relationship, but no one could prove it, and it wouldn't have mattered if they had. The Queen convinced the Hunters to fight for her and began targeting the AniMages, flushing us out of our homelands. Your parents were among the first to leave, and now I understand why. They left to save you. But at the time, a lot people were upset, thinking they had abandoned us. I can only imagine how hard that had to be for them. The rest of us tried to fight, but we were always outnumbered. Our wives and our children were dying around us. We've struggled to grow our numbers since. And yet, during all of this, the Queen had the Prince. No one even knew she was pregnant, which only furthered our intrigue around Cane. She kept the Prince hidden away and surrounded by Hunters his whole life, except when she apparently let him run off to college."

Elias scowled and I found my face matching his as I thought about Micah. What I wouldn't give for a few rounds of bare fists with that guy.

Elias grimaced, but then continued. "Those who could get away went as far as their feet or wings could take them. Many of them found their way to North America. There's so much space here and it was easy to blend in when we wanted to, yet live in places where we could shift and be ourselves when we needed to."

And this prophecy everyone talks about?" I asked.

"The Elders told Julia one of their own would stop her, with your help. At least, we believe it's you," he said.

I sat back and absorbed Elias's statement. There was so much information there, but my mind could only focus on one thing.

"It wasn't a burglary, was it?" I asked, mostly to myself. Elias quirked a brow and I explained what I knew of my parents death and the supposed robbery of our home, leaving them dead but me alive.

"I would guess not. What I don't understand is if your parents were killed, why weren't you?" Elias rubbed a hand over his jaw and I could see his wheels spinning just as quickly as my own. Neither of us spoke for a few minutes.

"I can feel how conflicted you are, Aidan. Why don't you tell me what it is you want to know?"

I appreciated Elias allowing me to process all of this the way I needed to.

"Tell me more about my parents and the AniMages," I said.

He nodded. "The AniMages had their own figurehead. A family that governed and essentially ruled our people, which were the Montgomerys. Your father was our leader. He often went to the palace and worked directly with the royal family on any issues that arose. And your mother was also an AniMage. She was beautiful, kind, and had a wicked sense of humor." Elias stopped talking and a smirk developed as he stared off in the distance.

I had to laugh at his expression. I wished I could reach into his mind and steal his memories of her, the way Charlie had shown me his stories. I couldn't even picture her anymore. The only thing I still had was the melody of her song and the sound of her voice.

"You grew up together? You knew them well?" My voice was choked with emotion I hadn't allowed for years. I had stopped asking questions about my parents by the time I was five years old. It was clear no one knew them, or me, and it only made my foster families uncomfortable.

"I did. I knew them very well. Your father was my best friend. We grew up together. Where you found one of us, the other wasn't far. Your mother was always part of our pack. Growing up, a group of us scoured the woods together and got into more trouble than we should have. But we took care of each other. Which is just one part of why I'm sitting here now. Our people need you, but your father was like a brother to me. I want to help you.

"Now, what about you, Aidan? How did you realize you were an AniMage?" Elias asked.

I shrugged. "All I know is one day, I couldn't do any of this, and the next, I could. I've always felt like something was off, but I haven't been turning into a wolf my whole life...that one was quite a shock. Growing up, I always had a lot of energy and a lot of anger. I always knew when I was with a bad family or when I needed to run. But, then I met Amelia and she made me feel...right. I was drawn to her, to the peace she brought me. Like...she was the light to the darkness I was always fighting. But then things just kept getting more weird..." I trailed off, my rambling seeming incoherent to even me. Elias let me stew in my own thoughts once again.

"Can you explain how Amelia fits into all of this? I need to understand how I could possibly be this prophecy."

"You aren't a prophecy yourself, but we believe you are part of the prophecy coming true. Unfortunately, though, the details aren't as clear as we'd like. We know Julia captured and tortured Lavignia, an Elder we considered a seer, or someone who could see the future. As we have heard the story, the Queen wanted to know when she would die and how. Lavignia prophesied there would be just one Elder left, and she belonged to the ones who got away, which we believed to mean her parents also ran. Lavignia said the five families would merge inside her and only a man who was a King and companion could tame the wild and set her free. We have made guesses as to what it all means, but we know you are our rightful King—the King of the AniMages. We are also certain Amelia is an Elder. So..." Elias trailed off and we sat in silence.

A King. I was a King. Of people who turn into animals. I turned into an animal.

"You've got to be shitting me," I muttered to myself.

Elias laughed. "I wish I was, Aidan. But you are the one and we don't have time to lose. The question is, are you ready and willing to be the man we need you to be? The man she needs you to be? I will be there with you every step of the way."

I looked over at Elias and his solemn expression. It was clear he wasn't going to try to convince me. What he didn't understand was he didn't have to.

Everything about being an AniMage felt right. For years, I'd always known when I was walking into an abusive home, or when the kids at school were coming for me. I'd always trusted my sixth sense to tell me when I was making the right choice. It had led me to Amelia and it had led me here. Believing I was their King...that was a battle for another day. Forcing my mind back to the facts of why I was here to begin with, I cleared my throat and met his gaze.

"I came here to find out who I was and how you could help me save Amelia. Nothing has changed. Now I know who I am and I know you'll help me. Where do we start?"

Chapter 12
Amelia

I had spent more hours than I wanted to count over the past few days surrounded by books Micah wouldn't let me touch, claiming we had to wait for this mysterious Tragar to get back because he would direct us to the right places. Today was that day. I was antsy and kept opening my door to see whether Micah had opened his, signaling he was up and we would go to the library soon. After the third time, Baleon finally turned to me, and said, "Would you like me to wake him?"

It actually startled me a little. "Well, well, it's good to know you can actually see me!" I smiled and the corners of his lips quirked the tiniest bit before his face resumed its standard blank look. He stared down at me, waiting for an answer, and I laughed. "Yes, please, bodyguard of mine. Wake your master and tell him to get his butt over here."

I closed the door, but listened for Baleon's footsteps across the marble floor and his knock on Micah's door. Micah's sleepy voice followed and he hollered, "I'm coming, you slave driver. Did Bethany teach you to wake up this bloody early?"

I wrenched the door open at the mention of her name. It was the first time he had spoken of her. I had wanted so badly to bring her up, but we'd been getting along and I needed Micah's help. Micah stood across the hallway from me, looking just as surprised by his own outburst. His eyes were wide as he gripped his door with white knuckles. Baleon stood silently, his eyes slowly moving back and forth between us.

"Do you miss her, too?" I asked. "Just tell me, Micah, because I miss her so much and I don't want to believe you hurt her and don't feel something." My chest tightened as I watched him. He took a few shallow breaths before speaking quietly.

"Of course I miss her, Amelia. She is the only person who ever knew me as simply Micah. I wasn't the bastard Prince hidden behind Hunters or the subject of a prophecy. I wasn't Mikail. I was Micah and she wanted to be with me anyway." He started to shut the door, only pausing to say, "Be ready in ten minutes."

As he closed the door and I heard the click of the lock, I couldn't move except to whisper, "That's what she was to me, too." I looked up to find a sympathy I hadn't expected in Baleon's eyes. "Neither of us chose this. We don't want it."

"And yet, you are the only ones who can make it right," he replied as he resumed his post and turned his back on me.

It wasn't two seconds past ten minutes and Micah was rapping on my door. I opened it, but neither of us spoke. He turned and led me to the library with Baleon just behind us. We walked beside each other, understanding that the silence between us was our acknowledgment of the completely screwed up situation we had both been dropped into.

Instead, I focused on the paintings on the walls. The landscapes were so varied...everything from lush green mountains to rolling hills dotted with trees, to cliffs covered with vegetation jutting out into the ocean. It was gorgeous and I wanted to reach out and touch them. To run my fingers over the canvas and see what it would feel like to be close to my real home. I wondered whether anyone still lived on the grounds of the main castle, or if it was a ghost town, a long-abandoned relic.

As we walked into the library, I heard the mutterings of someone as loud *thuds* sounded, over and over again. A smile overtook Micah's face as his steps quickened, rushing to the man who had to be Tragar. His name had led me to believe Tragar would be another towering man. Instead, I found a slight man wearing robes two sizes too big. He had a cap of silver hair and a long beard. His fingertips were stained black and he scowled as he flipped pages at an insane speed, closing the book cover in seconds and tossing it on the ground.

"You're back! Welcome home, Tragar!" Micah approached him and Tragar finally looked up, a smile overtaking his face, transforming him from the grumpy little man to looking like a beaming grandfather.

"Mikail, my boy, there you are!" He hugged Micah and his eyes found me over Micah's shoulder. "And you've brought her to meet old Tragar, have you? Come on, dear, don't be shy. I'm the least likely to get salty with you around here." He laughed as he shot Baleon a look. Bale shook his head.

I approached him cautiously. Unsure of what I was supposed to do, I stuck out my hand and introduced myself. Tragar surprised me again as he grabbed my hand and yanked me in for a hug. "You have no idea how long I've waited for you, little one. Your mother told me you would come, and here you are."

He smelled like books. Like paper and ink. And as he spoke of my mother, goose bumps rose across my skin and my eyes filled with tears.

"There, there. I'm here to help you. To help you both. And I have stories you will both need and want." I sniffled and swallowed down the tears, nodding into his shoulder.

Tragar stepped back and moved to the stack of books in front of him. "Hunter, shut that door. Keep those demons out of here. We have work to do!" He threw a hand in the air and as his robe fell back on his arm, I noticed the symbols tattooed on his skin matched those on my cuff. I pulled at my sleeve, even though I knew the cuff was hidden.

Baleon pulled the door shut and Tragar resumed his muttering, "Hid the damn thing from myself, that's what I did. Knew this day was coming. Can't believe I lost Liana's journal."

"Her what? My mother's what?" I exclaimed.

"Journal, your mother's journal." He didn't even look up as he tossed another book onto the floor. "All of the Elders on the council kept one and hers was the only one I was able to preserve after…" His voice trailed off and Micah piped in next to me.

"After my mother lost it? You can just say it, Tragar."

"No need to be indelicate, Mikail. I taught you better than that. Your mother is simply…misguided."

Micah harrumphed a little. "How can we help? Where should we look?" he asked.

Tragar pointed to stacks totaling in the hundreds. "I pulled every book it made sense for me to hide it in, which, unfortunately, is many.

Feel free to start going through them. I had to unbind the pages, so you are looking for loose pages. I believe I spread them out over a few volumes." He turned to the next book, muttering again, "Just damn it if I can remember which one. I'm getting too old for this."

Micah and I stepped around Tragar and sat down in the stacks of books across from each other.

"How old is he?" I whispered as I reached for the book on the top of the stack closest to me.

"Hundreds of years old," Micah replied. "He's been the librarian and historian for as long as anyone can remember. It's the interesting thing about us. We're called Immortals, and we can live forever, but we can also be killed. I'm guessing this is basic information no one gave you, so stop me if you've heard it, but we age slowly and it takes hundreds of years for us to look the age of a seventy-year-old human. Our bodies will never give out on us so long as we have our magic. But, if attacked by another Immortal, their power has the ability to eradicate our own. Once that happens, our bodies can no longer sustain us."

My hand had stopped in mid-air as Micah spoke. The whole Immortal thing hadn't made a lot of sense to me considering it sounded like people were dying constantly, but this explanation brought it all together. Our power was a faucet constantly turned on. As long as it ran, we lived. But if it turned off, we were done.

As my hand finally came down on the book and my fingertips pressed into the binding, I jolted. The response I'd felt from my magic during our first trip to the library was back. A smile spread across my face as I turned to Micah. "I've got this. I can find these. Help me! Turn them on their sides so I can get to them easily."

I was scrambling to get up and Micah was staring at me confused. Tragar also looked up from his position, his eyes questioning. "My power, it recognizes my mother's. When I was in here the first day, I was touching the books and I was drawn to some of them. I felt it as soon as I touched them, but I had no idea what it meant. I can find the pages faster!"

I walked up to a stack of books on a table, looked back at both men, and then slowly ran my fingers over each spine, top to bottom. Nothing. I grimaced and heard a snort come from one of them. I moved to the next set and again, nothing. Frustrated, I dropped to my knees and ran my fingers over a stack on the floor. Finally, one at the very bottom sent my Keeper into a frenzy.

"Yes! Here!" I pushed the top of the stack off the book I needed and opened it, shaking the cover and giggling as two pages fell to the floor. One of them fell face up and my smile faltered as I took in my mother's gorgeous cursive handwriting. I was frozen, holding the book in the air as I stared at letters not forming words in my head. Micah came up beside me and gently took the book from my shaking hands.

"Are you going to pick it up?" he asked softly. I didn't move except to shift my eyes to his. Panic twisted my insides and I fought the instinct to run. Here I was, inches away from knowing my mother's innermost thoughts, and I couldn't reach out to pick up the pages.

"Do you want me to?" he asked, reaching a hand toward the pages.

My mind snapped back to attention and I lunged for them. "No! I have to. I have to do this." I stopped short of actually picking the pages up and looked back to Tragar.

"Do you know how many of these there are? How will we know what order they go in?"

"There are a few hundred. This is the journal she kept when her betrothal was announced. She spent a great deal of time in the castle library during those weeks before she ran away with Nathaniel. And the pages are numbered. Before I hid them, I did that myself."

I looked down and found I was staring at page thirty-two. "Then we will find them all. I will find them all and then read them. Not yet."

"Are you sure, Amelia? This is your mother's journal, don't you—"

I cut Micah off. "No. Not yet. I want it all. I need to understand it all. I'm...I'm..." I stumbled, trying to find the right way to explain it. I was afraid of what I would find in these pages. I wanted to find the mother I had always hoped for. The one I had heard about from Cole. But, nothing in my life had turned out as I expected and I had no idea what would lie within those pages.

"It's okay, Amelia. I understand. Let's find them all, then." He pulled me to my feet and then reached back down to pick up the pages, looking up at me for confirmation before he actually touched them. I nodded, a lump in my throat as the Keeper pushed at me, wanting me to take them, to not let him near my mother's innermost thoughts and fears. But, if I had any chance at all, I needed all the help I could get.

It didn't take as long as we expected. My Keeper was on the ball. As Tragar and Micah worked to line up the books, I walked along, my finger grazing each spine until I would feel the power spike, pull the book from the stack, and hand it to Micah. He would find the pages and hand them to Tragar, who put them in numerical order. In a matter of hours, I was sitting in a chair by the fire, a stack of pages in my hand I still didn't feel ready to read.

Micah had sent Bale to bring us lunch and he and Tragar were in the next room talking. They had left me to do this alone. It was both what I needed and the last thing I wanted. I wished Aidan were here. He was always so strong and sure. He didn't let me waffle and question. He just made decisions and acted. He forced me to see past the emotion and questions and made me find the truth. What would he have said to me right now?

He would have asked me why I wanted these pages.

Because I want to know my mother. And I believe these pages will tell me more about her and why I'm here.

And why do they scare you? I heard his voice in my head, asking me the question. He never wasted a word.

What if she's like so many others and not what she seems? What if this Keeper isn't something I can ever control? What if she wrote down what was going to happen to me in here and I don't like it?

Can you change any of it? It was his favorite question. I would drive him crazy with "what ifs" during our conversations and he would always end them by asking me if I could do anything about it. I pretty much never could. And now, I wouldn't be able to.

So, instead of arguing with myself, I flipped over the first page.

I'm hiding. I know it and Tragar knows it. But he allows me to hide here. They've told me I must marry. They say it will help bring our people further together as he is a Hunter and Elders on the council are required to mix magic to preserve the races. But no matter how necessary they say it is, I do not love him. I have loved Nathaniel for as long as I can remember. My heart has been his since we were children. I don't care if he is more Mage than anything else. But, alas, I am the only one who doesn't.

The visions have been coming stronger lately. I come to the castle library because I know Tragar will help me when they hit, and he will not tell Julia's father or the Elders. The scenes are clearer than they've ever been and I worry for what's to come. I see things that have sent me into the stacks, looking for explanations I cannot find.

Homes will burn. People will die. The races will suffer. I can't see why yet. I can't find the catalyst. But I know my time will come. I will have to make choices I don't want to make and the time will come for me to make the decision that can either save us all, or seal our fate.

I flipped to the next page, unable to stop myself.

Tragar has been helping me to understand where I come from. I have been drawn to the history of the Elders and our origins as an Immortal people. I cannot stop devouring the texts from our beginnings. They are so detailed in places and vague in others. Why can nothing ever be as easy as it should be?

I stopped, a small laugh erupting. It sounded like something I would have said. Or, had been saying, a lot lately.

I believe whole-heartedly in my sisters. I know I have the power and am expected to take my place on the Elder council to represent our family. I know the women I will join have all come to the council for specific reasons. But why do we even exist? Why do the people need us at all? Julia has been trying to get into our council meetings, she wants to ask these questions. I can feel the frustration she holds toward us and I can't blame her, but there must be a larger reason we're here. She cannot be right. She believes we have become unnecessary and I cannot believe that to be true. I only wish I were officially part of the council so they would share the truth with me.

The date draws nearer. I know I only have a short time left before everything will change. I only hope I can find the answers we need.

"Amelia," Micah interrupted. "I'm sorry, but we must get back. We still need to work with your power today and Bale tells me the other Hunters are questioning us being in here with Tragar. They've never been fans of his, nor he of them, so we must go."

"Can I take this with me?" I clutched the pages. After being inside my mother's head, the last thing I wanted was to leave them here.

Micah shook his head. "Unfortunately, no. We can't trust they will be safe in your room. At least here, we know Tragar will hide them and they will be here when we return." Micah took the pages from me and I crossed my arms across my chest, feeling a deep loneliness taking root. I had felt her with me and now I had to walk away. Part of me wanted to grab the pages and make a run for it, but I knew Bale would have me in an instant and then I couldn't guarantee they would give them back to me at all.

Tragar came up beside me as Micah handed him my most treasured possession. "Don't worry, little one, your mother has always been one of my favorite people. I will guard her secrets with my life. If you ever want them, you will find them here." He showed me the cover of a book bearing only a symbol. A circle around four interlocking loops. I'd seen that symbol before and was sure it was on my cuff.

"What does it mean?" I questioned.

"It is the symbol of the Elders. We may as well hide her in plain sight, don't you think?" He chuckled and I couldn't help but smile in return.

Chapter 13
Aidan

I spent the next several days going through Elias's version of bootcamp. There were moments he couldn't believe what I could do—uprooting trees, taking on multiple guys at once, and using MMA training to make my attacks even more targeted—and other moments when he couldn't believe what I didn't understand. One of the most shocking to him was my inability to remember my time as a wolf.

"You truly remember nothing?" he asked for at least the fifth time.

"Yes, Elias. Nothing." I was getting frustrated. I was tired from all the energy I'd expended figuring out my power allowed me to shoot magic bursts, levitate objects, and move in complete silence without disturbing anything. My beast was getting restless and I hoped a shift wouldn't come out of nowhere again.

"Dillon! DILLON!" Elias hollered the young boy's name and I heard him reply, "COMING, SIR!" Soon he was dragging poor Bethany across the clearing. She was hunched over, trying to keep up with him while he wouldn't let go of her hand. "I'm coming, sir. We'll be right there!" he yelled across, waving at us as he pulled on Bethany, urging her to move faster. Charlie came trotting out behind them, his giant paws easily eating up the ground.

"Why does he call you sir and me Mr. Aidan?" I asked. We both watched them, trying not to laugh as Bethany attempted to slow Dillon down. "Sweetie, you've got to calm down. They are *right there*. There's no fire. Goodness gracious."

Elias spoke quietly. "His parents died when he was young—maybe three years old. I found him hiding in a tree and it took me an hour to convince him I wouldn't hurt him. I had to change into three different animals to prove I wasn't a Hunter in disguise. Finally, after he told me he could shift into an owl, I did the same and landed on the branch beside him. We sat up there for another hour while he told me all about his parents. It wasn't until after his story he told me his name. I told him he could call me Elias and he said, 'My momma told me to always respect my elders. I will call you Mr. Elias so she stays proud of me.' And he's done it with everyone he's ever met. As I'm sure you've noticed, Dillon is the only child with us. He's the only child we know of. Though, there are AniMages spread across the globe, so there could likely be others. He's something special. And, his powers allow him to sense the animal side of you more clearly than the rest of us."

It was clear Elias cared for Dillon and so did the other AniMages. People yelled hello as he passed them and he always replied with a chipper, "Hello to you, too!" and a wave.

As he and Bethany finally reached us, Dillon postured up and stood with his hands locked behind him. "Good afternoon, sir. What can I do for you?"

Elias reached down and ruffled Dillon's hair, a move garnering the first real scowl I'd seen since he led me home after my last shift. "Dillon, when you were out with Mr. Aidan, could you talk to him?"

He shook his head quickly. "No, sir, I couldn't. I tried and tried but something wouldn't let me in. I had to follow him around the whole stinkin' forest, waiting for him to come back to himself." He lowered his voice and leaned into Elias. "Sir, are you sure he's the one?" I caught a sideways look and couldn't decide whether I wanted to laugh at the kid questioning my manhood or jump on his side of the argument.

"He just needs a little time. What do you say we all go out running tonight? We'll get this sorted out and you can be our eyes in the sky?"

Dillon pumped a fist in the air. "Heck, yes! I mean, of course, sir." He looked back at Bethany and it reaffirmed a lot of the "yes, sir…no, sir" was for her benefit.

"Alright, then. Meet us after dinner," Elias said. Dillon nodded and took off. He got about four running steps before he turned back. "Goodbye, Miss Bethany. I'll see you soon." His ears burned red as he took off.

He wasn't ten feet away before she was in our faces. "Do either of you know how utterly exhausting it is to be relegated to hanging out with ten-year-olds and dogs? Miss Bethany this and Miss Bethany that. Let's play ball, or Frisbee, or I'll just head-butt you until you do. I'm going to drag you here and there to meet people or smell every inch of the forest floor. All I want is a little quiet and some coffee. Speaking of, how much longer are we staying? I've got a perfectly good bed not far from here and my kitchen is stocked with the essentials. Also, I would like to make sure my family knows I'm alive and that I haven't been fired. It's only been a few days, but I'm someone people notice and they are gonna notice my absence."

She flashed a huge smile. "Bless your heart, Elias, you've been entirely hospitable," and then she turned to me with a scowl, "But, truly…" The chick stance was back and her arms were crossed. "I don't do camping. This is *barely* above camping."

I started to speak, but Elias beat me to it.

"Do you completely understand the predicament you are in, Miss Jackson?" The sharpness in his tone made us both recoil a little. "I understand you have grown comfortable with the AniMages, but do you remember what happened when you encountered the Hunters?

Do you realize you are likely on their watch list? And as close as you are to Amelia, they will have the same idea we did, except not be such gracious hosts."

Bethany paled, swallowed, and then paled further. "Can't you keep me away from them?"

"No, I can't," he spat, and I could feel the tension building around us. Charlie must have, too, because he stepped up next to Bethany as Elias continued. "Because I don't have the resources or the manpower to spare any of my people just so you can sleep in your bed and have coffee. I can send someone for your cell phone, but outside of that, your life is only as important as you make it. Right now, your only value is they want you more than we do and I refuse to give those bastards anything they want."

"Are you telling me I'm a prisoner, Elias?" She tried to stand tall, to regain some control over the conversation, but I could see her hands shaking as she clenched her fists.

I stepped between them and put out my hands. "Come on. We don't need to do this. Bethany, of course you aren't a prisoner. But I told you what I am to them and what that can mean for Amelia. You've got to work with me here. There's something I'm missing. Something I'm not doing that I need to. I can feel it. I'm so close, but...I just can't find it yet."

I was surprised to hear Charlie bark. He so rarely did, I jumped and turned to him. "Quiet down, Charlie." Which only set him off further. His deep *woofs* were nonstop and he slammed his head into my thigh. "Come on, dog. Can't you see we're in the middle of something here?"

I stooped down to get eye level with him and with a satisfied snort, he lifted his paw and dropped it onto the exposed flesh above my knee. This time, I wasn't falling into his head, I was hearing him. I was staring into a dog's eyes and he was talking to me.

He's told you, you have to embrace it.

"Embrace what? What do you mean?" I barely registered the fact that Bethany and Elias were staring open-mouthed at me as I spoke out loud to Charlie.

The beast inside you. You can't control him, you have to let him control you. He won't be a beast then, he'll be you.

"But how?"

Let him tell you.

166

I was about to ask who when I looked in the direction Charlie had turned. Dillon was standing in the tree line. I didn't hesitate and took off toward him. "Dillon, I need your help," I said loudly as I approached.

"Uh, sure, Mr. Aidan. How can I help you?" Dillon looked around me and didn't seem thrilled at the bewildered looks on Elias and Bethany's face.

"Can you talk to your owl?" I wasn't sure what I was asking.

Dillon cocked his head. "That would be weird. Then I would be talking to myself." I immediately felt like an idiot.

He smiled a small smile at my bewildered expression. "But you have to let it talk to you. That's the weirder part."

"What do you mean?" I was completely confused.

"My owl tells me things. He tells me when Hunters are coming close and when people are good or bad. He makes sure I'm safe. He never uses words, but he tells me. That's why I don't talk to him, because he wouldn't understand. I just listen." Dillon looked up at me with wise eyes I was sure had seen too much after Elias's story.

"My owl should be able to hear your wolf, but he can't."

"What does your owl say about me?" I asked.

He shrugged. "Your wolf wants out—bad. He's been howling a long time and you don't hear him. Someone made it so you can't hear him."

One of the other AniMages yelled for him and Dillon took off around me. "Gotta go. See you, Mr. Aidan!"

"See you, Dillon," I muttered, wondering why my best, and most confusing, advice so far had come from a dog and a kid.

Bethany stomped around our small room. She didn't speak, but she stomped. And she threw things into piles. And she exhaled loudly. I was a guy, but I wasn't an idiot.

"B, talk to me." Her head snapped in my direction.

"About what? What do you want to talk about, Aidan? How we've been here for days and nothing has changed? How you leave me with Charlie and Dillon all day? How I spend a majority of the day getting glared at by the animals and listening to people like Melinda make fun of me for being 'just a human' every time I walk past? We aren't any closer to finding Amelia, which is why we came here to start with, and you have no idea where Cole is. The last time we saw his place, it was destroyed and you know Hunters took him. What the hell are we doing?"

I wanted to argue, but she was right. "I don't know, I'm missing something. They want me to be some kind of leader and I have no idea how. It feels right, like this is where I belong, but I have no idea how to unlock whatever is inside of me. Dillon told me someone made it so I can't hear my wolf. What the hell does that even mean?"

Bethany stood up and turned back toward me. "He said someone made it so you can't hear your wolf?" She spoke slowly, a smile tugging at her lips.

"Yeah, what the hell, right?" I scratched the back of my head and she laughed, smacking my arm as she walked past.

"We need to find Elias. I think I know what's wrong with you."

Of course. It took a dog, a kid, and a chick to get me where I needed to go. I tossed my hands in the air and rolled my eyes at the empty room.

When I got back outside, I found Bethany and Elias in the middle of a very animated discussion. Well, at least she was. Her arms were flying around in wide gestures and she was talking nonstop. Elias simply stood back with his head cocked to one side, giving her small nods of encouragement. When I finally got within range to hear the steady stream of words she was spouting, I heard, "I'm telling you, Elias, it's the same thing. It's got to be. Those Hunters did something similar to Amelia's dad. He's *still* that way. I'll just bet they did it to Aidan, too. How's that for adding value?" All I could see was her back, but I was sure her signature satisfied smile was in place.

Elias looked over her shoulder at me, his eyebrows drawn together as he rubbed a hand over his jaw. "Feisty one, eh?"

I snorted my agreement. "I don't really get what she's talking about, though. And if a Hunter did this, who the heck is going to get rid of it?"

Elias was still rubbing his hand back and forth, clearly not listening and lost in his own train of thought. "Yo, Elias. You're the only guy with possible answers here." I snapped my fingers in front of his face and he jolted.

"Sorry. I was just thinking—"

"You need to find Will." A voice I'd never forget interrupted him and Melinda stepped around the corner. She'd made herself somewhat scarce up to this point, but now she stood not two feet from me in her traditional outfit of skintight everything. While I could appreciate her from the neck down, I couldn't look into her eyes for long. Every time she'd caught me from across the grounds, she looked like she was not only undressing me, but plotting her next move. And her perfect smile was too stretched, too fake.

I was hoping she'd stay near Elias, but she strutted herself right into my space and traced her finger across my chest. "It's about time we found the right man for the job, sugar. Had I known whom I was playing with, I wouldn't have been so rough. Unless…that's how you like it." Her voice was low, blatant in words and tone.

"Oh, come off it," Bethany broke in, her condescension slicing through Melinda's wiles. "Do you actually think you stand a chance? You're way out of your league, and a tramp. He loves Amelia. They are freaking destined for each other. Back off."

Bethany's outburst shocked everyone but Melinda, whose eyes narrowed, but her smile never faltered. She chucked me under the chin with that same finger, saying, "You get tired of waiting around for her, you know where to find me."

Melinda turned to glare at Bethany. "At least I wasn't used up and left behind," she sneered.

Bethany took a step toward Melinda just as Elias stepped between them. "Enough. Both of you. Melinda, take it somewhere else. He's not a toy, he's your Alpha, and he deserves respect." Elias gestured Melinda away as I pulled Bethany back next to me.

Melinda's eyes lit up in a nauseating way. "Oh, I respect him, Elias. I just don't think he needs some half-possessed Elder to fulfill his potential."

"This is your last warning, Melinda," Elias growled through clenched teeth. His eyes were glowing and he suddenly took up all of the space in the vicinity. His body hadn't changed size, but the air around us expanded, making it feel like he was everywhere at once.

Melinda shrunk, bowing slightly. "Yes, sir." Without another look at us, she walked away.

Bethany and I looked at each other through sideways glances, neither of us comfortable with looking toward Elias. I felt the moment he was back to normal and he didn't waste time. He dragged his hands back through his hair and said, "She's actually right. We need to find Will and we better do it fast. He's the only one who could help you and you're no good to us, Amelia, or yourself, if you can't access your full range of power. We'll shift tonight and head toward his place. He's not fond of visitors, but he'll have to get over it."

"Who's Will?" we asked simultaneously. I had been itching to ask since Melinda brought him up and Elias had finally taken a breath that gave me the opening. Bethany turned to me with a small smile, and tipped her head, signaling me to continue. "You keep talking about Will, but why do we need him?"

"You know how I can hear your thoughts and that's not something every AniMage can do? We each have a unique ability, and Will's is removing magic from people that doesn't belong. Specifically, he can break Hunter bonds, which sounds like your problem."

Elias turned to Bethany, who I could feel was still simmering with adrenaline. "We might be gone a few days. Would you prefer to stay here, or we can take you back to your apartment with Charlie and a few guards?"

Her adrenaline turned to irritation. "Just take the lowly human back to her apartment so she can resume her pathetically boring life. And I don't need guards, I have Charlie." She didn't wait for a response, just called out for Charlie and strode away.

"You can't worry about her." Elias's voice broke my train of thought and brought my eyes back to him. "I'm sorry she doesn't feel included, but she doesn't understand the enormity of what we're up against. This isn't fun and games, Aidan. This is a war we're prepping for."

"What do I need to do?" I knew I should have felt scared, or at least worried, but all that mattered was finding Amelia. Every day I didn't get to her was another day I had no idea what she was going through. If anything happened to her that I could have prevented, I'd never forgive myself.

Chapter 14
Amelia

Micah was supposed to be taking me to the library. I wanted more time with my mother's journals and I was getting antsy waiting for him. I opened my door to find Baleon standing directly in my path, his black leathered frame blocking me from going anywhere. I tapped him on the shoulder a few times, and said, "Excuse me, coming through. Places to be. You know, there's this Prince who's waiting for me in the library?"

I was pretty sure he knew I was lying, yet he stepped to the side anyway. "After you," he said. I wondered if this was some kind of test, but ultimately didn't care. I needed movement. I needed to do *something*.

Unable to resist the opportunity, I brought both hands to my chest in faux shock. "He speaks! And to a lowly prisoner! I can't believe it."

Baleon's eyes narrowed, but I saw the glitter of amusement he tried to squash. Without another word, he pulled the door closed and started toward the library.

"You know, Bale, I'm on to your game. You want to talk to me. I can see it. I bet you and Micah talk all the time. I'm not so different. Want to know some things about me?" I didn't wait for him to answer, I just continued talking to his back while he walked in front of me. I didn't have a real plan, but I had to start somewhere.

"You know what I miss most right now, Bale? I miss music. I miss all my favorite songs. The ones I'd dance and sing to in the kitchen and blare on bad days. Do you like music? I'm sure you do. Everybody likes music. My brother always liked rap. Eminem. Dr. Dre. All that noise. Bethany...she likes pop and country. She really likes old country. Dolly Parton and Merle Haggard. Johnny Cash. You know, the man in black? You should know who he is, for obvious reasons. She loves it all. You'd love B, Bale. I mean, you both have the same initial, she'd fill all the empty space you leave, and really, everyone likes her. It's pretty impossible not to."

"What is it you find so appealing about humans and their trappings? It's painful to listen to." Rhi's voice interrupted my rambling and I almost tripped in surprise. Baleon spun around and shoved me behind him before Rhi had finished speaking.

He held me with one hand and had me pressed into the wall.

"What do you want, Rhi?" he asked.

Rhi took easy steps toward us, smirking. "I only aim to understand the almighty prophesied one. What's it to you, old man?" It was the least formal I had ever heard Rhi and I was puzzled by his insult. Though, it was basically impossible to guess an Immortal's age, so I shouldn't have been surprised.

"She's my charge, Rhi. The Prince has asked me to accompany her *safely*, and I shall." Baleon's fingers dug into my arm tighter. I was sure he knew I was planning to move out from behind him. I had a few choice words of my own for Rhi.

Rhi raised his hand and orange fire erupted in his palm. He tossed the ball of magic in the air, his head cocked, clearly challenging Baleon.

"I do not need your parlor tricks, Rhi. I have the power our people were meant to have, not whatever she has done to you now." The disgust Bale had for Rhi was unexpected.

Rhi's smirk disappeared and the cold, glittering hate I normally saw in his eyes returned.

"She? Do you mean our Queen, Baleon? Did you forget to whom you are speaking? You will address her with the respect she deserves or you will regret it. I will enjoy making you regret it." Rhi's voice was low and I reflexively ducked back behind Bale.

Baleon took a step forward, his voice dropping to a whisper. "When will this madness end, Rhi? You know she is not right, yet you walk alongside her, thinking that someday she will make you King. It will never happen. You are misguided in so many ways. You always have been."

I didn't expect the verbal explosion that came from Rhi or the rough hands throwing me to the ground. I looked up to find Baleon and Rhi going at it without magic. They fought hand to hand, and it was like watching *The Matrix* live. Their movements were a blur, their coats made snapping sounds as leather sliced through the air, and I heard nothing but grunts and *thuds* as their limbs connected. They kicked, punched, hip-tossed…it was MMA meets ninja. I was happy neither of them had swords.

At one point, Rhi gained the upper hand and had Baleon pinned against the wall, his arm twisted behind him in a gross way that had me wincing. He pulled him back and then shoved Bale into the wall again. "Do you yield, old man?"

"Stop it. Rhi, back away." I pushed myself to my feet, my palms filled with violet fire. I stood in a fighting stance and though there was no way I would go hand-to-hand, I was ready to use what I had. Baleon had fought for me and I wouldn't let Rhi hurt him.

Rhi started to laugh and took a half step back from Baleon. That was all the space Bale needed to kick up and back, connecting squarely between Rhi's legs. I had to stifle a laugh. I had never seen a guy use that trick, but it was effective. As Rhi doubled over, Bale grabbed him by the throat and held him a good six inches off the ground. He knocked him back against the wall a few times, Rhi's head making a hollow *thunk*. The hand around Rhi's throat glowed orange and I barely heard Bale whisper, "I can break this. I can remove it and you will be free of her. But I can see that you relish her madness. Have her then. But you will leave us be or I will end you." He had to be talking about the collar.

Baleon let Rhi slide to the ground and without turning back, he gestured down the hall. "The library is this way." I glanced back at Rhi in time to hear him yell behind us that Baleon would pay for this.

We rounded a corner and I turned to Bale. "What does he mean? Will you be okay? Why didn't you fight with magic?"

He looked down at me and sighed. "I will likely be punished, but it will be fine. I have brothers who heal and they will sustain me. It will not be the first time he and I have come to blows. We fight without magic because it is the way of our people. You were not allowed to guard the royal family until you can best another Hunter, hand to hand. We fight with honor, at least...among each other."

"And—"

Baleon stopped, putting his hand on my arm as he cut me off. "No more questions. We are almost there and I would rather Prince Mikail not know of this. He needn't be concerned."

I nodded and put my hand over his. "Thank you, Baleon. Thank you for keeping him away from me. I don't know what I'm doing. I didn't ask for this and I don't want to be here. I'm afraid, I have so many questions, and I'm just trying to survive. So, thank you."

"Surviving is what we are all trying to do." He dropped his hand from my arm and continued walking down the hall, though he kept his steps slow, allowing me to walk next to him instead of behind him.

When Baleon and I finally arrived at the library, I knew the Queen was back. I could see it in the tenseness of Micah's posture and the way his eyebrows pulled together as he attempted a pathetic smile. I was still reeling a bit from the incident with Rhi, but Bale had asked me not to say anything and I finally felt like I had a team. Micah, Bale, Tragar, and me...we were in this together.

"She's—" I started.

"She is," he interrupted.

"So, we—" I tried again.

"We work. It's all we can do," he cut in again. I wanted to be annoyed at him, but the steadiness of his tone was forced and I was sure he was going to grind his teeth into dust with the way he was tensing his jaw.

Micah immediately focused on working with my power. I could feel his concern over the Queen being home and what that meant for me. We didn't talk about it anymore, we didn't have to. But, I stayed focused on the same drills we'd been doing, going at them, over and over, until my mind was tired and my nerves were tattered. Micah finally allowed me a break and I was back in my chair by the fire, just finishing a new passage, which had only created more questions. I got up and found Micah with his head in a book of his own.

"Can I talk to you? Is there somewhere we can go where I can ask you some *questions*?" I put emphasis on the on word so he'd get my drift. His amused smile confirmed he had.

"Certainly. There's a place I've been wanting to show you anyway. I couldn't until Tragar was back, though. Hunters would still come in if it was just Bale, but they are terrified of Tragar." Micah smirked as he stood and turned to where

Tragar had last been seen. "We're headed out, let me know if there's trouble," he yelled in that direction.

"Oh, you know I will," Tragar said, his voice carrying over stacks of books taller than he was. "Those damn demons had best stay out of my way, though. They know better than to come in here." Tragar continued his rant against the Hunters as Micah shook his head and led me to a dark corner of the library. He grabbed a book, pulling it toward him by the top of the spine. Directly to his right, the wall of books popped open and sunlight burst into the room.

We were going outside. *Outside*. Where I could smell the trees and feel the wind and have the sun on my face. It had only been a few weeks since I was first stuck in that room at Esmerelda's, yet I felt like it had been months since I'd been outside. Micah motioned at me with a quick quirk of his head and I stepped out ahead of him. I had to shield my eyes but once they adjusted, I was staring at an eight-foot-tall hedge. I spun around to find Micah pulling at another hedge, which must have hidden the door. His hand buried in the foliage as he yanked it closed.

"What is this place?" I asked, as I turned to look around.

I turned back to what had been the door and it was gone, replaced by more greenery.

"It's a maze. A labyrinth of sorts. The Elders had it built and enchanted it far before my grandfather was even the King. It will only lead you where you are meant to go. It knows the heart of those inside and if your intentions are good, it will give you what you need in the time you need it. It won't let you in, or out, if it believes you are trying to use it to do harm. You can see the sky, but look." He stopped and shot a blast of power up. It dissipated and the air above me rippled, a sheen that hadn't been there becoming visible as it absorbed the power. My head snapped back toward Micah as he continued. "You can't get in from the top or bottom, only through the hedge. My mother and her Hunters stay far away from here. Those collars mean they want what she wants, and pretty much everyone knows what she wants is insane. But I'm rambling, and you said you had questions, so please, go ahead."

I bit the inside of my lip, hoping my questions wouldn't be too ridiculous.

"How does Rynna play into all of this? No one talks about her. There aren't pictures of her. Why is she on the...um, other side of this?" I looked around, unsure of exactly what I should or shouldn't say out here. Protection or not, I was learning from my mistakes.

"Ah. I wondered when we would get there." Micah started to walk and I fell in step beside him.

"Aunt Ryannon never quite fit in. She loved being out among our people but really wanted nothing to do with the royal dealings. From what Tragar has explained, she was forever sneaking out to go meet her friends—which included your parents. She had been allowed to befriend your mother because everyone knew Liana was the next Elder in line for the council, but Aunt Ryn took their friendship outside the library, which is where my grandfather wanted it to stay.

"The way I understand it, when my father— who was a Hunter—was killed and my mother lost her mind, Aunt Ryn tried to help. She tried to stop my mother, to get her to listen and realize what had just happened, but my mother refused to believe my father was using her to get to the throne. It seems so obvious, as it was explained to me, he saw the opportunity to put Hunters in a position of power and was merely using my mother to do so, but she couldn't fathom it. She was suddenly convinced that Aunt Ryn had partnered with the AniMage responsible for my father's death, so she exiled her. Aunt Ryannon is never allowed to enter the main castle again." Micah snorted, his amused chuckle seeming out of place given the sad story.

He turned to me with a sly smile. "What Mother didn't realize was Aunt Ryn wanted exactly that. So she traveled with your parents when they left for America and then took care of you and Cole as your mother had requested. All the while, she was waiting for me to grow up. When I turned eighteen, Aunt Ryn showed up inside this maze. Tragar had sent me out here and I found her waiting on a bench. She explained to me what was truly happening—what my mother was doing, what she had done to you, and what was to come. She asked me whether I wanted to fight for our people or against them. Since then, she's been working to convince the others I can be trusted. In the meantime, I used my mother's obsession with you as a way to get to Brighton to help you. As soon as you told your father you were leaving, I moved there. I knew no one else would be able to get you to a place where you could withstand what was to come. I told you I was there to help, and I was."

I gnawed on my lower lip as I thought through his explanation. It was simple. It seemed legit. And then something he had said clicked in my mind. "How old are you, Micah?"

He smiled. "I wondered whether you were going to put that together. I'm actually twenty-eight, closer to your brother's age than yours." I knew Immortals tended to age slower than humans, but I was impressed by how young he looked. I would have never guessed.

"And your father, you've mentioned him a few times, but that, ah, doesn't seem to be a pleasant topic." I looked up at him with quick glances, realizing I might be treading into deep water.

Micah sighed. Just one puff of air filled with pain, frustration, and sadness. "I've been called many things, but the bastard son of Cane seems to be the one people like most. They are too ignorant to realize my father didn't leave, he was killed, so the words don't actually make sense." He shook his head, his lips in a tight grimace.

"But the bottom line is that my father wanted my mother for no other reason than her lineage and birthright. To this moment, she still believes he loved her and they had a love for the ages, but it is simply one of her delusions. Once the prophecy was made and Rhi actually found you, she decided I needed protection. That was her code for putting me in a place where I could never learn the truth and would always do her bidding." Micah paused, and smiled a genuine smile.

"Too bad for her, I had Bale and Tragar on my side. Her compulsion doesn't work on Bale—his unique ability is to resist all forms of compulsion—and Tragar hasn't trusted my mother since she was a child."

I thought of Baleon and what had happened today with Rhi. I felt guilty for not telling Micah and worried about when the punishment would come down on Bale. Micah mistook my guilt for confusion and paused.

"Every Immortal has at least one ability that falls outside of the normal realm of their race," he said. "We don't know if they are genetic abnormalities, or what brings them about, but we each have one. Mine protects my mind, making it impossible for the Hunters or my mother to hear my thoughts. It kind of goes along with how some Mages have green or red power. Typically, families have the same source power, but not always. Not all of our history is documented and Tragar continues to find conflicting information. I assume it is genetics, but enough about that. What else do you need to know?"

I wanted to ask more about these abilities and what other types were out there, but instead, I reverted back to the questions my mother's journals had sparked. "Have you met Elias? My Uncle Derreck? Do you know what their plan is?"

Micah shook his head. "I don't know them or the plan. When we were attacked, I didn't initially put the pieces together that those doing the attacking were the same ones working with Aunt Ryannon. Had we been working together, it all could have gone so much more smoothly and no one would have had to get hurt." He sighed and I knew we were both thinking of Bethany.

"But because mother cloistered me away here at Cresthaven and no one knew who I was or what I looked like, there was no way for them to even realize we were all on the same team. Aunt Ryn was busy with your father and I was busy with you. I expect to hear from her soon, though.

We communicate every few weeks as Tragar travels and she promised to keep me apprised of the plan."

I felt marginally better knowing there was a plan. And that Rynna was pulling all the sides of this together. It also helped to build my trust in Micah. He hadn't held back. He told me the truth as soon as I had asked him. I still had so many questions, but we were getting somewhere.

"Okay, I have another question. Why are there both Elders and a royal family? My mother wrote a lot about your mother, saying she spent a lot of time talking about wanting to change things. Your mom wanted the Elders to allow the royal family to decide how to rule. She thought they should help the family, not the other way around."

"The Elders never wanted to rule our people. They simply wanted to do what they were meant to, which was to guide us, help us, and sustain us. They foretold events to come and were part of births, deaths, and marriages. My mother refused—still refuses—to believe they held our best interests at heart. The Elders encouraged intermarriage between the races. We talked about Immortals having various unique qualities and the

Elders realized if we were going to continue to evolve, we had to mix power and genes. Elders on the council were required to intermarry, and those were often set up in arranged marriages.

"My mother believed the Elders should work for the royal family, not have the ability to direct it. She wanted them to act as her personal counsel. One she could disregard at will. But with the people believing in them and not her, it wasn't possible."

Micah stopped again, pulling his lower lip in and sinking his teeth into it. He opened his mouth, closed it, and then opened it again. Looking at me, and then away before he spoke. "I believe the Elders held a higher function, though. Something no one really understood that made them invaluable. Because once they were gone, it became harder and harder for any of the races to conceive and continue their lines. Tragar spends a lot of time visiting Mage communities established around the globe, trying to find old relics and books. As the children our age have grown up, he has seen very few new ones born. We can't confirm that the same problems are happening for AniMages, because they stay hidden, but I know the Hunters also have this issue. I am surrounded by Hunters, both male and female, and I haven't seen a child since we came here." He stared down at the ground, his sadness radiating from him, permeating the air around us and laying a veil of grief on me before he even explained himself. "Our races are dying."

My mind went automatically to Elias and Nell. I saw that horrific day and heard the words they exchanged. *It had been years since an AniMage had been born.* "Is there anything to be done?"

He looked back at me, hope in his eyes. "I hope so. That's why you're here. It is the only good thing to come from Rhi's ridiculous meddling. You're here, and together, we can change all of this."

I stepped backward. "The betrothal. You think we can change this? Do you think..." I couldn't form the words. I couldn't ask if Micah thought he was my mate out loud. It couldn't be that easy...could it?

Before he could confirm or deny his thoughts, I was talking again. Spitting out the words rapid fire, not giving him the chance to speak for fear of what he'd say. "That's all. You answered my question. Let's go back inside. I'd like to go back to my room. I know your mother will want me soon and I want to be ready." I was fidgety and Micah gave me a curious look.

"That's all? Okay, Amelia," he said. He turned and plunged a hand into the hedge wall. It popped open, revealing the library. I rushed ahead of him and straight to Baleon. "Please take me to my room," I requested. I didn't say goodbye to Tragar or Micah, just hurried behind Bale's long strides.

Once I closed my door behind me, I finally let my piling thoughts loose.

Could it be Micah?

"No," I said out loud. "No, it can't be. That doesn't make sense." The prophecy rolled around in my head. He would be King. He had been trying to help me with my power. He was my friend. But, the thought of feeling romantically about him wrinkled my nose. First, it broke the girl code. I couldn't be with my best friend's ex-boyfriend. And second, it was just...gross. He was my *friend*. I paced my room while the thoughts tumbled over each other and finally threw myself onto the bed. I needed to do something productive and I hadn't visited my Keeper today.

I relaxed against a mountain of pillows on my bed, closed my eyes, and went inside myself. It was getting easier, and less strange, to seek out this separate entity taking up real estate in my mind and soul. I approached the door to the room where the Keeper stayed and was shocked to find it wide open with all of them still inside. They could have come and gone. They could have invaded my mind and my heart and done who knows what. I didn't know what it meant, but I still didn't completely trust that these peaceful pieces of power wouldn't suddenly slam together into the darkness I knew the Keeper capable of.

I stood in the doorway and stared at the lustrous orbs floating around the room. When they reacted to my presence, all but the white ball bounced around the room, blasting me with waves of happiness and joy. I walked the room and did what I had done previously, letting my fingers graze the balls of energy floating past me. Again, I was jolted with power. My little flame felt like a bonfire inside me as each one gave a small piece of itself. I was infused with each of their powers and felt renewed.

On a whim, I sat in the middle of the room. "What are we doing? How does this work? What am I supposed to do with you all?"

I didn't expect them to answer me, and they didn't. But the white orb brightened. It glowed and grew, and for the first time, came closer. I stared into the brilliance of it, and while I had to squint against the light assaulting my eyes, I knew it wasn't my eyes playing tricks when I saw myself. I was in a room, surrounded by Hunters. I could feel a sudden influx of power and then saw what was happening inside me. I saw the orbs fly from the room, infiltrating my body, breaking apart and letting their power flow through my veins. Fear hitched my breath as I watched myself convulse a few times, before I slowly stood. I opened my eyes and they glowed bright. My palms filled with orange and violet power, a crackling ball of light. My expression was fierce. The Hunters closed in and I threw both arms out from my body, lifting them from the ground and pinning them to the walls.

The orb snapped and the scene faded. "I have to use you. I understand. But how do I without the Queen knowing? If she realizes I have the power she wants, I'm even less safe than I am now." Of course, the white ball of energy showed me nothing more; just floated back to the top corner of the room.

I opened my eyes and stared at the ceiling of my room, somehow knowing the Queen would summon me soon. If not tonight, tomorrow. I forced myself into the shower and was surprised when emotion filled me. I hadn't cried yet. I had told myself I wouldn't. But I had no idea what was going to happen to me. I missed Bethany and Cole. I missed Aidan. I had so many things I wanted to tell my father and even Rynna. I leaned forward and rested my head against the tile of the shower wall. Tears tracked down my cheeks, getting lost in the rivulets of water until I couldn't tell whether it was me or the showerhead. These were not sobs. I was not hysterical. But I was scared and alone. I cried for me. I cried for my family. I cried for the AniMages and the enslaved Hunters. I cried for Micah, who showed me a little more of himself every day and was nowhere near the put-together socialite he portrayed himself to be. For just a few minutes, I allowed myself this emotional break, because I couldn't afford for it to happen in front of the Queen.

196

Slowly, the tears stopped. I turned the water off and stood in the shower. My long hair was soaked, dripping a steady stream toward the drain. I slid open the door, wrapped myself in a towel, and stared at my reflection in the mirror, focusing on the cuff and finding the Elder symbol Tragar had shown me on the book cover. Just to its left, was another symbol. A circle, with two closed fists inside and lines radiating outward. Its meaning clicked and I knew what I needed to do. I smiled, silently thanking my mother for her clues and protection. I closed my eyes and went back to the room, beckoning the light to join me. The balls bounced around the room, anxiety and excitement filling the air. Finally, the violet and orange ball made its way to me. It floated in line with my chest. I took a deep breath, hoping I wasn't about to make a huge mistake, plunged both fists inside the ball, and yanked them apart.

It was like lightning and thunder combined. The light blinded me and the loud snap was deafening. As I blinked my eyes back into focus, I saw thousands of tiny violet and orange balls of energy. They blinked like twinkling stars and scattered. Their power merged with my own for a brief moment but then it was gone. All of the energy melded back together in a split second and the glowing orb was back intact. The drain of power made me feel like something was now missing from myself.

I opened my eyes and slammed my hand down on the bathroom counter, frustrated. The granite cracked and crumbled. I slowly lifted my hand, turning it left and right. Not a mark. Clearly, I was supposed to be able to use the power. To diffuse it into my own. But why wouldn't it stay? How was it supposed to protect me if I couldn't reach it?

Chapter 15
Aidan

It had taken some time to shift on my own accord. It didn't help that I was with other AniMages, impatiently waiting for me to force something they could do with a thought. As I got more angry at myself, the beast finally made his presence known and I was able to let him take over. Because I would have no idea what was happening, I had to trust Elias when he said he would be able to keep me with them. It could have been minutes or hours we ran. When I woke up, Elias and Dillon were standing with their backs to me and we were alone in a patch of trees.

"Are we there?" My voice was raspy and my thoughts muddled. It always took me a few minutes to disengage and become myself again.

They both turned and Dillon beat Elias to the punch. "We've been here, Mr. Aidan. Just waiting on you. Hopefully Mr. Will can help you because, sheesh."

"Now, Dillon, don't be rude. What would your mother think?" Elias scolded Dillon and his shamed expression made me feel guilty.

"It's okay, Dillon. I appreciate you watching out for me while I figure all this out. Did your owl tell you anything else about me while we were out tonight?" I got dressed with the clothes Elias pulled from the pack he had carried as Dillon scrunched his face, thinking.

"During the run, he could feel you weren't there. You were with us, but you weren't. It didn't make sense, but he kept telling me you were somewhere else and we needed to watch out for you. But you were right there, so maybe he was wrong."

Elias and I exchanged perplexed looks and he changed the subject. "The last time I saw Will, he was staying in this area. There's a small cabin within a mile of here. It's likely he already knows we're here, so, if he's still around, I imagine we'll see him before long. I've also sent for a few friends who are supposed to meet us here. They should be able to help us get to Amelia."

He had piqued my interest but I tried to stay cool. I nodded and fell in step with Elias, my thoughts a whirlwind in my head. I had always been drawn to Amelia, I could recognize that, but I could separate the pull to her from *her*. It had been nagging at my mind, wondering if my attraction could be a product of this prophecy, but when I thought of her, I didn't think of her as drawing me in against my will. I thought of her laugh. I thought of the way she hid so much of herself until she knew me, trusted me. I remembered all those days I spent pursuing her, working to build her trust and climbing over her walls. The vision of her laughing in the parking lot when she accused me of being a stalker, but her smile giving away her excitement over seeing me. Fate may have brought us together, but we could have pushed against it and we didn't. We had something. We just needed time to keep figuring out what it was for ourselves.

Rustling in the trees brought me out of my head and Elias, Dillon, and I immediately stopped and circled, our backs to each other. Elias tried to push Dillon between us but he was having none of that. He jumped back into his position and glared up at Elias.

"Show yourself!" Elias's voice boomed out across the forest. My anxiety was rising and I could feel Dillon's fear, even though he was working so hard to suppress it. I stepped a little closer to him as my senses sharpened and the feeling of my cells slamming into each other, reshaping, and preparing to shift started to take hold. My breathing was shallow and Elias looked out of the corner of his eyes at me. "Stay calm, Aidan. Focus. Allow him to be a part of you, not take you over."

The rustling intensified and a female voice floated over to us. "Oh, calm down, Elias. It is just us. Call off your dogs. Or cats. Or whatever it is you were about to become."

She laughed and he instantly relaxed. I took the opportunity to focus on his directive. I tried to relax while keeping the beast present within me. I failed. As soon as my fear melted, so did his presence. Frustrated, I swore.

"A lady is coming, Mr. Aidan. Mind yourself." And now I was being scolded by a child.

Finally, the three people pushed through the tree line. The woman was small, both in height and build. She had long brown hair braided down her back and held a branch for the men behind her. As the first man maneuvered past her, I got a look at his face and found myself staring at the man from Charlie's vision.

"Derreck," I breathed out.

He looked up at me, confusion drawing his brows together. "Do we know each other?" he asked.

"No. Sorry. It's...complicated." I wasn't sure what to say or why he was here. Charlie's vision had said he was friends with Elias, but how could he and this woman help get to Amelia? He had abandoned her. Lied to her. My anger rose and as I took a step forward, I was met face to face with Elias, who stepped in my path.

"No, Aidan. I'll apologize in advance for listening in, but he is not what you think. Your story is incomplete. They are on our side," he said.

The second man came through the trees and moved around Derreck and the woman Elias had yet to introduce. He was thin and looked exhausted, but I could feel relief and excitement pouring off him. A need for action. He didn't hesitate as he shook hands with Elias, a broad grin exchanging between them.

"It's good to have you back, old friend," Elias said. The man nodded and then pulled Elias in for a hug. "You have no idea, Elias. It's been far too long. But I thought we had a plan? Why am I walking toward Will instead of as far away from him as I can get?"

I stepped toward him, interjecting. "That would be my fault, sir. I need Will's help. My name is Aidan, Aidan Montgomery. Maybe you knew my parents, too? Zen—"

"Zendrick? You are Zen and Kayla's son?" He turned to Elias, and then to the woman and Derreck. "Did you know he existed? I had no idea!" The man turned back to me and took my outstretched hand, shaking it as his excitement radiated through our connection.

"Nice to meet you, son. I'm Nathaniel Bradbury."

My mouth went dry. I was shaking hands with Amelia's father. I had just been introduced to Amelia's father.

"Nice to meet you, sir." It was the best I could do under the circumstances—my brain had basically shut off.

He stepped backwards as Elias attempted to stifle a grin. The woman stepped up next and extended her hand. "I'm Rynna. Very nice to meet you, Aidan. I was close friends with your mother when we were young. I'm so sorry for your loss."

"Rynna? You're Rynna? Amelia's Rynna?" My voice came back and though I likely should have been more excited to meet Amelia's father, she hadn't had many kind words to say about him. Rynna, on the other hand, she had always spoken highly of.

She nodded, still wearing a puzzled expression. "I'm going to find her," I said. "I'm going to find her and bring her home."

My words brought out a full-fledged smile from Rynna and before I knew it, I was captured in a hug. She wrapped her arms around my chest as she whispered, "You are the one. You are her one."

I knew what she meant, but Mr. Bradbury must not have. He stepped toward me, scowling. "Ryannon, what do you mean he's the one? He's my daughter's one what, exactly?"

Rynna laughed. "Nathaniel, calm down. You haven't been yourself in a very long time and a lot has happened. Amelia spoke with me about choosing her duty or her heart. And, clearly, Aidan is meant to take Zendrick's place in leading the AniMages. It's clear from his declaration, and his position, he is the one. He is her mate and the other half of Lavignia's prophecy. Aidan is the reason she has taken a stand and likely the reason she will fight."

Derreck came up and put a hand on Mr. Bradbury's shoulder. "One thing at a time, Nathaniel. You've had a trying few days. The binds have only just been removed. Give your mind and your power some time to balance before you have a heart attack over meeting your daughter's boyfriend."

"I don't know that I'm actually her boyfriend anymore, Mr. Bradbury." I couldn't truly make any claims. She had left me. "But I'm going after her, sir. You can count on me to bring her back."

"Nathaniel," he corrected. "Please, just call me Nathaniel. And let's not talk about boyfriends or not-boyfriends for a few minutes, okay?"

I nodded. "Yes, sir. Mr. Bradbury...er, Nathaniel." Dillon was standing next to Rynna and looked so embarrassed for me. I was sure my face was three different shades of red, so I tried to change the subject.

"Where exactly are we going? Where is this Will?" We needed to refocus on the task at hand.

"Ah, yes. Let's go. He's probably waiting. Nathaniel just came from Will's. They've both been recuperating from the unbinding, so he should be in great spirits." I didn't miss Elias's sarcasm and wondered exactly how pleasant this Will was going to be. I wanted to ask Amelia's father how his unbinding had gone, but it was a pretty personal question and we had known each other all of five minutes.

Elias, Derreck, and Nathaniel walked back through the trees the group had just come from, with Dillon just behind them. For a second, I could only watch them walk away. I wanted to stop moving for a minute and give my brain time to sort through all the information streaming in over the course of the past few days.

"It's a lot, I know. But you can do this. And so can she. I've seen her, you know, and she's strong. She's determined and she knows we're coming for her. Well, not you—I didn't know about you—but the rest of us."

Rynna's soft voice took a moment to register in my mind and I whipped my head in her direction. "You've seen her? When? Tell me."

"Walk with me. We need to get you to Will." She looped her arm through mine and I felt like a giant next to her. I could feel her warmth, both in body heat and love for Amelia. Her happiness at finding me here and her underlying fear for Amelia. My ability to sense emotions was getting stronger, but knowing people's innermost emotions was still really strange.

"I saw Amelia the morning she left for Washington. She is with Mikail and he will help keep her safe. She also has a protective charm from her mother. It will help control the Keeper."

"Micah? The lying Prince who pretended to be her friend and hurt Bethany?" I couldn't restrain myself at the mention of his name. The visual of my fist connecting with his face was the only comforting thought I had.

Rynna patted my arm. "Now, now. What neither you nor Amelia have had time to realize is what's happening now was set in motion years ago. We have never stopped trying to undo the damage Julia has done. Mikail is just another innocent who was born into a situation he didn't ask for. He is not like his mother and he is not out to take Amelia from you." She looked toward Elias, her features pinched in annoyance. "You aren't the only one who has a hard time believing Mikail is on our side. I've been trying to convince Elias for months."

I was silent, not wanting to offend her, but silently siding with Elias. "Was she really okay?" I finally asked. I hadn't spent much time really allowing myself to think about Amelia and the situation she was in. I had intentionally tried to focus on myself for that reason. If not, I would obsess over her safety and what might be happening wherever she was. She and I were so alike in some ways. I knew she would sacrifice herself for everyone else. She'd done it, over and over, since we'd met. She'd told me a version of her life story while we were getting to know each other and adding in everything I'd learned recently, it was clear her pattern was to think she could take things on so others didn't have to. Thinking of the rash decisions she could make and what that could mean for her was more than I could handle.

"She was okay. She's scared, which is probably good. We both know how her temper can take hold and cause her to do some irrational things." I couldn't see the smile, but I heard it in her words. She definitely knew Amelia. "The protective charm I told you about will help her manage the Keeper power and as long as she listens to Mikail and steers clear of Julia, we should be able to get to her before anything can really happen. We set a few things in motion and pulled the Queen away from Cresthaven. It bought us some time. Not much, but some."

"You don't sound as confident as I'd like you to," I said, pushing through branches. I wanted to ask more, but as we got to the other side, the guys were waiting, talking with a man I assumed was Will.

I expected some kind of greeting, but got nothing. Will stared at me, his face a mask of indifference, as we all stood awkwardly in the clearing near his cabin. He was big. He probably should have been a lumberjack or heavyweight fighter. He had close-cropped hair, looking like he owned his own clippers and did the job himself. His sleeves were rolled up his forearms and thin white scars crisscrossed his skin, along with what looked like burn scars around both wrists. I was puzzling over the perfect circles of scarring when pressure pushed at the base of my skull. Suddenly, my ears were ringing and my head felt like it was splitting open. I dropped to my knees, clasping my hands to my ears.

"What. The. Hell?" I could barely push out the words and seconds later, the change began. The too-tight feeling was everywhere at once, my insides swelling and rearranging as fur sprouted in various places.

"Will. Come on, man. Go easy on him." I barely registered the words and had no idea who said them, but the pressure instantly backed off and the shift reversed. I groaned as things found their proper home inside me, wincing from the pain of muscles and bones moving. As quickly as the pain had come, it was gone. I still couldn't come to grips with how I was able to withstand my body completely rearranging itself. I slowly sat up and found Dillon hiding behind Rynna as she glared at Will.

"William Ryder, was that really necessary?" Her tone was sharp, reminiscent of the various foster mothers who were always yelling at me for whatever fight I'd been in at the time. But I could feel her concern, where they never cared that I was always protecting the other smaller children. They were too focused on the attention I was bringing to them and myself.

Through my squinted eyes, I watched Will give Rynna a sideways look, his eyes narrowed. "Would you like me to invite him in for tea, Ryannon? Or would you like me to undo whatever Rhi has done to him?" There was no sarcasm; he simply spoke the words as facts.

I pushed myself up and stepped toward him, still a little lightheaded. "I've heard of Rhi. The Hunter, right? What did he do to me?"

Amelia's father snorted. "It's apparently his specialty. But if anyone can help you, it's Will. He helped me."

Will glanced around and then gestured toward his door. "Come inside. You never know who might be listening."

We filed into Will's cabin and I was surprised at how large the inside looked compared to the outside. Support columns were spaced across the open layout and it was clear Will didn't get out much. Books were stacked by the dozen, the couch was old with one side sunk in, and dirty dishes were piled in the sink. This was clearly a bachelor pad.

"We're protected here?" Derreck asked.

Will grunted and responded, "Of course. They will never find me again. I've made sure of it. Sit," he said, directing me to the chair next to his. He looked up at Rynna. "You need to remove the child. He shouldn't be here. Actually, none of you should stay aside from Elias. Nathaniel still needs rest."

Nathaniel was the first to disagree. "I don't need a damn thing but to find my daughter, Will. I've spent all these years trying to protect her and now she's alone. Julia has exactly what she wants and I won't have it. I want to go—now."

Rynna stepped up and put her hand on his arm, her words soft. "Nathaniel, we need Aidan. If we're going to get to Amelia, we need all the help we can get. Let's leave Will to his work. A few more days will give us time to plan our entrance into Cresthaven."

Nathaniel turned to glare at me. "We don't have time to waste. Do you understand?" I could only nod.

For the first time, Derreck stepped toward me and I stood, still leery of him. He reached out a hand, saying, "I owe you an apology. I had no idea who you were and Amelia pulling away from you is partly my fault. Had I known..." His words drifted off and a weary sadness radiated from him. For a split second, I saw a man so much older than the one standing before me. How long had they been fighting this war?

I clasped his hand in mine, unable to stop myself from gripping a little harder than necessary. "We're here now and she needs us. Go make your plans. Hopefully this won't take long."

Will's voice cut in. "Oh, it won't take long, but you won't be going anywhere for a few days. And it isn't going to be pleasant." You would have expected sarcasm, but again, it was facts. His tone was level and the solemnness of it rattled me.

Nathaniel came up and shook my hand again. "Good luck, son. For my daughter's sake, I hope you are the one."

"Thank you, sir," I responded. He nodded, turned, and left.

Dillon broke away from Rynna and ran to stand in front of me. He looked up expectantly and crouched down. "What's up, Little Man?"

He looked around, clearly uncomfortable, and then threw his arms around my neck. "Be careful, Mr. Aidan. My owl says this is where you'll meet your wolf, but he's worried about you. I'll take care of Miss Bethany while you're gone. I'll make sure she went home and that she and Charlie are okay." He pulled away and ran to Rynna as she opened the door. She didn't say anything, just gave me an encouraging smile and then pulled the door closed behind them.

I dropped back into the chair, both filled with adrenaline and exhausted all at once. "What now?" I asked, looking between the two men.

Elias stopped pacing the perimeter of the room, but wouldn't meet my eyes. Instead, he looked at Will. They maintained eye contact for too long, making me think there were words I couldn't hear being exchanged. Then Will moved his gaze to mine, and steely determination stared back at me. "Now, I'm going to restrain you so you can't hurt yourself or me. I'm going to invade your mind and body and break every bond Rhi has put on you. It's going to take time, but nowhere near as much as you'll need in recovery. This is going to hurt—a lot. You're going to scream and curse my name, but if you are truly Zendrick's son and Amelia's mate, you will withstand it. Follow me."

Chapter 16
Amelia

It was time. As I had suspected, not long after my shower, I was summoned. Now I was pacing. I was wearing a long, ornate, deep purple dress, one of the few hanging in my closet with long sleeves, and had twisted my hair into a ballerina-style bun. The run-in with the Keeper had left me energized, but jittery. I was talking to myself as I paced, trying to practice what I could say. Trying to envision what the conversation might be like. Micah had warned me to keep my sarcasm buttoned up and to be nice.

The soft knock on the door made me jump and I was surprised when Micah stepped through. He was dressed to the nines. I wasn't sure how I ended up in medieval dresses while he got to wear tailored suits, but he looked amazing. His hair was pulled into a low ponytail and his bright purple tie was a nice contrast to his black suit and dress shirt, matching my dress perfectly. I cocked my head.

It was an educated guess. His voice rang clearly in my head.

Are there cameras in here? Because, seriously, Micah.

He laughed out loud. "No, of course not. Going into this night, I thought you might like the visual reinforcement of your power. Because you do have power, Amelia. And you can handle tonight. You can handle her." His laughter had died and his words were serious. I looked into Micah's eyes and saw hope. And pride.

I wanted to believe him. I was so close to believing him. But my hands were shaking and I was scared.

"Whatever you do, Amelia, be deferential. Don't provoke her. I haven't seen her yet today, so I don't know what kind of mood she's in. Tread lightly. Try not to offend her in the first three breaths." He waggled his eyebrows a little, clearly trying to make me laugh as we both remembered my tirade our first day. It felt like a million years ago, not just a week.

"Let's go." I was finding it hard to speak. The words lodged themselves in my throat and it was as if I had swallowed a cup of sand.

Micah opened the door and nodded to Baleon, who preceded us. He reached down and pulled my hand into the crook of his elbow, squeezing it.

You are stronger than you know.

They were Rynna's words, but Micah's voice in my head was calming. I wasn't alone, not entirely.

Bale opened the door and his eyes connected with mine as I passed. They didn't hold the normal indifference I had come to expect and I felt his worry. It didn't help. The dining room was massive and lit with candle chandeliers, sending shimmering shadows across the walls. The only furniture in the room was a table able to seat forty people. Micah had to slow his step and latch down on my hand to keep me from tripping over my own two feet as we crossed the room. At the end of the too-long table sat Queen Julia. She looked every bit the Queen in her silver gown and matching crown.

219

"Welcome, Amelia. I'm so sorry I've been away. Won't you sit?" The words she used were pleasant, but her tone was ice. Her face was expressionless and her only movement was to take a small sip of her wine. My mouth wouldn't work and could have been stuffed with cotton balls for the all the good it was doing me.

"Good evening, Mother. I trust your trip went well and business was taken care of?" Micah pulled back my chair and helped me sit, giving me time to collect my brain from where it had obviously fallen out of my body.

She waved away his question. "Someday those buffoons are going to realize I'm right and stop pining away for their beloved Elders. They only focus on the reproductive issues we're facing and not on ensuring our bloodlines are pure and we have eradicated all those animals." She shook her head and then scowled. "This is not appropriate dinner talk, though, Mikail. I want to talk about Amelia. How are you finding our humble home, dear?"

I couldn't reconcile the words I heard with the mask of indifference she wore. She was putting on a show and doing a horrible job of it.

I sputtered a little, but finally found my voice. "Y-Your home is beautiful, your highness. Mi...Prince Mikail has shown me around and I haven't found an area I don't love, especially the library. I enjoy books and you have a wonderful collection." I struggled to look into her eyes for more than a few seconds at a time.

She nodded slightly. "Indeed, we do. Mikail spent far too much of his time in that drafty old library with the ancient Tragar. Had he spent his time in the training yard with the Hunters, he may be more of a force to be reckoned with, but we cannot control the genetics our children inherit, now can we?"

She arched an eyebrow and Micah sighed, his shoulders slumping. This couldn't have been the first time they'd had this exchange.

"It's been unfortunate I've had to be away in your first few days with us, Amelia, but I do hope you and Mikail were able to spend some quality time together." Her smile made me uncomfortable. The thought of marrying Micah, not some unknown Prince, and the insinuation of what I would have to do after the wedding, made me squirm in my chair. I forced a smile and nodded.

Thankfully, she continued. "But now there is no time to waste. In the hopes one good turn might be received with another, I have a surprise for you. An incentive, we'll call it. I've brought you a guest. Would you like to see who it is?" Julia leaned back in her chair, taking another larger drink from her goblet. From the corner of my eye, I saw Micah's expression tighten and dread filled me.

"Of course, your highness. How nice of you to think of me." The ache inside me grew and my power flared in warning for the first time in a long time. Fear, anger, and determination swelled within. All of the Keeper magic sat in the back of my mind, but I still didn't understand how to activate it or how helpful it would be to me. And, I knew that was the exact reaction she was looking for, so I swallowed the lump of emotions and produced another smile.

"Rhi. Bring out our guest." Her icy smile and sneering tone as she said the word 'guest' sent me into an internal tailspin. There were so many people she could use to hurt me. I only prayed it wasn't Bethany again. Not here, not with the Queen pushing me toward Micah. The door we had come through opened again and I gasped as

Cole was shoved through. His hands were bound and his left eye was black. His clothes looked to be days old. I dug my nails into the armrest of my chair and tried to stay seated as Cole shuffled forward. Rhi yanked the chair next to mine from the table and barely gave Cole time to drop into it before he shoved it forward again, sending Cole reeling and knocking into the table.

"Now, Rhi, you don't have to be so rough. And unbind the poor child. We're having a civilized dinner."

I couldn't take my eyes from Cole. He had yet to look at me as he glared up at Rhi, muttering something I couldn't hear. Rhi snickered evilly as he removed the cuffs from my brother's wrists.

"Your day will come, Mage. You have no idea what we have in store for you." Rhi's words were a gruff whisper, but not quite low enough to go unnoticed by Micah and me.

Finally, my brother turned to me and without a word, I quickly scanned as much of him as I could. His face was swollen, clearly healing from a previous injury. His wrists were raw, bracelets of purple and black bruising. His shirt was torn and his jeans were stained. Dirt streaked his skin. He should have been able to heal himself, so something must have been done to bind his power.

The longer I stared into Cole's eyes, the more my fury built. My breathing picked up and the roaring began in my head. The Keeper magic stayed where it was supposed to, but I could feel them crying out their willingness to help, if only I understood how.

"Don't, Ame. It's what she wants. I'm okay." Cole's words were raw, his voice hoarse. I closed my eyes, knowing he was right and hating that I couldn't defend him as he had always done for me.

I turned back to my right, toward the Queen, only to find her studying us. She was leaned back in her chair, her elbows on the armrests and fingertips steepled together. She looked amused. *Amused.*

Calm. Stay calm, I told myself.

I refused to take my eyes from Julia's. "Thank you, your highness. How kind of you to invite my brother to stay with me. I can only imagine what an imposition it's been for you to get him all the way to Washington. I expect he'll be staying near me so we can catch up?" I gritted out the words and we both knew the game was being played.

Her eyes couldn't hide her delight and mine likely gave away the anger I couldn't completely tamp down. "Of course, dear. I'm sure the two of you have lots to say to each other. Just remember, your brother is here as a courtesy. And I expect that courtesy to be returned. Soon."

What she didn't say was, "or else," but we all heard it. His wounds were visible on purpose. The stories he would tell me would purposefully make my blood boil. His pain was intentional. But what exactly did she want from me? My agreement to consummate a marriage I didn't want? I couldn't give her access to power I couldn't control. What was her end game?

"Shall we eat?" Micah interrupted the silent war between his mother and me.

"Of course," she replied, snapping her fingers, causing Hunters to file in with various dishes. I nodded and they piled my plate high with fish, vegetables, and breads. My glass was filled with water and for once, I wished it were wine. As I tried to take in what was happening around me, I realized the only Hunter in the room I could feel was Baleon. The rest were blank. It piqued my curiosity, but I didn't have long to ponder over it since Micah's worry radiated from his side of the table and my brother felt like a volcano ready to burst. I reached out toward the Queen, trying to pinpoint her aura to see if it would tell me anything useful. Unfortunately, she was like a radio tuned between two stations—a ball of static sending so many emotions my way, I couldn't begin to sort through them. I pulled away and picked up my silverware.

I ate mechanically, easing my left hand down between Cole and me. In seconds, his finger gripped mine and I almost choked as his true feelings assaulted me. My brother—the one who healed me, who calmed my storm—was battered but raging. His body had bruises I couldn't see and his power was bound somehow, indeed. I could feel parts of him reaching for me, as they always did, but something was blocking them. I squeezed his hand, hoping to convey I would help, and his tightened around mine again.

"Amelia, I am going to be blunt. I want to see what you can do. I want to confirm for myself you have what I expect you have—what I need you to have. I saw a taste at Esmerelda's, but if you are what they say, then there is so much more. How cooperative do you plan to be?"

I tried to keep my voice level. "Would you like me to put on some kind of display? It doesn't work like that. I don't know what you want from me, but I can't just snap my fingers and make things happen. I don't know what I am, or what I'm not, but I'm not hiding anything from you. You know very well what my childhood was like. You were watching. You know I wasn't properly trained. You know what I know and there is nothing more."

She laughed, a low, throaty chuckle. "Nothing more? What do you call the display at Esmerelda's? It's quite more than any Mage can do and you bear all the markings of an Elder. I just need to know whether you have the power. Did Liana find a way to give it to you?" She leaned in, her excitement unnerving.

"Don't you say our mother's name. You don't deserve to even know her name!" Cole's raspy voice boomed through the room and he swayed back and forth on his feet.

"Oh, sit down." Julia waved at him as if she were swatting away a fly and shook her head at the Hunters, who had moved toward my brother.

"No need to get so worked up, Mr. Bradbury. I've known your mother for years. There was a time when we were even friends. But times change and priorities shift. She was a traitor. She made my sister a traitor. And your sister is the proof of her ultimate betrayal. The question simply is, will the two of you continue your mother's foolish ways or will you join the right side of this war?"

"I am no one's pawn, your highness. And you have given me no reason to choose your side outside of threatening the people I love. Why don't you try telling me exactly what it is you're fighting for?" Micah looked surprised at my response, as did his mother.

"You are no one's pawn? Is that what you truly think, child?" Her tone was sharp, her eyebrows arched. "A pawn is all you have ever been. Your father tried to control and hide you to keep you from me. My son dated your little human friend simply to get close to you. Your mother used you as a vessel to hold the only magic that could supposedly stop me from trying to save us. My Hunter betrothed you to Mikail to ensure no matter what, you landed right where you are. You are nothing, if *not* a pawn.

"But I will humor you. Your family is a mix of Elder and Mage. Elders always mixed their magic with the other races and claimed it would benefit us all. What really happened is they diluted the Mage bloodlines and diminished our power. They allowed animals to pollute us and servants to believe they could rise above their ranks—that their power was theirs to have and not ours to manage. Whether the Mage inherits green or red power is as irrelevant as their eye color. What matters is that Mages rule the Immortals and ensure our survival. I have spent my life trying to cleanse our people of these mixed races and put the classes back where they belong. Don't you see?"

I gripped Cole's hand, trying to control my temper and the power building in my body. I had been draining myself for days, but the feeling of it growing, unfolding and stretching through my system, like the warmth of a latte on a cool morning, made me feel strong and confident.

My words were even and tempered. "Can you tell me, your highness, how Elders who ruled our people for hundreds of years in peace and harmony had it so wrong? How your methods have made us better and not worse? I realize I came from a simple place and was not well educated, so it isn't clear to me."

Her eyes narrowed slightly and her lips flattened into a thin line, but she didn't scold me as I had anticipated. "My methods, as you call them, are making us better because they are ensuring Mages will dominate the Immortal race. They will be the ones to procreate again and they will have the most pure and powerful magic our people have ever known."

"And where are the children, your highness?" I asked quietly. "Where are the Mage children who will be our saving grace?"

She smiled an evil smile, her lips so thin they seemed to disappear but for the tiny red lipstick rim around her teeth. "They will come. You see, dear, I don't want your power simply for myself. Somewhere in you is the key to unlock the ability for our people to reproduce again. I will find it and I will use it for the Mages to rebuild our numbers. I am no longer bound by the rules of the old ones and I do not have to hand over my crown just yet. I will spend every minute I have exploring every part of what you hold inside you. I will take you apart piece by piece if I have to."

I stared into her eyes as she spoke. As her passion intensified, I watched red overtake her blue irises and all I saw was blood spreading across ice. This time, though, I wondered whether it would be mine.

Cole wanted me to run. We had been arguing for over an hour, our voices hushed as we sat across from each other and I tried to explain for the tenth time why it made no sense.

"There are Hunters everywhere. And Rynna is coming, Cole. She told me herself. I've already explained all of this. Yes, she's the queen's sister, but she's been looking out for us all along. She's bringing people together and they are going to get me out of here—get *us* out of here. We just have to give them time."

His face only got redder and the bruise around his eye blended with the dark brown of his irises. "How can you be sure they'll get here, Ame? How do you know they can get in, get to you, and get you out? Exactly how are they going to be any match for all of these Hunters? Look what they did to me. Not only did they spend a few days beating me to a pulp, they bound me in some way. I can't heal myself, I can't help you...I can't do *anything*."

"I hear you, Cole, but what other choice do we have? Now you're here, too. Who's next? Dad?" As soon as I mentioned our father, Cole shrunk, his anger deflating as guilt took over. I could feel it.

"Cole? What aren't you telling me? What happened to Dad?" Fear snaked its way up my spine and I had to stop myself from shaking my brother and demanding an answer.

It seemed like an eternity passed before he'd look me in the eyes. "I talked to him. After we left Esmerelda's and got Bethany out of there, I confronted him."

I had never known exactly what happened between my father and my brother to cause the rift neither of them would breach. Clearly, Cole hadn't gone looking for reconciliation.

"And?" It was all I could muster. One word held so much meaning in that moment.

"Things happened right after you were born I never wanted you to know. Things Dad did to me—things I thought he did to me—that made me hate him. It turns out I was wrong. God,

Ame, I was so wrong." I watched tears fill my brother's eyes. I moved next to him and pulled him into a hug. Cole wrapped both his arms around me and wave after wave of emotion rolled from him—the ache of being wrong, the agony of lost time, and the pain of what he had done to our father.

I pulled back, holding his hands in mine, wanting to maintain contact. "Talk to me. Tell me what happened."

"While Mom was pregnant with you, things were different. She wasn't as happy. She and Dad had all these arguments and Rynna would find excuses to get me out of the house. But there was a day I remember with complete clarity." Cole paused, his eyes shining with more unshed tears. "At least, I thought I did. Mom wouldn't look at me. She wouldn't touch me. She avoided me all day. And that night, Dad told me we were going camping. Of course, I was excited, so I packed my gear and off we went. While I slept, Dad took me out of the tent. The memory always got fuzzy here, but I remembered pain. Searing, white hot, stabbing knives of pain throughout my entire body. Someone was holding my head and all I could see was Dad holding me down, telling me to be strong, and it would be over soon. He held me down while someone tortured me, that's all I ever knew. And when it was over, while I was curled in the corner of the tent, all he said was he was sorry and we would never speak of it again. He made me swear I wouldn't ask a single question.

"I blamed him. My power went through the roof and I felt everything from everyone. All their pain and their sadness—every emotion anyone had. It took years for me to gain control and separate myself from it, and he refused to help me. By then, Mom had died. You were there and all he did was lock himself away. I couldn't leave you with him, I thought he was a monster, and with my crazy power, I could feel yours. I knew when you were going to have a meltdown, and somehow, I was always able to divert it—to calm you. After we left you at Esmerelda's, he told me it was Mom. Mom was holding my head. She was the one who put the power in me, just like they put the Keeper in you. She gave me the singular purpose of being able to temper your power and keep you alive. She made him help. He didn't want to. He didn't want to take away both of our choices. But he didn't want to ruin my memory of her either, so he allowed me to blame him. All these years, he let me hate him."

I was stunned. Questions flew through my mind but the words were captive in my throat. Our father was nothing we had believed him to be. He had given up everything for us and we believed the exact opposite our whole lives. He allowed us to think terrible things so we would think well of Mom and so I wouldn't be found. Yet, here we were, invalidating it all.

Cole took my silence as a signal to continue. "We have to get out of here, Ame. Everything he went through was to keep this very thing from happening, yet, here you sit, giving the Queen exactly what she wants. You're a sitting duck and you have no idea what she's going to put you through. You heard her. She's not going to stop. She's demented. Right now, let's go. We'll run for it."

I opened my mouth to respond. To tell him he was right, that I was insane for thinking I should just wait around for Rynna when my parents clearly gave up everything to keep me from this place.

"That would be a very poor idea, Cole. Very poor, indeed." We both turned to find Micah leaning against the doorframe of my room. "You'd be dead before you reached the front door."

It was hard to keep Cole quiet as Micah ushered us through the halls with Baleon leading the way. We made it to the library in record time and Bale stood watch as Micah led us into the maze. I tried to get a better look at which book on which shelf he pulled to open the door, but Micah moved too quickly and used his body to block my view.

Once outside, Cole finally let loose. He grabbed Micah by the front of his shirt and pinned him to the hedge wall. "You had better start talking, *Prince*."

Micah looked down at him and placed his own hands over Cole's. "I think you need to release me, Cole. You are not at full strength and this is not productive." Micah's eyes glowed red and I saw the flash of power in his palms as he made his point. Cole dropped him and shook out his hands, scowling.

Micah smoothed down his shirt and took a step back. "After tonight's dinner, it's clear my mother is moving faster than even I had expected. I had no idea you were even here, Cole. Or that she would stoop to these levels already." He turned to me. "We do not have time to work together anymore. Where you are is where you are. And I cannot overtly help you. You simply aren't ready." His last statement was more to himself and Micah started pacing. Cole and I exchanged looks and then it occurred to me. There was one x-factor in all of this.

I hesitated for a second and then decided I might as well go for it. I pulled my sleeve up to reveal the silver cuff tightened around my forearm. "But, I have this and it helps. I just can't take it off."

Micah's swift intake of air and his saucer-sized pupils had me worried. I yanked my sleeve back down, clutching my arm to my chest. Cole looked at me, clearly confused. Micah leaned across the space between us, his eyes still on my arm. "Can you show me again?" he asked. I pulled away a little, bothered by the look on his face. "I won't touch you. I promise," he said. His words were barely above a whisper and his behavior was alarming, but I had come this far, so I slowly eased my arm out and slid the fabric up again.

The silver cuff was tight on my forearm, close to my elbow. As I looked between Micah and the cuff, with all of its intricate designs and emblems, I couldn't help but ask, "Do you know what this is?"

"A miracle," he whispered. Shooting straight up, he was suddenly very anxious. "Cover it. Cover it now. Don't ever show it again. Not to me, not to anyone. Especially not my mother. I don't know how she could even use it, but she would try." Then, he started muttering as he locked his palms behind his head and stared skyward. "Is this how you've kept control? Why we had to start over? It's helping you temper the Keeper, isn't it?"

Cole piped in. "What are you guys talking about? What does mom's cuff have to do with any of this?" He moved to stand closer, motioning for me to pull up my sleeve again. Micah reached out, stopping just before he touched my arm. "No. Don't. Even though I believe this is a safe place, there is no place safe enough to have that anywhere others can see."

"Hold on, Cole. Micah, how did you know?" I asked.

"It's been obvious something changed. Your power was dramatically less and I felt less...emotional upheaval in you. I just couldn't determine what had changed. I thought maybe getting you away from..." He trailed off and wouldn't meet my eyes, pressing his lips closed as he stopped himself.

I stepped toward him, realizing exactly what he didn't say. "Aidan? You thought Aidan was the reason I was so emotional? You didn't stop to think maybe having the magic from the most powerful Elders stuck in a little room inside me might have contributed to all this? Or maybe having my entire life shot to hell over the course of just a few weeks had a little something to do with it?"

Having to say his name sent an ache through me. Longing for Aidan I had kept shoved down and out of my mind surfaced in a tidal wave of emotion. My eyes filled and I blinked back the tears as I allowed anger to replace my heartache. It was easier that way.

Cole stepped between us. My brother, ever the mediator. "Stop it. Both of you. This isn't getting us anywhere. Can we back up just a minute for the guy who hasn't been around to know what you're talking about?"

Micah spoke, his sentences punctuated with frustration and fact. "If my mother realizes Amelia is maintaining control through the cuff, then she will find some way to remove it to see what Amelia is truly capable of. There were only a handful of Mages able to create a piece like that and the amount of power held in those runes…I only hope you are the only one who can access it. But, she believes exactly what she said, no matter what you do or don't have. She wants to see exactly how much power you hold, then she can determine how much of it she wants. She thinks you have the power to give our people children again, and she is certain you are meant to end her. She will do whatever she has to do in order to break you, and then use you however she sees fit. It is why she's forcing the marriage issue…" he stumbled as he realized it was my brother he was talking to, "and, uh, everything that comes with that, or she could have something much worse in mind."

Cole's eyes darkened and his hostility built so fast, it had me amped up as well. "So what are we going to do about it?" he demanded.

Micah actually laughed a short bark devoid of any amusement. "So far, the plan has been simply to get Amelia to a place where she has a remote chance of surviving whatever it is my mother has planned. Based on what I saw last night, my mother isn't up to her normal mind games, which is worrisome. If I can't anticipate her next move, I can't help either of you. Our only saving grace is she believes I am not worthy of worrying about, which gives me access and freedom to try to figure out her game."

Micah was pacing, stopping every few steps like he was going to say something, but then shaking his head and continuing on. Cole stood, clenching and unclenching his fists, looking back and forth between Micah and me. I should have been coming up with a plan or brainstorming in some way, but my mind could only focus on one thing. For the first time since I had walked away from Aidan, I couldn't put him out of my mind. His face was all I could see. His declarations of love all I could hear. Had anyone explained what had happened to him? Was he okay? Had he found the other AniMages? I was scared to consider whether he missed me or had moved on. I wanted him to move on, didn't I?

Lost in my own thoughts, I barely caught Cole in my peripheral vision. He stumbled backward into the maze wall, gripping his throat. His mouth was open wide and I could see him trying desperately to pull in air. As both Micah and I ran the few steps to him, he dropped to the ground and began convulsing. His eyes rolled back into his head and I found myself screaming his name.

"What's happening? Micah, what the hell is happening?" I had no idea what to do or how to help him. "Cole? Cole! Stay with me, Cole!"

We were losing precious seconds and Micah was frozen in place. He suddenly looked up and swore violently. My eyes followed his and found Rhi standing in the window, a gloating smile on his face. *You will watch him die.*

Rhi's lips didn't move, but I heard the words as if he had stood next to me, whispering them in my ear.

"The hell I will!" I screamed the words up at him as I yanked my sleeve up, not even hesitating before I tore the cuff from my arm and grabbed my brother's face with both hands.

I vaguely heard Micah yell, "NO! Don't!" but she wouldn't be stopped. Cole couldn't die. We wouldn't allow it.

No sooner than the cuff hit the ground, I felt and heard the explosion in my mind. I screamed as the pain of the Keeper merging back together and the sudden infiltration of her power rocked my system. Everything I had done to break the five parts of the Keeper apart and keep them calm was undone in seconds. The darkness of the untethered Keeper filled me, layering on top of my own power, creating a bonfire roaring from my center outward. My cells were alive, dancing with electricity, while my mind spun in a hundred directions at once. I looked up at the window and the smile was gone from Rhi's face. His hands were pressed against the glass as he stared down at me intently. His face held no expression, but I could see the shock in his eyes. My head was filled with her and her pride at his reaction. I cocked my head slightly and smiled my own gloating smile. I started to stand, but I was still holding Cole's head.

That realization sliced through her domination of my mind and I shook my head, trying to regain control and direct the situation. I didn't have time for this. *He* didn't have time. I smashed my eyelids together and screamed inside my own head.

Cole. We have to help Cole! You have to stop the Hunter.

I felt her joy at being given a purpose and a fight. All of her focus switched to Cole. The pressure in my head rose, my body filling and my hands shaking as I tried to keep them on Cole. I was swaying back and forth as the violet smoke not only appeared around my hands, but surrounded me and Cole entirely. She had encased us and I could feel her explaining the need to attack from all sides, to prepare myself for our best work yet. Micah was moving around the barrier she'd erected, yelling at me, but I could hear him and I didn't care.

I barely managed to stay on my knees as our combined power flowed through my fingers and into my brother. My vision was filled with the inner workings of his body. I saw his damaged cells—the orange layered over his green magic—and wound my way through his system, unsure of what to do, but allowing her to guide me. She had to know. I trusted her to know how to save him. We zipped along his bloodstream from area to area, his body wrecked by the orange power attacking every piece of him. In his heart, though, is where we found the worst of the damage.

Orange electricity wrapped its way around his heart—a rope squeezing tighter and tighter, minimizing his blood flow and killing him. I was watching my brother die from the inside out.

Help him! Help me help him!

I could feel her confusion and frustration. She had brought me to the right place, but there was something I wasn't doing. Something only I could do. I had never stopped to think she would need me for anything. But, she was there, telling me she had given me the power to do what needed to be done. I heard her words inside my head—*Get to the rope.*

I opened my eyes and stared down at my hands, gripping each of Cole's cheeks. His face was tinged blue and I knew I had to do something. I couldn't stop staring at my hands and I was screaming out loud when everything changed. My hands weren't surrounded by violet smoke, they were made of it. Cole's body wasn't skin and clothes, I could see inside him. My hands disappeared inside his head and I yanked them back them out—finally understanding what we had to do. Fear filled me, but she was in the back of my mind yelling for me to go, to act now. He was dying.

Tears filled my eyes as I prayed I was making the right decision. I plunged my hands into his chest, dug my fingers between Rhi's bind and Cole's heart, and wrapped the cord inside my grip. I took a breath, simultaneously calling for as much power as possible. Tears streamed down my face as I screamed, pushing all of the power available to me at the orange glowing cord and then pulling it apart.

Power ricocheted through me as the cord snapped and somewhere above me, I heard a bellowing roar. Cole's heart started beating and I could see the blood pushing through his veins and arteries. But it wasn't enough. Rhi's binds were everywhere. I was exhausted, lightheaded…barely able to stay upright. But I couldn't stop. I gently wrapped my hands around my brother's heart and slowly pushed my power into his bloodstream. I watched the violet smoke fill him, spreading outward to the tips of his toes and his fingers with each beat from his heart. As each area was overtaken, I watched the orange layer peel away and disappear. I felt the pain, but his own power came back and tamped it down. Then, his breaths deepened and evened out. It could have been minutes or hours, but I didn't stop until I couldn't find another shred of orange light inside Cole.

When I finally pulled my hands away, I opened my eyes to find both my body and his back in their normal state. The smoke around us had dissipated and the Keeper was elated. She filled my body with strength I shouldn't have and cooed words of excitement to be back and promises of what we could accomplish in my head. I looked up to the window where Rhi had stood to find him gone.

Hatred filled me along with the need to hurt Rhi, to grab his heart with my own hands and squeeze it until it exploded in my palm. I struggled to my feet, my legs filled with pins and needles from being on my knees for so long. But I forced them to move, sending my own power through me to stop the pain. She goaded me, whispering all the ways we could make him pay into my ear. I stumbled forward and was about to shove my hand into the hedge, looking for the door out so I get to him, when arms came around me and something pinched around my forearm.

I vaguely comprehended the words "I'm sorry" as her shrill screams filled my head. And then, I heard nothing.

Chapter 17
Aidan

Twenty minutes after everyone left, I found myself lying in a four-post bed. Except this bed had a frame made of a black metal-like material I'd never seen with leather restraints coming from each post—restraints currently being strapped to my extremities. I wanted to make a joke about the setup, but I couldn't even string together the words, suddenly overwhelmed.

"Wait. Wait!" I yanked myself up, pulling my one free arm out of Elias's hands. Will was buckling the restraint around my left ankle and looked at me, eyebrows raised, silently questioning my outburst. I was holding my arm to my body, as if controlling one piece of me somehow made a difference.

"What the hell am I doing?" I asked, looking back and forth between Elias and Will. "We've got to talk about this. I don't even understand what Will is about to do to me. And, Elias, you just want me to believe this guy is going to help me? This whole thing has been built on lies and betrayals. How do I know you aren't going to kill me? I'm supposed to just allow myself to be tortured? And for what? Who is this guy?" I looked down at Will, who had sat back on his heels and was looking at me with barely-restrained hostility. "Who are you?"

Will looked over at Elias and again, something was exchanged. Elias nodded and Will came to my bedside. He reached a hand toward me and I recoiled a bit. "I'm not going to hurt you. I'm going to show you what you want to know." I wasn't sure what he meant, but then he touched his fingertips to my temple and I was staring at the inside of a dark room.

I was standing to the side, watching a scene play out, as I had done with Charlie, except this time, I was myself and Will was screaming. I've never heard those sounds come from a person. He was hanging in the center of a room, chains falling from the ceiling, holding his wrists apart.

Every few seconds, he screamed as his body lurched from one side to the other, looking as if he was trying to get away from an invisible attacker. The cuffs holding his wrists glowed bright red and the smell of burnt flesh filled my nostrils, making my stomach convulse. His screams turned into screeching howls as I watched him partially change. His eyes grew round and filled with yellow, short pointed ears sprouted from his head, and his arms were covered in the striped fur of a tiger. When the change hit the cuffs, the howls intensified, mixing with his human screams.

A low chuckle came from the dark corner of the room as a man walked toward Will. He flicked his hand right and then left and Will's body instantly reacted. I could barely register the slashing welts across his naked chest before they were scars. "Half-breed, when will you stop this nonsense and just tell me what I need to know?" he asked. His voice was achingly familiar and I recognized him from Charlie's memories. Was this the infamous Rhi?

Will's breath heaved in an out as he slowly swayed in the air. Finally, he looked up and met Rhi's gaze. "I don't have the information you seek, Rhi. And even if I did, there is anything you could do to force me to give it to you."

"Is that so?" Rhi spoke slowly as he raised both of his arms from his sides, his palms up. Orange fire burned brightly in his palms and his face twisted into a satisfied, terrifying smile. With the flick of his fingers, the screams started again. Will's legs reshaped and tucked into his body, his feet becoming paws and his barrel chest growing fur, but as soon as the shift made its way to the cuffs, the process instantly reversed. His screams became bellowing roars mixed with the high-pitched yowls of a big cat as bones lengthened, muscles reknit, and his cells fought to maintain one form or another. Tears streamed down Will's face as Rhi repeated the process, over and over, adding slashing welts to his back and legs as he forced the shift again and again. Will's body was broken, bruised, and confused, yet he kept healing. It had to be part of his abilities.

I knew I couldn't do anything to help him, this was only a memory, but my own beast was barely contained as I watched minute after long minute of the scene playing out in front of me. Rhi approached Will, his hand stretched in front of him. "You have one last chance, half-breed.

We will wipe each and every one of you from this planet one way or another. That is a guarantee. You can either tell me where to find Zendrick or I will take the thing you hold most dear."

Will simply hung there for a moment, his head dangling and his breathing ragged. With his chest heaving in and out and tears still dropping on their own accord, he slowly looked up. As his eyes connected with Rhi's, he spit blood at his feet. "He is gone. That is all I know. And I have nothing left. Your men burned my home to the ground with my wife and children in it."

"Indeed, they did. We are one step closer to cleansing our world of your mixed magic and evil breed." Rhi took the last step toward Will and cupped the back of his head in his large hand. As he neared Will, I barely caught his whispered words. "And now, animal, I will take your freedom and you will truly have nothing left."

As I came to, I knew those last screams would be ones I never forgot. Will had stepped away from me and stood, his arms crossed. "That is who I am, Aidan. I survived him and went on to find a way to remove the binds allowing Rhi access to my mind. He wanted to use me as a spy and assumed I couldn't find him inside me. But I did. He tried to wipe my memories, but he couldn't. I isolated myself until I found the way to remove every speck of his magic from me. I removed similar binds from Nathaniel, but I am the only one who has survived him, and you are the only one who can give me the revenge I desire."

"Revenge?" I couldn't fathom why anyone would want to go a second round with that guy.

Will smiled for the first time, a slow grin developing over seconds, sending a shiver down my spine. "Oh, yes. I will find him and I will kill him. I will take him apart piece by piece because I know how. I know exactly how. But you are the key. Without you to lead us and unite our people, I will never have that day. And I must."

I nodded slowly, my stomach lurching at the gravity of his words. How many other people had been waiting for me? How many others had stories to share and would expect me to help them? All I really wanted was to get to Amelia, but it was clear this was so much more than I'd imagined. Elias stood next to the bed, holding the last cuff, waiting for my reaction. I took a breath and extended my arm.

As Elias leaned in, he held my stare. "Focus on her. Not the rest of it. Just her. You'll get through this."

Will sat at the head of the bed in an old kitchen table chair. He leaned over me and touched his forehead to mine, placing his hands on my temples. I closed my eyes, needing to forget the awkwardness of his closeness. "Elias is here to help control you. Don't worry about how much you move or scream. We will make sure you don't hurt yourself. And the restraints are reinforced with my power, so they will help."

I kept my eyes closed and tried to block out his words. I couldn't hear them tell me again how much I was going to hurt or scream. My beast was strangely silent, as if he knew we were where we needed to be. Hopefully Dillon was right. Hopefully this is where I would meet my wolf. I tried to relax against the mattress and did as Elias had instructed—I focused on Amelia.

I brought her image into my mind. Her smile. The way her eyes gave away everything she was thinking. The purple dress she was wearing the night she told me she wanted to give us a try. I thought of all the time we spent on her couch playing twenty questions, just trying to get to know each other and realizing though we were so different, we had lived similar lives. We had just never known exactly how similar until it was too late.

Since I had started figuring out what I was, I spent a lot of time trying to put myself in her shoes. I tried to understand what it had to be like to hide yourself from the world, to try to live two lives and be two people in the same body. And the more I learned about the Queen and the history of her—our—people, I respected Amelia even more for the choices she made. Bethany had been right. I couldn't judge anything Amelia had done until I understood it. Now, I did. And the only thing that mattered was getting her back. I'd get her away from the Queen and I'd protect her. I'd be whatever she needed because I wanted to be the choice she made. So much in both of our lives hadn't been a choice, and I wanted the time they took from us. She would choose me this time. I knew she would. I had to believe that.

I knew the second Will entered my mind. The pressure in my head increased and my wolf reacted to the perceived threat. My senses sharpened and I wondered how I could stop myself from attacking him, but he simply sat in the back of my head, waiting it out. Slowly, my wolf calmed and Will started to move. He probed around, looking for something. I spent minutes feeling him making his way through me, a warmth spreading to each cell and extremity as he passed through. I braced myself, expecting pain, but so far, it had felt like a warm blanket, soothing my system and dulling my senses to a twilight feeling where I wasn't sure whether I was awake or asleep.

Then hands pressed down on my chest and the first shot of pain ripped through me. I struggled to breathe and tried to sit up only to be shoved back down. It felt like my heart was exploding. My body seized and I ripped at the restraints. I couldn't form words as my skin felt like it was being ripped from my muscles one centimeter at a time—a razor scraping between the two layers, leaving raw, open wounds in its place.

Will's hands gripped my head like a vise. His forehead pressed into mine, the connection point between our skin burning. I bucked and tossed on the bed while Elias straddled my hips, trying to keep me still. I could hear them yelling back and forth as I pulled at the restraints and roared wordless promises of retribution. My screams were short bursts of sound as each bone in my body was broken and reset. As each fingernail was removed and replaced. I would swear he ripped out each hair on my body individually and replaced it with new. I couldn't think of anything but the pain—never-ending, all-consuming pain. It could have been minutes, or hours, or days, I had no idea. I screamed until my voice gave out and my throat was raw from the attempts.

Time stretched on, until finally, something inside me snapped and broke open. Relief flooded my system and euphoria drowned out the pain. The wolf's memories assaulted me, a barrage of images, sounds, and words hitting my mind all at once, like a family video showing every scene simultaneously as his mind merged with mine. I saw the world from his eyes. I saw Amelia. I saw her apartment building, her sitting on the couch at Cole's with Charlie, and the gym. They weren't my memories, yet they were. I must have been watching her. Her arms were wrapped around my wolf form and I heard her words as she cried into my coat. I saw her laughing as she lay with her head on my chest, her fingers twirling in my fur. Somehow, she and I had been together while I was shifted and I had no memory of it until now.

I heard the low yips and barks from my wolf as he celebrated us finally being one. I could no longer separate myself from him and I felt...everything.

My hyper-senses were on overload. Smelling the sweat coating our bodies, feeling the fear we all held, and knowing the trash needed to be emptied from the kitchen. Then, the memories took hold once again, and I saw the first clear memory I could remember of my parents. They were holding a small wolf pup, laughing as they congratulated me on my first successful shift. I saw the loving looks they exchanged and confirmed I truly was the spitting image of my father.

Then I saw Rhi. I saw him fling my mother across the room, her body flying through a window and the glass puncturing her skin. I saw the pleasure he took in holding my father locked in place while he drained my mother's life. He stood there, smiling, his hand outstretched and orange flames connecting him to her. I had been upstairs, watching through the crack of a door, where I had hidden when I heard my mother's screams. Another Hunter found me, cowering in the back of my closet, where I had shifted in response to my fear. The large hood from his jacket fell over his face, like the reaper, as he held me by the scruff of my coat and then pulled me to his chest, whispering, "You must live. You are the one. I will do what I can to protect you. This will only hurt for a moment. Quiet now."

Finally, darkness pulled at the edges of my mind and I welcomed the reprieve. I couldn't fight anymore, so I let it take me under.

I had been awake for a while, but was afraid to move. Nothing hurt, which was more worrisome than I expected. After what I had been through, I was afraid if I did more than breathe, the pain would return. There was just no way I was going to be able to get up and walk around after that ordeal.

"Yes, you can. Well, theoretically you should be fine." Elias's voice came from somewhere else in the room and I sighed.

"I thought you were staying out of my head?" I asked, moving only my mouth and nothing else.

"We had to make sure you were healing properly so I didn't have a choice. You shouldn't even be awake yet, but from what we've been able to tell, you're fine." His voice had moved closer and I turned my head slightly to see him standing at the edge of the bed.

"You're sure?" I was unconvinced.

"As sure as we can be. Try to sit up," he suggested.

I moved slower than I needed to. With every inch I pushed myself up, I expected a reaction I didn't get. Finally, I was sitting fully upright and decided to stand. I swiveled my body on the bed and took Elias's outstretched hand, allowing him to slowly pull me to my feet.

There was nothing but a tinge of dizziness. And then my stomach growled. Elias laughed. "Well, outside of hungry, how do you feel?"

I stretched my arms out to the side, allowing my body to expand while I tried to get a read on each group of muscles. "I feel...amazing. Like I could run a marathon. Or go five rounds." I couldn't help but return Elias's smile as I pulled my fists up into a fighter's stance and bounced on the balls of my feet.

"Where's Will?" I asked, looking around.

Elias's smile faltered. "He needs to rest, so he's in the other room. He...well, he was a little shocked at what we found inside you. We both were. Let's get some breakfast and I'll explain."

Elias led me into a small kitchen and gestured for me to sit at the table. I took one of the chairs and he set a glass of water and orange juice down in front of me before pulling out eggs, pre-cooked bacon, and bread. I downed both glasses and he refilled them as he started cooking. I waited for him to speak, aware on some level he was nervous about what he was about to say. The senses that had gone ballistic during the unbinding were still at level ten and I was barraged with smells, sounds, and emotions.

Elias set the plates on the table, sat down, and finally spoke. "It's only been four hours, Aidan. You should have been out for days, maybe a week. In four hours, your body has completely healed and your mind seems to have recovered every moment you lost. We didn't intend to spy on your memories, but you can do things our people shouldn't be able to do. And this bind wasn't placed on you by Rhi. It wasn't done to hurt you. A Hunter did this to protect you."

Elias paused, running a hand through his red hair before saying, "He didn't just bind you, Aidan. The Hunter gave you a part of him. He shared his power with you. You are part AniMage and part Hunter. Right now, we don't know what that means, who he was, or why one of them would ever help one of us. All we know is you are something we've never seen before, and if there was any question before, there is none now. You are our King."

I was their King. Being an AniMage felt right. Being their King felt ludicrous. And knowing I had the most evil power out there running through me was deflating at best, depressing at worst. But now was the time to deal in facts, rather than dwelling over more unknowns. And the fact was, I was whole, I was free, and I had everything I needed to get to Amelia.

Chapter 18
Amelia

I opened my eyes to find myself in the woods, lying on bed of leaves and staring up through empty branches. I exhaled a shaking breath, wondering whether these dreams were a matter of protection. Did my head bring me here because it knew I couldn't handle the real world anymore? But Cole was fine. He had to be. When I got up from his body, he was breathing and his power was unbound. I was certain of it.

Micah had to have put the cuff back on my arm. It was the only explanation for the reaction from my Keeper. I silently thanked whoever was up there for the Keeper, but also for Micah doing what he had. I would have gone after Rhi. I would have broken down every door and killed whomever was in my way to get to him. There was no question. And I wasn't a killer. That was what scared me most about her. She turned me into someone I wasn't and made me want to be that person. She made me crave the destruction she loved.

I lay back against the leaves, hearing them crunch beneath me as I waited for Aidan to come. So far, every time I'd woken up here, he had been there as well. I needed the relief my mind had been giving me and smiled at the thought of him—even in wolf form. I wanted to curl into his chest and splay my fingers in his fur while I told him what had happened today. I needed his reassurance that I had made the right choice and it was going to be okay—that whatever I woke up to, I could face.

But he wasn't here, and the longer I sat there, the more frustrated I became. This was my dream, damn it. I sat up, saying as much. "Come on! These are supposed to be the dreams I want to have, so give him to me!" I wasn't sure how I was supposed to communicate with my own subconscious, but my heart was still racing and I was so agitated. The after-effects of the Keeper were a mad rush in my system and all I wanted was the proximity to Aidan I knew would bring me balance.

I shoved myself up from the ground and decided to go searching. He had to be here somewhere. As I worked my way through the bare trees, I could hear something. The sound went from an echo on the wind to drumming in my ears and my heartbeat raced. Cries wrought with pain filled my mind and stole my breath. I worried the Keeper had taken some of Cole's memories of Rhi's torture, but those weren't Cole's cries. They were Aidan's. Every fiber of my being reacted to his bellowing howls as adrenaline shot through me. He was here somewhere and I had to get to him.

I ran, yelling Aidan's name as I tore through the forest in search of him. His agony was torture. My lungs ached and my muscles burned as I ran harder, but it didn't matter how far I ran or loud I hollered his name, the sounds coming from Aidan never changed in volume. I couldn't determine whether I was getting closer or farther away. I stopped, using a thick trunk to hold myself up as I heaved breaths in and out.

Trying to decide which path to take, I turned first right and then left, but the screams stopped. I stood still, a statue in the clearing. I took shallow breaths as I strained to find the sounds again, but there was nothing. I sat down in the exact spot I stood, my legs crossed and my hands in my lap. I tried not to make a sound as I scanned from one edge of my vision to the other. I waited, jumping at every rustle of leaves or snap of a twig. I waited for Aidan to appear, or the sounds to begin again, but neither happened. As the sun slowly started to go down, I lay down, pulling myself into a fetal position as tears slid from my eyes.

I couldn't feel him. My power sought his, expanding out of me and searching everywhere it could reach. I had no idea where Aidan was or what had happened, but I was suddenly certain these were not dreams. I had felt the echoes of his pain ricocheting through my own body and it was very real. I pulled myself into the smallest ball possible, silent sobs wracking my frame. I had told myself I could protect him by making this choice. Now I had no idea if he was even alive.

Pounding on my door woke me and I was confused to be in my bed. My eyes were swollen from crying and I was still tucked into a ball on my side. I heard Micah on the other side, yelling, "I'm coming in!"

I sat up, pulled the covers around me, and rubbed my eyes, unsure of what was real and what was in my head. Had I finally lost it?

Micah looked concerned and my head finally caught up to reality. "Cole?" My voice was a croak in my throat and my stomach clenched as I spoke.

"He's sleeping in my room. It was the only safe place for him." Micah stood back and looked at me with a puzzled expression.

"What?" I threw the covers off and stalked to the bathroom. It was satisfying not to wait for his answer, and even more so to let the bathroom door slam behind me. I wasn't mad at Micah, but I was a mess.

My heart ached with worry and guilt for Aidan and my brother. They were both in danger because of me and there was nothing I could do about it. Aidan could actually…no, I couldn't go there. He had to be okay. He just had to be. I stared into the mirror and wondered who this girl was. This girl who was challenging Hunters and

Queens and fighting with power she didn't understand. I wished I could have taken my mother's journals from the library. There had to be information in them I could use. I sighed and tried to focus on the issue at hand. Micah was in my bedroom, looking stressed, which only meant something bad was about to happen.

It took a few minutes to brush my teeth, wash my face, and pull my hair into a knot on top of my head. When I came back out, Micah was sitting at the small table in the corner. I came up behind him and saw his leg bouncing up and down as he tapped his hand on the table.

I tucked myself into the chair opposite him, pulling one leg under me. "He saw me. He saw everything. They know about the cuff and what I can do, don't they?"

He nodded, his expression solemn. When his eyes finally connected with mine, for the first time, I saw fear. Micah had been preparing me ever since I arrived but he had never let on that he was afraid for me. It was part of what gave me strength. He was concerned about how I would handle things, but he had never been afraid *for me*.

A lump formed in my throat. My mouth went dry and my tongue felt huge. My stomach rolled and I thought I was going to throw up right there. I swallowed down the acidic taste and took a deep breath.

"What do I do?" I asked quietly.

Micah didn't speak for a moment. "She's asked for you. Just you, in her chambers. I'm not allowed to join you. I don't know what's about to happen, Amelia. But she knows. Rhi saw everything. He felt the bonds breaking, which has only happened to him one other time, and he's spent his life searching for the man who broke his spell. I've…I've just never seen anything like it. Did you know you had those abilities?"

I shook my head, jerky motions that didn't stop as my mind spun in circles, trying to guess what was about to happen. I was staring over Micah's shoulder, my head still bobbing back and forth when he reached out and grabbed my hand.

"It's going to be okay, Amelia." It was a lie and we both knew it. He couldn't know whether it would be okay. "I can keep Cole safe for now. Bale is with him. You don't have to worry. He's already so much better. I think he'll be awake in the next few hours and I think I can get him out of here. But you have to get ready and you have to have your wits about you."

"Can you find Aidan?" The question slipped between my lips like a secret I wasn't supposed to tell. I smashed my lips together as soon as it was out, but I couldn't take it back. I needed to know if what I'd gone through last night meant anything. I had to know whether he was alive.

Micah's nostrils flared as his eyes turned cold. "Aidan? Why? Do you really think he's the person you need to be worried about right now?"

I shook my head. Aidan couldn't matter right now and Micah probably wouldn't believe me if I tried to explain. Besides, there was a chance Micah could be my mate. I needed to stay focused. "No. Just...never mind. It doesn't matter. How long do I have?"

"One hour. That's the best I could do." Micah stood, staring down at me as his eyes softened. "Good luck, Amelia."

I stood as well. We were just a few feet apart and there were so many words we could have said, but we said none of them. Finally, Micah nodded and moved to step around me toward the door. Before I could stop myself, I stepped directly in his path, my eyes filled with unshed tears as fear overtook my system and my mind ran rampant with the possibilities of what might happen. I looked up at him, my mind and heart a fractured, broken heap. Facts, emotions, and suppositions piled on top of each other so quickly, I couldn't distinguish one from the next. I hadn't even recovered from the day and night, let alone pulled myself together enough to handle the Queen.

Micah didn't speak as he looked down at me, eyes filled with compassion and regret. He simply wrapped his arms around me and pulled me into his chest. The tears slowly slid down my cheeks and disappeared into his jacket as he held the back of my head against him. My own arms stayed down at my sides as I absorbed the heat from his body and the moment of safety he gave me. I couldn't bear to pull myself from him and the sanctuary he provided, allowing me to be as broken as I'd felt for weeks.

Finally, he whispered, "You have faced everything head on, Amelia. You have persevered against all of the odds. You have controlled the uncontrollable. You have broken the unbreakable. You have given yourself—all of you—to this cause. You are stronger than you believe. You are more than we ever expected. You will survive this, too."

I expected Baleon to walk me all the way to Julia's chambers. He was sworn to protect me and I could have used the reassurance of at least one friendly face, even it was expressionless and silent. Instead, an unknown Hunter intercepted me and took me the rest of the way. I didn't try to speak to him, but a part of me wanted to rage at him. To scream he was the one who was wrong. I was the good guy in all of this. But, it didn't matter. So, I just followed him as he led me down hallway after hallway until we reached her door.

He knocked twice and her muffled invitation to enter came back in response. He swung the door inward and gestured me inside. Some part of me had hoped he would come in as well. Even if he wasn't on my side, I would have felt better knowing I wasn't facing her alone. But he stood, holding the door, finally glaring down at me until I moved.

I took cautious steps into a large sitting room. The drapes were drawn closed, blocking out the daylight, and a fire burned in the fireplace as Julia stood at the mantle, staring down into the flames. She was wearing another gown, this time a deep scarlet, a stark contrast to her blond hair.

As I looked around, I couldn't help but wonder when the Immortals planned to fully join the twenty-first century. Her clothes were medieval, as were the decorations all over Cresthaven. Even this room was filled with high-backed furniture in drab patterns, dark woodwork, and heavy tapestries.

She finally spoke, interrupting my musings. "You think I am a crazed woman. A tyrant who's lost her mind. But you haven't seen what I have, child." Sadness permeated the space as she turned to face me.

"You hear their stories of the terrors I've ordered, but they don't tell you of the losses before I took control. You hear of the terrible atrocities my Hunters have committed, but not of the races turning on each other. You idolize the Elders you come from, but you don't understand what they withheld from us simply to maintain their hold on our people. I am not the monster everyone believes—even Mikail." I couldn't stop my eyes from widening and I cursed myself for confirming her statement.

She simply laughed. "I know what he sees when he looks at me. I know my son, Amelia."

Julia gestured to a couch near me as she sat in a high-backed chair.

I glanced from side to side, trying to get my bearings in the room before turning my back to half of it. My mind raced, trying to determine her angle. There had to be one. Micah had told me she was all about head games. I had to find a way to play her game.

I sat slowly, forcing myself to relax into the couch cushions. It was hard and uncomfortable, as I imagined she had intended. I swallowed. "I've heard many sides, your highness, but not yours. Is that why you've called for me?"

She closed her eyes for a moment, and for a split second, I both saw and felt her exhaustion and concern. It flooded the room, the emotion becoming thick in the air. She had to be opening herself up to me. I felt that she truly loved her people. She had been fighting for so long and couldn't find the answers she needed, but she kept going. She refused to give up on them. She wanted my help and she was making it plainly clear.

"You are so young." Her words startled me. While she still sat perfectly straight, she rested her chin in her palm, her elbow on the arm of the chair. She studied me and I could only do the same. "I was young once, too. I looked around at the world and thought I could make a difference. I thought I could live my dreams and have the life I wanted, but it was taken from me, brutally ripped from my hands and tossed in my face.

"I made choices, Amelia. Choices that didn't feel like choices at all. My anger and my grief sent me down paths I hadn't known existed and once I was there, it was too late. Do you know what it takes to control these Hunters?"

Her question surprised me even more than the honesty she was sharing. "N-No, your highness." I stumbled over the words and forced myself to swallow, sitting straighter myself. "I can't imagine, your grace."

The corner of her painted lips rose in a wry smile. "Of course you don't, because you are a child with power you don't deserve." I recoiled a little, but she continued. "The collars they wear link them to me. At any time, I can use them to control their actions or see their thoughts. They are an army belonging to me. But it requires power I thought was lifelong. It is not. And I need your cuff so I can continue. I need you to give it to me, Amelia."

"Excuse me?" There were no respectful pleasantries. The words just fell out of my mouth as I stared at her. I couldn't reconcile her confession of waning power, or her belief I would hand over my cuff simply because she asked.

"Rhi saw what you did yesterday, Amelia. You need to use your power. You need to embrace it and channel it. You don't need the cuff for control. You don't need control. You just need to try harder. You're an Elder, which means your power can be used at will. This is an opportunity and you have to stop running from it."

I couldn't even speak. She had absolutely no clue what she was saying. All along, I thought she understood the prophecy and what was happening, but she thought I was actually choosing not to use my power rather than actively working to figure out how.

"You need to look around you, child, and realize you are lucky. You will marry my son. You will have glorious little babies filled with the most powerful magic ever known and you will be the beginning of a new era. You will continue to build the Mages to their rightful place and we will create the next dynasty." She looked so sure, so eager. I could only continue to stare at her as the words replayed in my head. I tried to connect the excitement and hope I saw in her eyes with the realities of what she'd outlined.

I swallowed. It was a dry, worthless act, but it made me think before I spoke. "Do you truly believe it is so simple? Do you even understand what I have inside me? And you think I'm just going to go along with this demented plan of yours simply because you said so? I'm just going to marry Micah and pop out some babies and the world will be right? Have you lost your mind?"

I had wanted to be deferential and appropriate, but the panic lodged in my chest and the subsequent anger over her ignorance took over the connection between my mind and my mouth.

The Queen sighed and stood. "As I suspected, you are still a foolish child. With everything you've seen and what you know I can do to you and those you love, you still refuse to do your duty. You are willful and disrespectful and everything I despised about your mother. She refused to fall in line and play her part as well." Julia closed her eyes for a brief second and I heard the door open.

I jumped to my feet just as arms closed around me from the back. I struggled, kicking and shooting blasts at the feet of whomever was restraining me, screaming out for Micah and Baleon. I got half of Micah's name out before my limbs were locked at my side and my mouth snapped shut. Julia's fingers pinched my chin and turned my face to hers. I was just inches from her and her bright red eyes.

"I want you to understand I tried to do this the nice way," she hissed. "I tried to give you the benefit of the doubt, as my son asked me to. Mikail obviously did not do a good enough job convincing you during your time together. And you don't even appreciate having your brother returned to you." She shook her head slowly, a low "Tsk, tsk, tsk," accompanying the movement.

Arguments and counter points were swirling in my mind as Rhi moved from behind me and stepped next to the Queen. I had instantly known it was him controlling me. With a tight-lipped smile, looking far too satisfied, he yanked my sleeve up. As he reached for the cuff, the Queen stopped him.

"No. Let me." She looked like a kid in a candy store, her eyes wide as she stared. I waited,

279

staring at her, knowing if she removed the cuff, I would destroy everything. I would end them and this could all be over. They didn't realize this. She didn't know what was truly inside of me. I stopped resisting and instead, hoped she would. I was tired of it all.

Just as Queen Julia's palm wrapped around the cuff, she started screaming. My movements were under my control again and I looked down to see the cuff glowing white as she howled in pain, shaking her hand back and forth. Her palm was bright red, the runes visible in the burn.

"Get her out of here!" Rhi yelled. As the Hunter pulled me backwards toward the door, I could only smile at the Queen and Rhi.

Chapter 19
Aidan

I walked the woods outside Will's cabin, picking my way through the trees as my mind churned through the last twenty-four hours. Every now and again, I would stop, close my eyes, and connect to my wolf. He was always there now. I only had to link to him to feel his intuition and emotion. Dillon had described it perfectly. I wasn't really able to talk to him, but he spoke to me in his own ways.

I probably should have felt odd to have someone else inside my head, but this felt right. Together, we were Aidan the AniMage. I was no longer Aidan the human with a beast living inside me. To test my theory, I stopped and held my hand out in front of me. As fast as I thought the words, my hand shifted into a paw. In another blink, it was simply a hand again. There was no pain. The stretching and breaking I had previously felt was now a seamless melding of bones and sinew. Elias had explained that without my full AniMage abilities, which now included healing, I had felt each part of the shift. That wasn't how it was supposed to be, and I wouldn't miss the pain.

I laughed out loud. I could feel his pride inside me. His relief that we were finally as we needed to be. But what was the Hunter piece of it all? Elias said the Hunter who had bound the AniMage in me had done it to protect me, but he had also infused a piece of himself. What did that mean? How did I access that? Again, I held my hands out in front of me and allowed the power to build. Small blue orbs of crackling light gathered in my palms. I tried to picture them as orange, like the power I'd seen in Will's memory, but nothing happened except a snort of displeasure from my wolf. I shook my head and kept going. I needed to use the physical exertion to let my mind wander. There were answers here, I could feel it. I just needed to give my brain time to sort through it all.

As I pushed up steep inclines, I no longer became winded or tired. Energy would fill me and adrenaline kept me going. As I thought about my parents, I could now access footage of when I was young and what it had felt like to be loved by them—when I was accepted for who and what I was, and knew I was safe. As my mind bounced to Amelia—to the moment my wolf had come alive inside me—I saw that night at the theater and finally understood. She had broken the first binds. She hadn't meant to, but that night while she held my hand and attacked Melinda, her power had inadvertently flooded my system and the first door was opened. That was the first night I shifted and the first night my wolf had overtaken me.

Amelia. I sighed. And then my wolf was tugging at my mind, his frantic energy filling me as he made it clear he had information for me. I closed my eyes and rescinded my control. Visions of Amelia in the woods as she cried into my fur filled my head. Then it flashed to me stretched out, her head on my belly as she spoke. Her words filled my head. She told me what she and Micah had been doing—the mental training and the journals she had found from her mother. She told me of her guard, the Hunter Baleon, and how he irritated her to no end because he refused to speak to her, but she knew she was getting under his skin. She got quiet as she described having to face Queen Julia for the first time and the idiotic ways she had provoked her.

I felt her fear and I hated myself for having to lay there while she hurt. I saw her twist the ends of her hair as she spoke, the words not stopping until she fell asleep, curling onto her side, her fingers twisting in my coat. The last scene he showed me was just days before the binds had been broken. I hadn't remembered it until now, but she was so clear in my mind. Her words sliced me to the core as she cried, her arms wrapped around me. "I've missed you so much, Aidan." What I didn't expect was for her voice to continue, saying words I hadn't heard or expected. "This is the only place I feel safe. Every day, I wake up and wonder what I'll have to face. I never feel like I've made the right choice. Being away from you hurts all the time—I have to force myself to block you from my mind. I'm sorry for the choices I had to make. I'm sorry I couldn't return your words."

I stood still, afraid to even breathe, lest she disappear and the words stop. She had heard me. She had told me we were over and I was nothing, but I knew she didn't mean it. We had shared too much of ourselves and I knew those weren't words she'd use, even if she felt them. They were forced and she had refused to tell me the truth. She walked away and hid inside her apartment. As I had pounded on the door and called for her, the words slipped from my mouth before I could stop them.

I hadn't actively thought about it before then, but being faced with losing her made our connection more real. Afterward, I had thought it was ridiculous. We'd known each other just a few months. And while we had spent every second we could together, or connected through texts and emails, it seemed over the top to think we could be in love. Looking back, I could fill in the pieces of stories she'd told me where magic should have played a part, but we'd both laid ourselves bare, sharing about our parents, our upbringing, our fears...connecting on a level neither of us had expected.

Now, I saw my overprotectiveness for what it was. If we were the subjects of this prophecy then it seemed only logical that my innate response to her would be protection. And as a man who was part wolf, I wasn't going to be able to stop the dominating part of me. I chuckled a little, remembering that night on the beach when she finally admitted to wanting to be kissed as much as I wanted to kiss her. Not even a millisecond later, I had her in my arms and didn't let her go until we were both breathless. The glazed look in her eyes and her swollen lips told me she clearly liked the dominating side of me. Something tickled in the back of my mind...a niggling little thought that I couldn't quite grab. There was something here I was missing. I nudged at my wolf to see if it was him, but his response was an annoyed exhale.

I started walking again, this time back toward Will's. All these thoughts of Amelia made our end goal of getting to her push to the forefront of my mind again. I needed to figure myself out, but I had to move faster. She had given me information. I stopped in my tracks, my mouth falling open.

Montgomery, you're an idiot.

It had been there the whole time—she had given me the information. Somehow, we had ended up in the same place and she had told me. I had to get back there. If I could get there, she could help me to help her. I took off running toward the cabin, praying Elias and Will would know how I could find her again.

One of the perks of being an AniMage was super-speed, apparently, because I made it back to the cabin in record time. I flung open the door and Will turned to me slowly, one eyebrow arched, while Elias showed no reaction.

"You're in my head again, aren't you?" I asked dryly.

Elias flicked his gaze up to mine. "It would help if you weren't broadcasting it as far and loud as possible," he said as he stood and moved toward me. "But we need to get back to camp. If you're one hundred percent, let's shift and get going. We can talk while we cover ground."

I gave Elias a short nod and he walked outside. Will followed, still not speaking to me. He actually kept some distance between us and I was mildly offended. The guy had seen the inner workings of my mind and body, yet, since he knew a Hunter had helped me, he wouldn't acknowledge my existence. I shook my head a little and followed them outside. Elias was already down to his shorts and Will was pulling off his shirt as I approached. I'd spent years in locker rooms with half-naked guys, but stripping before shifting was still awkward. Often, before they shifted, the AniMages would throw their clothes in a pack and carry it in their mouths or with their claws, depending on their animal of choice. Will and Elias had tossed theirs to the ground, so apparently we would find new clothes once we got back to camp.

I looked around a little and sidestepped behind a larger tree trunk. In the time it took me to get my jeans off, I could hear the rumble of big cats. I looked around the tree to see Elias had taken the form of a sleek panther and Will a massive tiger. There wasn't time for debate, so I yanked my shirt over my head and whispered under my breath, "Let's do this," trying to reassure myself as I prayed the shift would work.

I inhaled a deep breath and the exhale was a snort from my muzzle. Just like that, I was in my wolf form. I blinked a few times, trying to adjust to the feeling of being contained in a body with four legs. I stretched, pulling backward and then pushing forward, my back arching as the muscles tightened and contracted. The dirt under my paws was gritty and moist, and the scents of the woods were sharper in my nose. I could smell a rabbit and heard the rustle of what I knew was a deer in the vicinity.

Let's go.

I heard Elias's voice in my head and turned to see the two animals looking at me expectantly.

Um...can you hear me?

Will's voice was loud and perturbed. *Of course we can hear you. This is how we communicate.*

And clearly, the guy who's actually present for the first time in his animal form would know that, right?

I couldn't stop the response and felt my blood pressure rise with the exchange. Something in me was building, making me want to assert my dominance over Will. I wanted his respect. I heard the whisper in my own mind saying I deserved it. Shaking my head in an attempt to clear the chaos and stop a response guaranteeing to start a standoff, I echoed Elias. *Let's go*, I said, and took off.

I probably should have let the other two lead, but I knew exactly how to get where we were going. My wolf had been aware during our trip out here, so the path was ingrained in my mind. It was the first time I had experienced the freedom of running. My paws gripped the ground and I loped through the trees, feeling worry free for the first time. Nothing mattered but the air in my lungs and the burn in my muscles. I allowed myself the time to enjoy the simple happiness until Elias was in my mind again.

You came back wanting to talk. What about?

How is it possible I was able to connect with Amelia in wolf form? Do you know how I can get to her again? I need to talk to her. I'm pretty sure she thinks those were dreams. She kept saying she didn't want the dream to stop. But they weren't. We can share information and use our connection to help her escape. At least, I hope we can.

Elias was silent. It was Will who responded.

Show us.

The thought of sharing our intimate moments rose my hackles and a low growl formed in the back of my throat.

Calm down, kid. We just need to see what you mean. What you're saying isn't something we know how to do.

Will's lack of patience for my learning curve was really starting to piss me off, but I saw his point. If this wasn't an AniMage trick, maybe it was the first display of my Hunter ties.

Fine. I pulled at the memory. It felt like opening someone else's filing cabinet and removing their personal files, but I did it. I only let a portion play inside my mind, keeping Amelia's secrets between us. I cut the memory off and waited. This time, Elias spoke as we dodged between fir trees and through ravines and creeks.

That definitely isn't something you got naturally. AniMages don't have those skills. Honestly, I don't know of any race capable of it. But you are something different entirely. My best guess is it comes from the mixed magic inside you, combined with your connection to Amelia.

The best you can do is guess? Is there anyone who would know? I have to find a way back to her. The need to get to Amelia was overwhelming. It was hard to stay focused on anything but her, but I needed answers. I needed more than a guess.

You don't get it, kid. Will's gruff tone cut in. *What you are isn't normal. You weren't born from a Hunter and AniMage, yet you carry both inside you. I was only able to give you access to this power. There is no way to remove the Hunter from you. You're on your own. No one can help you, but you.*

The silence between the three of us lasted until we approached the caves and the AniMages' hiding place. Elias had explained they had likely been here too long, but they had known Amelia was in Brighton and were determined to get to her before the Queen did. They had spent their lives outrunning Hunters, but over the last few years, the Queen had been less interested in them. They just weren't sure where her focus had gone. It gave them the opportunity to stay in one place for longer, though their wariness still kept them on edge. We heard the hooting of an owl above us and I looked up to see Dillon.

Mr. Aidan! Mr. Elias! I'm so glad you're here. Braxton is causing all sorts of problems, sir. He has everyone very upset. And he made me go get Miss Bethany and Charlie, even though you told me they were supposed to stay away. Are you going to punish him, sir? Can I help?

Dillon's voice gained volume and pitch as he hurried through his update. He was clearly anxious and had been searching the woods for some sign of us.

Elias responded. *Calm down, Dillon. Let's all get back to human form and then we can talk. Okay?*

The owl dove toward the ground, flying right over us and behind a bush. Dillon sprang up, his red hair sticking out every which way as he tried to pull his pants on, not drop his pack, hop toward us, and talk at the same time.

"But, sir, it's bad. He's got everyone really upset and wondering why we're waiting on Mr. Aidan instead of going to attack Cresthaven. He doesn't believe in Mr. Aidan and now they sound like they don't either. But, we still do, sir. Mr. Aidan is the one, right?" Dillon eyes shifted from Elias, to me, to Will. At this point, we all had pulled on sweats left in the trees and thankfully, Elias spoke, because I had no idea what to say to Dillon.

"Breathe, Dillon. Why don't you tell me where Braxton is and we'll just go find out exactly what's happening? And yes, I don't just *believe* Aidan is our leader. I *know* he is. You trust me, don't you?" Elias crouched down, getting on Dillon's level. He held up a closed fist and Dillon smiled, bumping it with his own.

"I sure do, sir. Let's go get 'em. He's talking in the clearing." Dillon stopped and muttered, "Trying too damn hard to be like you, sir, if you ask me."

I struggled to keep a straight face and so did Elias. I even saw Will press his lips together.

Through clenched teeth, Elias tried to reprimand Dillon's swearing, but failed miserably. Instead, he said, "Let's just go."

We all snuck along the perimeter quietly, wanting to hear exactly what this Braxton character was up to. I had no clue who he was, but Elias hadn't seemed surprised that he was causing trouble. We didn't have to go far before we could hear him.

"Are we really going to trust some guy who showed up out of nowhere and can barely maintain his own shift? A guy who claims to be the discarded boyfriend of the Keeper? Why aren't we mobilizing and making our way to Cresthaven? We know the Keeper is there and so is the Queen. We could be getting the girl and even finding a way to take out the Queen!" We could hear the muddled questions and hollers of agreement in response to Braxton's accusations.

"We're going to entrust our lives and our futures to a stranger? Elias's vision is clouded. This Aidan is not our leader. He claims he looks like the long lost Zendrick, but none of us knew Zendrick. There is no one to corroborate his story—"

Just as my blood pressure rose and my wolf stirred, I heard a man's voice carry over the crowd. "Excuse me."

Braxton's response to being interrupted was filled with fury. I could feel his barely contained rage before I even heard his words. "What? Who are you? You aren't an AniMage. You have no right to speak here."

"Don't I?" he responded. "You speak of the Keeper. A girl who is prophesized to change our future, and is being kept captive by the Queen. You think she can help you and give you back your place in the world. That girl is not just *some girl*. She is not *just* the Keeper. She is *my daughter*."

I had known it was Nathaniel speaking before he finished. I only wished Amelia could be here to see her father fight for her.

The crowd quieted and Nathaniel continued.

"You say you don't believe in Elias or Aidan? I can tell you the three of us were just as close to Zendrick as Elias was, and we will also vouch for his son. I have been a friend of the AniMages my whole life. My wife and I ran from our home, not only to escape Julia and keep our children safe, but to fight on the side of those we believed in— you. My Liana died at the hands of a Hunter, on orders from the Queen, while she was bringing our daughter into this world. I have spent the last eighteen years bound by Rhi. The Queen holds both my daughter and my son captive. We share a common enemy and a common goal. I'm telling you there is no one else who can help us."

We were just around the corner at this point and Elias looked back toward me, his eyes glowing blue. He was holding back his panther, but the power was flowing through him all the same. I knew the feeling. My power was slowly becoming a familiar piece of me. As it uncoiled and spread through my veins, I could feel the change. I was lighter on my feet, more alert and attuned to the emotions and movement around me.

Elias moved back to me and whispered, "I think you need to face them—to face him. If you don't establish your dominance now, all is lost. And we need fighters if we're going to get to Amelia."

I wanted to argue, but his logic was sound. Whether or not I believed I was their leader— which I was still on the fence—if I didn't stand up now, I'd never have their support. This wasn't about me, it was about Amelia.

I moved to the corner and peeked around at the man standing in front of the group. Immediately, I thought, *I know him*. But, I couldn't place him. It didn't matter. I took a quick breath in and out and sauntered around the corner, as if nothing in the world was wrong and I wasn't about to face down fifty AniMages who could rip me to shreds. Literally. With their claws.

Chapter 20
Amelia

I had spent the afternoon working with my contained Keeper power. After being deposited back in my room, I heard a knock and opened it expecting Baleon. Instead, I found an unknown Hunter who wore a terrifying smile and shoved my tray at me. Instantly, I knew Rhi must have Bale and I was sick to my stomach. Baleon hadn't been there this morning and he wasn't here now. I had no idea what was happening to him, but I knew it was my fault. Guilt weighed me down.

I threw the tray onto a table and tried to call for Micah via our connection, but I couldn't find him. I hoped him being unavailable meant he was either trying find Bale or getting Cole out of here. I needed to know my brother was safe.

I had to distract myself somehow, so I focused on my Keeper. A certain nervousness always came over me when I was intentionally engaging with the Keeper power. I didn't fear it as I had before, so long as my cuff was securely in place, but I still didn't entirely trust it either. There was too much at risk and too many unknowns.

It took me some time to calm down and focus long enough to withdraw inside myself. I found all five entities separate again and floating around the room. The door was once again wide open and they simply existed, moving about the room and emitting relief at being in their preferred form. It didn't seem like they enjoyed the dark and dangerous being they became when combined.

I wanted to make progress. I *had* to make progress. So, I tried mimicking the cuff symbol again by inserting my fists and trying to separate the mixed Hunter power. Within seconds, it melded back into its magical orb and moved from my grasp. The white orb was elusive as always, staying near the ceiling and mocking me. I knew she was the key and not being able to get to her frustrated me. I couldn't afford to get worked up, though, so I left them alone and spent the rest of the time staring at the ceiling, wondering what was to come.

I hadn't expected to be summoned again by the Queen, especially not just hours after our first encounter. But another new Hunter stood outside my door, this one actually introducing himself.

"I am Joran. I am here to take you to the Queen." His head was bald and covered in tattoos, but his voice was surprisingly soft. There was pity in his eyes I hadn't expected, yet I still felt no emotions from him. Baleon was nowhere in sight and I hoped he was behind Micah's door with Cole.

"It's nice to meet you, Joran." He was the only Hunter outside of Bale to show me any kindness and I didn't want to give him a reason to change his mind. He gave me a small smile and gestured into the hall. I nodded and we fell in step together.

"Where is Baleon?" I asked. I wasn't sure whether Joran was the right person to ask, but he was the only person to ask.

"He is otherwise engaged." Joran's tone reeked of disgust and my stomach fell. Rhi had Bale and it was my fault.

"Will he be okay?" I clenched my fists, digging my nails into my palms as I waited for his answer.

"He will survive. The Queen will not allow otherwise." Joran turned away from me and I knew that line of conversation was closed.

Once we hit a point I didn't recognize, I let Joran lead, but my anxiety grew. He turned in directions I wasn't familiar with and I found myself going underground.

I had never considered myself particularly phobic of anything, but as we went down flight after flight of stairs, the darkness overwhelming the space outside of the orange flame erupting from Joran's palm, my fear elevated. If I were walking into some sort of ambush, I knew I could at least remove the cuff and protect myself, but it was a last resort. I couldn't guarantee I could stop the Keeper once she got started again.

As we reached the bottom of the staircase, Joran stopped and turned to me. "This will only be temporary," he said apologetically before waving a hand in front of my face, making me blind. I turned my head in every direction and saw nothing. Blank. Black. Darkness. No shapes, no colors…nothing. I was paralyzed, my power lashing out, but whatever Joran had done to me was more than my own magic could combat.

"Be calm, Keeper. I'm not hurting you. I simply must not allow you to understand the rest of our journey." He placed his large hand on my shoulder and another at the small of my back. "I will lead you and let no harm come to you. I swear it."

With his touch and words, my mind and body sprung back into action. I whipped around, unable to see him but well aware of where his voice had been. I lashed out, using every bit of training Cole had taught me. I struck out with my left hand, hoping the butt of my hand might connect with his nose, as I lunged in with a right cross. Both missed the mark and I heard his chuckle to my right. I pivoted on my heel, planted, and threw out a left sidekick, barely grazing him. I dropped back into my stance and stood still, listening for him.

"Keeper, we can do this forever if you'd like. But I can see you and you can't see me. It isn't a fair fight. If you'd let me take you where you need to go, I can remove the bind that took your sight." I hated how his logic was sound and even more, the humor laced in his voice.

"Where are you taking me? Tell me and I'll play along." I considered trying to get one solid roundhouse kick in before I did, but I knew if anyone got hurt, it would likely be me.

"My gift is recognizing truth and because I know you speak it now, I will concede," he said. I wasn't sure if he could see my eyes, but I rolled them, realizing the last thing I needed was a Hunter who would know when I was lying. Even if he didn't seem to hate my guts like the rest of them.

Joran continued. "The Queen has determined you cannot be convinced of her true motives until you see them for yourself. If you will allow me, I will take you to her." Joran slowly curled his fingers over my shoulder, though he didn't dig them in to prove his superiority, as I would have assumed.

"I know you do not trust me, and that is fine. It's likely for the best. But I hear the truths you speak, Keeper. They are louder than your words. There are more truths inside you than you even understand, but there are also many lies."

"What does that even mean?" I asked, frustrated on many levels as I started forward, cautiously putting one foot in front of the other.

We walked for some time before I felt his warm breath on my neck as he leaned down, his words a light whisper in my ear. "Sometimes we convince ourselves lies are truth and truths are lies. We convince ourselves so vehemently, we cannot tell the difference. You have been told many things and it can only be you who finds the real truth. Now, hush, we must not speak anymore. Just walk."

I turned his words in my mind, over and over. I couldn't argue with him. Elias had told me a version of the same thing and he had been right, too. So much of what I saw as facts were most often withheld secrets or misinformation. Things I had taken to be absolute truths were nothing close to reality. I had once told Cole we just needed to listen to everyone and figure out who was worth believing. Right now, I had no idea who to trust. From what Joran had just said, I wasn't sure I could even trust myself.

Finally, he stopped me and I heard a door open. Placing his hand on my lower back once more, he guided me into a room. I heard the loud *thud* of the door being closed and the *snick* of the lock. I focused on the sounds. Beeps at regular intervals. The *ting* of metal on metal. Quiet feminine voices. A television in the background. The sound of muffled tears.

My nose wrinkled at the smell of bleach. Anxiety crept through my system. "Joran?" I said his name quietly, unsure of who else was in the room, but knowing there was no way we were alone. He didn't respond, but the air shifted as what had to be a hand moved across my face. And, just like drapes being pulled to one side, my vision returned.

My mouth gaped open and I gasped as I took in the scene around me. There were women everywhere—there had to be twenty of them—all in hospital beds, hooked up to multiple machines. Each one looked at me in fear, their eyes wide as they pulled themselves to the furthest corners of their beds. Only one looked at me passively—indifferent even. She had long, deep red hair pulled to the side in a braid that interrupted the blue-checkered pattern of her hospital gown. She stared into my eyes with such intensity, such hate, I could hardly maintain the contact. She didn't know me or why I was here, but it didn't matter.

My eyes travelled the cavernous room, with rows of beds and scared women, finally landing on barred doors lining the walls. One look at the animals struggling to move to the back of their cells and I knew what was in front of me. I had seen enough pregnant stray cats growing up to recognize it right away. I walked slowly through the room, looking at each woman, even though most wouldn't look at me. Joran didn't try to stop me, but he stood still, his face blank as he looked in the opposite direction of the women. Then I came to the cages.

In the first cell was a cheetah. Her coat was dull and patchy, her frame small but clearly bloating with pending kittens. A collar around her throat was anchored to the wall, giving her only a few feet of chain to work with—just enough to lay on the floor as she labored to breath. Next to hers was a cage far too small for the tigress contained in it. She, too, was chained to the wall, her belly swollen with kittens. She huddled in the back of the cage, baring her teeth at me as I wrapped my hands around the bars of her cell. A low growl rumbled in her throat and tears welled in my eyes. Her fear was only slightly outmatched by her determination to protect her kittens.

Not wanting to scare her, or anyone, further, I pulled away and stood. Seeing the two pregnant AniMage females made me look harder at the women around me. Each one protectively wrapped their arms around their bellies. The women were all in varying stages of pregnancy—a few weren't even showing. I was certain I had found myself in Julia's personal breeding center. Our conversations suddenly made sense now. She was up front about the fertility challenges the Immortals had been facing and had alluded to finding the solution, but I never imagined this.

Anger rushed through my veins and I debated removing the cuff right then and there, ripping the doors off the AniMages' cages and getting both the women and animals out, but I had to be smart. I had no idea where I was, I had no help, and I wouldn't have any clue what to do with these poor women when I got them free. I had to remind myself these were women carrying children. I couldn't put them in more danger than they were already in.

"Where is she?" I demanded as I strode to face Joran. He opened his mouth to answer as I heard the door open. I turned to find Rhi enter the room. I crossed my arms over my chest as I watched him move toward us. Rhi stared me directly in the eyes, gloating over my rage. His mouth twisted into an evil smile and he ran his hands over the foot of the women's beds as he passed. He didn't spare them a look, but his smile grew as they cowered away. He enjoyed their fear and it made me want to break him. I clenched my fists and reminded myself *again*, now was not the time.

As he got closer, Joran adjusted his position so he was standing beside me. He moved only inches, but I felt his presence and it gave me confidence. Between his earlier words and his behavior now, I knew he was at least a partial ally. Right now, I would take whatever I could get. Unfortunately, Rhi also noticed his movement.

"Do you stand with the Keeper now, Joran? Do you betray your people and your Queen?" Rhi walked around us in a tight circle. He took slow, measured steps as he eyed not only me, but Joran. His eyebrows rose over his bright orange eyes as he appraised me. His eyes met my own, traveling to my toes and back again. As he walked a second circle, he stopped in front of me, leaning in so his face was only inches from mine. Power rippled through me and from the way my Keeper bounced around frantically inside me, I was sure his swirling orange eyes were met with the deep violet of my own. Violet smoke I couldn't stop gathered in my palms as I struggled to stand still.

"You are an abomination, girl. What's inside you should never have been, and we will get it out. One way or another, the Elder power will be put in the hands of the Queen and used for its rightful purpose. You may think otherwise, but you are only a pawn in this game. You mean nothing. You are nothing." He smiled and then a flash of surprise crossed his face as I smiled in return. A wide grin formed as I leaned into him this time, whispering my own threats.

"That's where you're wrong, Hunter. I broke your binds once. I have more power inside me than you've ever had in you." His eyes narrowed and his smile melted into a thin line as his jaw clenched. I continued. "You can't begin to know what I'm capable of. And bringing me here to see this was the wrong move. I didn't know firsthand what you were doing. I didn't understand. But I see it now. You've just made this my fight, and I will fight you with every ounce of what's inside me until you beg me to stop."

"Enough." Her clipped tone cut through the tension between us, and both Rhi and I pulled back, turning to see the Queen standing just inside the door. She walked toward us, wearing a pantsuit, her heels clicking across the cement floor. It was the first time I'd seen her in anything but a formal dress. She looked like woman ready to go into the office instead of a manipulative mastermind. Every hair was perfectly in place, pulled up in a loose chignon. Her face was made up flawlessly, down to the smoky eye shadow making her blue eyes seem even brighter.

She made her way to us, stopping every so often to tap the end of a bed and tell a woman she looked healthy, to comment her baby was growing so well, or to ask her how she felt. They murmured responses without meeting her eyes and Julia didn't acknowledge their fear or the complete silence overtaking the rest of the room. She finally made her way to stand in front of me, but before she could speak, I did.

"What's going on here?" I demanded. "What are you doing to them? I thought our people couldn't get pregnant."

I scanned the women once again and only the redhead would meet my eyes. Now her look was different. She looked at me with interest—hope even. Our eyes locked and I wished I had time to create a connection with her, but I had to focus.

"I knew after last night you wouldn't listen to words. I wasn't going to be able to convince you of anything unless you saw it for yourself." She turned to survey the room and I could feel pride radiating from her. She truly believed what she was doing was the right thing.

"What I see are women being held against their will." Violet smoke still surrounded my hands and I took a few breaths in an attempt to temper my power and calm the emotional storm brewing inside me. I was outraged on so many levels but Micah had warned me she was unstable. I had to play the game.

Julia faced me again. "When Mikail's father died, all I wanted was revenge. I wanted to see the AniMages punished for their crimes. They were always the weakest link and the Elders allowed their magic to pollute ours. They claimed the mixing of magic furthered our abilities and evolved our lines, but the truth was, the Elder control inhibited our growth." I wanted to interrupt. But, though Julia was speaking to me, she clearly wasn't present. Her far-off gaze and hollow words made it obvious it wouldn't matter what I said. She wanted to tell her story, so I bit my lip and let her.

"Mages were put in charge of the people because we are the purest lines. We are not animals. Our instincts are not to hunt and destroy. So, yes, at first, I took my revenge upon the AniMages. It wasn't easy, mind you. First, I had to convince the Hunters and other Mages I was correct. I needed them to believe AniMages weren't worth saving. And then, I tried to convince the Elders, but in the end, I just used their love of people against them." Julia smiled to herself, a satisfied quirk of her lips.

I hadn't known how disturbing a smile could be until it was attached to stories of murder and genocide.

"The Elders serving on the council wouldn't leave their chamber in the main castle, so I attacked their mates to draw them out. I knew one couldn't fully function without the other, and I can be so creative with my torture techniques." Julia smiled to herself, the memories that turned my stomach and provided history I wanted to forget bringing her satisfaction once again.

"Once the Elders were no longer there to meddle in royal affairs, I drove the AniMages from our lands and disposed of their leaders. But I ordered my Hunters not to kill any children. I was pregnant with Mikail at the time and couldn't bear the thought. They were to bring the children to me in hopes I could cleanse them of their vile blood and they could help build the next Immortal generation. They were part Mage. I had hoped to simply make them all Mage. I had come to my senses and realized it made no sense to kill off an Immortal species simply because I could. It made far more sense to simply alter them to be what we all needed, which was to be fully Mage. Then, they could be trusted. They could be taught. But, as my Hunters swept the countryside of our homeland, they found there were few children and even fewer pregnant women—both AniMage and Mage. I knew then something had to be done. So, instead, I asked Rhi and his men to bring the pregnant women to me. All of them."

Her words sunk in as I scanned the room again. The women were of varying ages and lineage. "How long have they been here?" I asked.

"It depends. Once they can no longer conceive, they are of no use to me." Julia shrugged, as if her statement had no further implications.

"What happens to them when they can no longer conceive?" The words were slow to exit my mouth.

"That is no concern of mine. Rhi and the female Hunters handle such things." She spoke the words as if my questions were stupid as she waved a hand in the air, swatting the notion away like an annoying fly. As if I should have assumed not all of the women had been here for years, and of course, they would be disposed of once they were no longer useful. I looked toward Rhi and he was smiling again. A disgusting twisted grin confirming the poor women were dead.

"Does Prince Mikail know about this? Does he understand what you've been doing?" I prayed she would say no. I couldn't fathom Micah being a part of this.

"Of course not," she snapped. "My son has no idea and it will continue as such. He doesn't need to concern himself with this. He is not built to handle the pressure of ruling. Joran and Rhi are the only males allowed here. Female Hunters guard the women and Mikail has only seen the

Huntresses as servants. He would never consider I have alternative uses for them."

"And the Huntresses, do they have the same problem?" I caught Joran wince ever so slightly from my peripheral vision.

"Not that it matters, but since they have come to work for me, no, the Huntresses have borne no children." I turned to scan the room again, but really only wanted to see Joran's reaction. His features may as well have been stone, and he stood as if there were a metal rod in his back. There was more to Julia's story than her casual dismissal of their worth.

I took a minute, letting her words and his reaction sink in. Everything about this was too much. I wanted to free the women and AniMages right now. I wanted to stab Rhi in the heart with the nearest scalpel and pin Julia to the wall while I let the shifted AniMages feast on her body. Revulsion pooled in my stomach and bile built in the back of my throat.

"Why am I here?" It was the million-dollar question. I couldn't fathom what it was she expected me to do.

Julia's cold smile sent chills down my spine. "You, dear, are here because not one of these women can actually give birth to an Immortal child. They either miscarry or the poor thing is born human." The way she said human, with such disdain and loathing, made it clear she hated humans even more than AniMages.

"What happens to the human children?" The words slipped from my mouth as I exhaled, though I hadn't meant to say them.

"She kills them! She takes our babies and she kills them! MURDERER! SHE'S A MURDERER!" The shrill screams of one of the women made me jump. She pulled on her restraints, tears streaming down her face as she continued to scream, "MURDERER!" She was one who didn't have an obvious belly. I was sure she must have recently had a baby who had been taken.

Julia stared in her direction, entirely indifferent to the wailing accompanying her outburst. "Where are the guards? Sedate her before she riles the others."

Rhi didn't wait for guards, or call for anyone. Instead, he stalked toward the woman. Her screams stopped and she pulled herself into the corner of the bed, trying to become as small as possible. He grasped around her ankle, his hand glowing orange. She yelped and I heard his low words, a vibration filled with painful promises.

"You will be quiet and grateful, woman. You are alive. You will have more children. You will build the future."

Her eyes glazed over as he spoke and I heard her mutter, "I will be grateful. I will build the future."

"I-I don't understand. How can I possibly fix them?" My confidence was waning and the grief and fear emanating from the women was overwhelming my system. The longer I stood there, the more aware I became of the weak heartbeats of the mothers and the pattering beats of the babies growing inside them. Even with the cuff, my Keeper was reacting strongly to the situation. I worried I wouldn't be able to contain it, and had no idea what would happen if the five orbs were somehow triggered.

Meeting the Queen's eyes, I knew right then I wouldn't like her answer. A part of me had known all along I wouldn't, but I had to help these women. Somehow, I had to right this horrific wrong.

"You will either take off the cuff and use the power you demonstrated with your brother to give the fetuses back the power they should have, or I will take you to the room where the infamous prophecy was born and show you what it took to get Lavignia to share it with me. The choice is yours."

Chapter 21
Aidan

I approached the group of AniMages from the back. Braxton saw me before anyone else. He pushed his glasses up and with that one movement, I knew exactly where I'd seen him before. He had come into one of the classes Amelia and I shared to announce class was cancelled. I committed his face to memory, thinking he was some perverted professor with the way his eyes lingered on her.

I watched his chest puff up as he decided how to react to me. I intentionally walked through the center of the crowd, tapping the other AniMages on the shoulder and politely making my way through. As more caught on to me being there, they all turned and moved out of the way, making a path as they whispered to each other. I passed Nathaniel, Derreck, and Rynna, and Amelia's father gave me a short nod. I returned the sentiment, silently thanking him for standing up for me. By the time I made it to Braxton, Melinda had joined him. I wanted to laugh as she draped herself over him.

"Opportunistic, are we?" I addressed her first, knowing the slight would likely piss Braxton off even more. I preferred him to be off-kilter. She laughed loudly, clearly a show for the audience.

"Always choose the winning team, sugar. The odds are not in your favor," she said as she pecked Braxton on the cheek.

He wrapped an arm around her, clearly not realizing he had picked the most insane woman in the bunch. I was sizing him up, trying to decide whether I should punch first or try being diplomatic.

"Do you have something to say to me? I don't even know who you are, but I understand there's some question as to who I am." I could have had a PhD in mind games at this point. My second foster home was a constant stream of no-win scenarios and manipulations. I just needed to get this guy to make an ass of himself so I didn't have to do it for him.

"You don't know who I am?" He looked past me at the others, shaking his head. "He's supposed to lead us and he has no idea who *we are*. He doesn't even know how to shift. He can't remember what happens while he's gone. He isn't AniMage...not really. Who knows what he is."

As Braxton's insults piled on top of each other, I could feel the power in me building. The need to assert myself and prove my dominance was back. My breaths were coming deeper and I had to hold back my wolf.

"You know nothing about *me*." I decided to play his game and turned to the people staring at us. Some looked intrigued, some angry, some confused. My eyes landed on Dillon as he stood with his arms crossed, glaring at his fellow AniMages. I knew what it felt like to be an adult in a child's body. He had seen too much too young, and so had I. I pulled my eyes from Dillon and worked my way back across the crowd.

"He's right. I don't know you, but until yesterday, I didn't know myself. I was born to Zendrick and Kayla Montgomery. Yesterday, for the first time, I was able to see my own memories of my parents—to know what it was like to be a young pup. But I also saw them murdered by Hunters. The same men who killed your friends and family took mine. Not only did they take my family, but one bound the AniMage in me. Yesterday, those bonds were broken."

I took another step forward and held out my hands. With one internal command, blue power gathered in my palms, a mix of smoke and electricity. I closed my fists, reopened them, and fur sprouted. Seconds later, my hands were paws. And then they were hands once again. I got a few approving head nods from the crowd. "I can shift at will. And I now have all the memories I lost." As I turned back to Braxton, my wolf shared a critical piece of information. There was only way to settle this dispute. The way our people had been settling challenges like this for generations.

"But, if you would like to officially challenge me, I will accept. Right here. Right now. Man to man, for the pack to see and decide." My voice echoed and the crowd was silent.

Red crept up Braxton's neck. He clearly had no intentions of taking it this far and hadn't expected me to call him out.

"Come on, baby. You can take him. Show them. Show me," Melinda cooed in his ear, and Braxton had no choice but to accept. He would have been humiliated otherwise. He'd end up there anyway, but at least this way he could say he fought.

I smiled as he stepped away from her. Cole had always called it my ruthless smile. The one I saved for opponents in the ring moments before a fight. This smile told you I was more likely to let you break my arm than tap.

Elias broke through the crowd and stepped between us. "You fight fair—no shifting, no magic. If you're meant to lead this pack, you have to be able to do it as a man first. Got it?"

I gave him a curt nod and my smile grew as Braxton swallowed, his fear showing in the sweat on his brow and the shake of his hands. I kept smiling as realization hit me. He expected me to be scared of the unknown—of what we were. But nothing had felt more right than knowing I was an AniMage.

I dropped into my fighting stance and bounced on the balls of my feet. For the first time in weeks, I felt at home. My body and my mind were mine to control. I was whole and my wolf and I were one. He was excited. He was ready, too. I had wanted to punch something for weeks. This poor schmuck had no idea what he was in for.

A part of me knew I shouldn't actually want to hit Braxton, but I did. The need to prove myself to Elias and everyone else in the pack was overwhelming. I wanted them to know I was my father's son, that I belonged here. Somewhere in the last ten minutes, my whole mindset had shifted. I wasn't on the fence anymore. I wanted to make my father proud and continue our family legacy. And I wanted my pack to help me get Amelia back. I wanted her to know we belonged in this world together—fighting a common enemy who had taken too much from all of us.

Braxton attempted a fighting posture but it was clear he had no idea what he was doing. Like so many, he was all talk. Guilt crept into my mind. The realization that this guy was probably some book nerd who shifted into something fairly harmless came to the forefront. He was probably the last person I should be taking my pent up anger out on.

"Wait." I held out my hand, a stop gesture. I stepped toward him and was actually impressed when he didn't take a step back. I lowered my voice and turned my back to the crowd. "You don't want to do this and you don't have to. Just yield."

As I finished my statement, his eyes glowed blue and his fist shot out, connecting with my nose. I stumbled back a few feet and shook my head, wiping at the blood pouring from my face. Braxton wasted no time, not giving me more than a second to recover. He had played me and was taking full advantage. He leapt at my waist, attempting to take me down. I sprawled, putting my weight into my hips as I pushed him toward the ground. I hit my knees just as I gave myself the room I needed to wrap my right arm around his neck in a chokehold and my left under his right armpit. It was fairly obvious he was a street brawler with no formal fight training, which made this easier than it should have been. He had no idea how to get out of the hold I'd put him in, yanking and pulling in all the wrong ways. With a quick spin, I was on his back, tightening my arm into his throat and cutting off his blood supply.

I vaguely heard the yelling from the crowd, and registered "Look out!" just as claws tore into my back and teeth sunk into my shoulder.

Braxton was still underneath me as pain shot through my shoulder. I reached back, grabbing my attacker by the scruff of its neck, and tossing it over my head. The small, reddish wolf went flying. It was easier than it should have been. Was super-strength a Hunter trait? I knew staying human wasn't going to end this fight soon enough and these two already weren't playing fair. My wolf had been waiting and as soon as the thought formed, he took over. I shredded my clothes as I shifted, still on top of Braxton. I dug my nails into the back of his body, simply to make a point, and was rewarded with a howl of pain.

I leapt at the wolf, realizing it was Melinda who had come to Braxton's rescue. I was easily double her size and able to knock her onto her back. As I clamped my teeth around her neck, she brought her back legs up, kicking into my belly. Sharp claws sliced open my skin, forcing me to retaliate. I didn't want to kill the wolf, but I understood what was at stake. I quickly pulled back and snapped at her ear, tearing away the corner. She instantly started yelping, but she also stopped kicking. I moved off her, the blood from her wound in my muzzle and stuck to the fur around my mouth.

I looked up for the first time, only to realize all of the AniMages had shifted and fighting was everywhere. It was clear I had come into a house divided and Braxton's words had more impact than we expected.

Take control. They are your pack. Stop this madness.

It was the first time I had heard his words, but I knew it was my wolf.

But how? How can I stop this? I sat there, feeling powerless.

Nathaniel, Derreck, and Rynna were circled, their backs to each other, shooting bolts of magic at the group of AniMages surrounding them. I didn't envy them not having the ability to shift. Dillon was high in the air, fending off hawks and other birds diving at him. Elias and Will were shifted, but fighting together. They were completely encircled by all kinds of animals— from a hyena, to a mountain lion, to a grizzly bear.

Just tell them to stop. Command them.

Still in my wolf form, I did the only thing that made sense. I let out the deepest, longest howl I had in me. I infused the sound with the command to stop fighting, to listen to me, and to yield to their true leader. I stood on all four legs, my tail in the air and my ears pricked. I made myself as big as possible. When I started, my eyes were closed. I was focused on pulling up all the power I had inside me, collecting it, and sending it out in the sounds vibrating from my core. I continued howling until I heard nothing but my own voice.

When I opened my eyes, not only had everyone stopped fighting, but they were standing completely still, their heads tucked down into their chests. The birds had landed in the trees. Every animal showed me their submission. Even Braxton, still in his human form, had moved to the side and held one hand up, fisted over his heart, as he bowed his head in my direction. I surveyed the crowd and my eyes connected with Nathaniel's. I had no idea what to do now. He gave me a silent nod of encouragement.

Look at me. Every head came up and I was met with a clearing full of wide iridescent blue eyes. I pulled my gaze from one side to the other, and back again, making eye contact with each AniMage individually.

We are done with this. We are done fighting. There is a war going on and we are being hunted. It makes no sense for us to fight amongst ourselves. I am your leader and I'm telling you I can help fulfill the prophecy, but we must find Amelia. She is the key and she is in danger. Will you help me?

I continued scanning the crowd, unsure of what to expect. Dillon was first, hooting from the branch he sat on. Elias joined in, a screeching yowl. The bellow of Will's tiger followed. Soon, every animal was shouting their own version of encouragement.

I slowly let out a breath I'd been holding since I'd stopped talking. Adrenaline was coursing through me, but right alongside it was pride in what I'd just done and hope for what this meant for Amelia.

Quiet down, please. I waited for everyone to simmer down and then turned to Braxton and the small wolf who had attacked me.

You. Shift.

As I had expected, Melinda crouched next to Braxton. Her right ear trickled blood and she glared daggers at me. I shifted myself, refusing to acknowledge my naked state.

"I won't have you causing trouble in the pack. Do you submit, or will you leave? Those are your choices. Your only choices." My wolf was feeding me all the right words. I had no idea how to lead a pack of AniMages, but he knew exactly what I should say and how I should say it. I knew enough to understand if I didn't take command of every aspect of the pack, I would always be looking over my shoulder, and I didn't have time for that. I was done wasting time. I needed to find Amelia—now.

Braxton spoke immediately. "It's clear you are our alpha. Please forgive me. I submit." He dropped to one knee and once again, bowed his head.

I turned to look at Melinda, who had also pulled herself to stand. I allowed no expression on my face, but I refused to look away from her. Finally, she dropped to one knee as well. "I also submit. You are clearly our alpha," she said, begrudgingly.

She didn't apologize and neither did I. I turned to face the crowd once again. "Please, shift. Get dressed and we'll reconvene soon. We have a plan to make."

Animals started shifting into humans and the crowd started to scatter to the bins stationed near the cave entrances. In those first few days, I hadn't understood why the bins were there, but stacks of clean clothes could always be found in them. In general, the pack was better at anticipating the shift and not ruining clothes as often as I did, but it was always good to be prepared.

Dillon came running up to me and I'd never been so happy to see a pair of sweats in my life. As I pulled them on, I heard Dillon gasp. I looked up into his shocked expression. "What's up, Little Man?" I was bent over and though I'd pulled up my pants, I stayed there, not sure what he saw that I didn't.

"Your wounds, Mr. Aidan. They are healed." He hesitantly reached out and ran a finger over my back, where I knew the worst of the pain had come from. "There isn't even a scar, sir."

I stood up slowly and it was Will who caught my eyes this time. "I told you. You're like nothing we've ever seen before."

I didn't have time to digest what Dillon and Will had said before I heard my name. I had just enough time to register blond hair flying in my direction when Bethany shoved me.

"Ow! What the hell?" She caught me off guard and I took a step back from the impact. "Who taught you to be so violent, woman?"

She was in my face in an instant. "Do you have any idea the pickle you left me in, Aidan Montgomery? It was like being kidnapped all over again. Little Dillon shows up at my apartment, trembling and looking near tears, telling me I've got to come with him, and who do I find waiting outside? Oh, nobody in particular. Just the very same redheaded hussy who drove me crazy the last time. And what do you think she's been doing since you've just been off doing whatever in the Sam Hill it was you were doing? Telling me all sorts of lovely little stories, that's what she's been doin'."

I could hardly keep up with Bethany's tirade. Her accent was getting thicker the faster she spoke and the more worked up she got. "Hey!" I cut her off before she could start again. "What stories? What are you talking about?"

Bethany glared at me with a mixture of what felt like disgust and anger. "She told me you can't be who they say you are because these people can't have kids. There hasn't been a child born to an AniMage in years. They don't even know where Dillon actually came from. Clearly, he's a kid, but he's the first one they've seen in ten years.

That's why they all look at him like they do—he's a miracle.

"And it doesn't even matter if you are somebody's son who's supposed to rule this damn zoo, you can't get to Amelia. There's no way into Cresthaven. It's impenetrable. There are Hunters everywhere and they are not going to let Amelia walk out of there alive. And what in the world am I supposed to do while all this is happening even if y'all do go? Just sit back in my apartment and wait for everyone I know and care about to be poofed, or zapped, or whatever the hell y'all do to each other?"

Her eyes had filled and her voice thickened. I sighed. "So, that's what this is really about. It's not the stories, you don't want to be left behind." I reached a hand out and waited for her to decide. Slowly, Bethany uncurled her arms from her chest and put her hand into mine. I pulled her in for a hug. It still amazed me how someone who was barely even a friend a month ago had become my partner in crime. I had the same protective instincts for Bethany as I had for the rest of my pack.

I dropped my voice to a whisper so our conversation stayed between us. "It's alright, B,

I'm scared, too. I don't even know what the hell I'm doing and I *am* supposed to be managing this zoo." She sniffled and laughed simultaneously into my chest. "But I won't leave you here. I promise. I won't bring you into Cresthaven, because I'd worry about you getting yourself killed, but you won't be stuck here. Okay?"

I pulled away from her and she sniffled again. "We're going to get her out. We have a secret weapon." I turned to Rynna, who was standing a few feet away, and gestured her toward me. As she approached, I said, "Bethany, this is Rynna. She helped raise Amelia and knows her way into Cresthaven. Rynna…Amelia's best friend, Bethany."

The two women shook hands. "Bethany, it is so lovely to finally meet you. Amelia has had nothing but wonderful things to say about you. And I was thrilled to know she finally had the best friend she deserved." Rynna's words brought out the first smile I'd seen on Bethany in some time.

"Same goes for you, ma'am. She loves you. But…how is it you know how we can get into Cresthaven, if you don't mind my asking?"

Bethany used her sleeve to wipe away the mascara trails leaving black streaks down her cheeks.

I stuttered, taken aback. I hadn't thought to ask the question myself.

Rynna simply shrugged and smiled. "Because Julia is my sister and I grew up finding ways to sneak out of Cresthaven. I was young once, too."

Chapter 22
Amelia

I backed away slowly, but didn't get far, bumping directly into Joran. As his fingers grasped around my arms to steady me, a small jolt ran through my system. I looked back at Joran and his face was blank. Something had just happened, but he wasn't telling me what.

Joran shoved me a little, pushing me back toward Julia and Rhi.

You will not leave here alive if you do not do as they ask.

His words were crystal clear in my mind.

How did you—

Focus. He cut me off. *I see the truth. They will either get what they need from you, or you will die as they take it. This is no threat. You must try. She believes you will either provide the answer or she will kill you to stop the prophecy from coming true. She may fear death, but she fears for her people more.*

The exchange had taken only a few seconds and I struggled to keep my own face blank. I looked around the room, finding the women staring back at me. They had heard Julia's explanation and I wondered if it was for the first time. They had also heard my disgust at her plans. Some looked fearful, some looked hopeful. The redhead who had caught my eye earlier looked at me with questions. I could see her brows furrowed as she bit her lip. I wanted desperately to know what she was thinking, if she knew something I needed to.

"Well?" The Queen's sharp tone cut into my thoughts.

I stuttered, trying to find words to stall her. "I-It's not that simple, your highness. I don't know how to activate this power. I can take off the cuff, but that doesn't mean I can fix anyone. I don't know how." What I wanted to say was I didn't actually know how to *do* anything. This power was a constant stream of reactions, but I didn't want to encourage her torture threats.

Julia didn't miss a beat. "Well, then, we should probably have some test subjects, shouldn't we? Why not start with the beasts? We've never heard of an AniMage able to successfully give birth outside of their human form anyway." She spun on her heel and took short, quick strides to the barred cell where the cheetah lay on the concrete floor.

"Open it," she commanded. Rhi's collar flared red for an instant and I watched him grit his teeth. It was the first time I had noticed her influence at work. With a flick of his wrist, he opened the cage door. I watched the exhausted, emaciated cheetah attempt to pull herself backward, away from the Queen. The chain wouldn't allow her to go far, so she curled herself into a tight ball, trying to protect the kittens in her belly. I heard a faint growl, likely all she had in her, as the Queen approached.

"Calm yourself, beast. I'm not coming in there." Julia looked down at the poor animal, as if it deserved its circumstances, and then turned to me. "But you are. In you go." She stood, holding the barred gate in her hand, a petulant sneer twisting her lips.

"Move, Keeper." Rhi was at my ear in an instant. He had been ten feet away and then right behind me. "You will move or I will move you. I would be happy to."

My vision went dark. The visual of him with his hands around my throat as he walked me across the room, throwing me into the cell with the starving cheetah, was all I could see. The vision faded and my own sight returned. I whipped around and he grinned. Against his light brown skin, the sight of his bright white teeth was unsettling.

"Keep your fantasies to yourself, Hunter." I coated the words with sarcasm and bite, and forced myself to take confident steps toward the cell. I stopped in front of Julia and faced her.

"You understand once I remove this cuff, I cannot guarantee what will happen. It's not mine to control. I could kill her, or you, or everyone in this room. Or, absolutely nothing could happen."

"We must start somewhere," she said with a shrug. "And while I'm perfectly certain I can stop anything you try, if I die, apparently you will have fulfilled your destiny. But I cannot fulfill mine unless I bring our people to their proper place in the world and we must be able to find a solution before that can happen." Emotion I didn't expect took hold in her features. Her eyes dropped from mine as her mouth turned down and her voice lowered. Waves of remorse and sadness came from her. The mighty Queen. The cold Queen. Something inside me was certain this was not the way she intended her life to go.

I swallowed words I knew would be worthless, or simply likely to frustrate Julia further. I turned to look at Rhi and Joran. Joran still stood at the door, a masque of indifference. Rhi, on the other hand, stood near the first line of beds and took pleasure in the women cowering. I shook my head and wished I could direct my Keeper to kick the shit out of him. Maybe later.

I turned to face the terrified AniMage in the cell before me. She still didn't trust me, and she had every reason not to. Her growl intensified and she bared her teeth as I slid to the ground and walked slowly on my hands and knees toward her. I jumped as the cell door behind me snapped shut with a loud clang of metal on metal. I hadn't expected to be locked inside, and fear had my power running rampant. I took measured breaths as I tried to stay calm, in hopes the old tales were true and animals would sense your own emotions.

I pushed out as much calming energy as I could, every signal saying I was trying to help.

"I'm sorry to scare you. I-I'm here to help you and your babies. To try to give them back their ability to be AniMages again. I don't know if I can, but I'd like to try." I spoke softly and though it shook more than I would have liked, I slowly extended my hand toward the cheetah. She snapped her teeth at me once and I yanked my hand back.

I sat back, closed my eyes, and tried to think. There was only one thing I could think to try before I took off the cuff, which was the last thing I wanted to do. I focused inside my mind and found my way to my Keeper's room. As was the norm lately, the door was wide open, the power floating around. I called to the violet and cerulean orb and it dropped down in front of me.

I need your help. I need you to help me with her. Can you do that? How do I use you? The orb hovered there, just as it always did. Frustrated, I decided it wouldn't hurt to try to break apart the orb and use what power I could from it. I shoved both of my fists into the orb and pulled them apart. It flew into a million droplets and there was a surge as the Keeper power layered on top of my own.

Before it could pull back together, or the Cheetah could react, I dove across the cell to her and grasped her paw—the only thing I could get to. I pushed every ounce of what had spread through me toward her.

I felt the transfer, the Keeper power draining out of me, but with it went my own. I let go of her paw and struggled to sit up. I shoved against the cold surface of the concrete and dropped my head back against the wall, exhausted. It vaguely occurred to me once again how inhumane these conditions were. But when I looked at the cheetah, she was beautiful. The missing hunks of her fur were back, her coat shone, and her frame was filled out. She looked like she was fresh from hunting in the jungles of Africa. Relief filled me.

"What did you do? What did you find? Tell me, girl!" Julia peered through the bars, demanding answers.

"Right now, I don't know what I've done except give this AniMage her strength and life back. Something vital to her having healthy children and something you should have done yourself." I was repulsed by the Queen and her disregard for these people's lives.

"I don't care what you've done for her. Did you fix the babies? Will her mongrels have magic? That is all that matters here. Why are you wasting time?" Her shrill tone grated on me. I was so busy wondering how I might be able to kill her from inside the cell, I didn't realize the cheetah had come to me. I heard a soft purr as she nudged my arm with her head and licked it.

I turned my back to Julia, ignoring her demands and focusing on the cheetah. "Hello. My name is Amelia. I'm here to help you and your babies." I could feel her love and need to protect her children. I reached out a hand and gestured toward her belly. It drooped as she stood in front of me, perfectly placed so I could reach it.

"May I?" I asked. She purred in response, standing still.

I slowly moved my hands toward her stomach until both were up against her warm fur. While I could feel the heartbeats of the babies, and the vibrations of their mother's love, I could feel nothing else. But I had no idea whether I could even sense magic in others. Their auras were easy to distinguish, but nothing else was clear.

I turned back to Julia and stood. I stumbled a little, still weak. "I can't do this. I can't just take off the cuff and hope for the best. I could kill her. I could hurt myself. I'm no good to you if I can't continue to do this, right? I need more time. I refuse to try this on anyone carrying a child of any kind. I won't do it."

Julia stood, eyeing me as if she were trying to decide whether I was bluffing.

"What you saw with my brother, I had to actively work to control the Keeper. Had I not focused her, she would have gone after Rhi. That's what she wanted. You don't understand. She does what *she* wants. You need me to control her and right now, if you force me to take off this cuff, I will not. I will let her tear this place apart. You don't have your army down here now. Do you want to take that chance?"

We continued to stare at each other until she finally said, "Open it." The door swung open again and I turned. I knelt in front of the Cheetah and whispered, "I will be back for you. I will set you free." I stared into her eyes, knowing she heard me and understood.

I moved out of the cell and stood before Julia. "Understand I am going to do this, but not for you. I'm going to do it for them. Because you have no right to hold them here, impregnate them, and steal their children. You are the worst kind of evil. The kind that holds some righteous notion your cause is greater than the lives you take. I will not let you take another innocent Immortal's life."

I heard a slow clap and turned to find Rhi, an amused smile on his lips as his hands came together and apart. "How touching, Keeper, but you act as if you have a choice."

"Don't I? You've heard the prophecy. You know what's inside of me. You have seen what I am capable of. I broke your bonds, didn't I? How many years have you been down here? How many failed attempts have been made? How many women and children have died? Without control and focus, it could be gone in an instant." I snapped my fingers and Julia's head twitched. I internally celebrated someone buying my story, because I was making threats I wasn't sure I could keep. I saw the darkness of the Keeper when I didn't wear the cuff, and while it was terrifying, I had no idea whether it could do what I was claiming.

"Joran, does she speak the truth?" Julia seemed to know the exact time to call me on my crap. I stood with my head held high, leaning slightly toward Julia in the aggressive stance Cole had taught me to use whenever I needed to appear stronger or more confident than I was. I waited for Joran to tell her the truth, to confirm I was lying through my teeth.

"She speaks the truth, your highness. The darkness must be tempered." Joran's words shocked me, but I let nothing show. I knew Rhi watched my every move.

A slow smile crept across Julia's lips and ice snaked down my back. "Rhi, let's show our guest the same hospitality we provide all mixed breeds, shall we?"

Before I could internalize her words, Rhi had locked his arms around me and we were across the room. "You play dangerous games, Keeper, and you cannot win. I always win." His breath was hot in my ear and the pads of his fingers burned into my arm, making me cry out as he threw me into the cell on the other side of the tiger.

I landed in a heap and didn't have a chance to duck before a pillow and blanket were thrown at me. I tangled in the blanket and ripped it away, only to hear the clang of the lock as the cell door closed. Rhi smiled from the other side and moved away as Julia came to the door.

"You have two days. You will find this control or I will find it for you." Julia's eyes blazed red. She hadn't used much magic in front of me and her display of emotion unnerved me.

I heard her heels click across the room as she commanded Rhi and Joran to follow her. I wanted to yell for Joran, but realized it wouldn't help me and might hurt him, so I stayed quiet.

I dropped my head into my hands, my fingertips massaging my forehead as I tried to figure out what I had just done and what the hell I was supposed to do about it. I tried calling out to Micah via our connection, but I couldn't find a trace of his power. I wished I had my mother's journals here with me so I could see whether she had left me any information I could use. Finally, I went back to the Keeper room and tried breaking apart the Hunter power mix, hoping it would give me the strength I needed to get out of the cell. But the orb slammed back together so quickly, I never had a chance to hit the bars with a blast of power.

I was so frustrated, I started shooting violet bursts at the lock, one after the other. I pushed everything I had into trying to get through the bars until I heard, "You can stop. It won't work. Nothing works. They are all made by Hunters."

Somehow I had forgotten about the women. I moved to the wall of the cell and looked out through the bars. Across the room, the woman with the braid was leaning toward me. She was one of the few I could actually see from my angle, and she couldn't move far, the restraints keeping her in the bed.

"How long have you been here?" I asked.

"Eight years," she responded. Her eyes flickered blue for just a second.

"Are you an AniMage? How are you out there?" I had just assumed the human-looking women were Mages.

"You typically stay in whatever form you came in here as, and AniMages give birth in human form. They wanted some of the women in their shifted form to see if it made a difference, but it doesn't. When they took all of us, we were pregnant, so they knew we had the ability to conceive. When the children are born human— which, if they are born at all, they are—they take them." Her voice was hard, the emotion gone. She had been here too long, been through it too many times, to grieve anymore. I could feel the numbness she'd forced on herself. The detachment she held in place. Right now, she didn't look pregnant and I wondered whether she held similar detachment when a tiny life was inside her.

"They keep inseminating us. We can only assume the fathers are Mage, but every child is either miscarried or born human. I have listened to women scream as their children are brought into this world and the Queen has tested her every theory on how to unlock the power she believes is still in them. She forces the female Hunters to attend our births and experiment on our babies."

I couldn't bring myself to ask what had happened to the children.

"Can you help us? I see what you did for Nell, but what can you do for us? For our children?" she asked.

It took a second for her question to register but as soon as it did, I was on my feet and yelling. "Nell? She was Nell? Elias's Nell?" I tried to see over to Nell's cell, but it was two down from mine and impossible to see anything but the bars in the door. The woman recoiled, as did those who had been quietly listening around her.

"I'm sorry," I dropped my voice and tried to be calm. "I didn't mean to scare you. I just know of her. Her husband thinks she's dead. But if that's her, then she's alive!" I was both elated and sickened to realize Elias had spent all those years believing his wife was dead.

"All of our husbands believe we are dead. It is why they haven't come for us. The Hunters raided the villages in search of us. They killed hundreds, both for sport, because Hunters are evil creatures, and to hide what they were really after," she said. "We are nothing but incubators and our children are lab rats. You have to help us."

"What's your name? I'm Amelia. And I honestly don't know if I can help you, but I'm going to try." I would try like hell. This was the first time the prophecy was tangible—sitting right in front of me and making it clear it wasn't about having a choice. These were my people and I would help them.

"Cora. My name is Cora. You are the Keeper. I believed in the Elders and their sight. If you have their power, you will find a way." She sat back onto her pillows, her head held high as she nodded at me. I wished I had her faith.

"Are you the only one who can speak? Are the others okay?" I strained my neck to see through the bars past Cora to the other women.

"I'm Nadine, a Mage. I've been here three years."

"Sully, an AniMage, five years."

"Willow, a Mage, seven years."

I leaned my head against the bars as the names continued. One after another, they told me who they were and how long they had been here. Lydia had been here the longest at ten years. It left me wondering how many women had been deemed useless to Julia and killed after being bred like animals?

"How do you do it?" I wanted to clarify the question, but I couldn't find the right words to ask how they could possibly keep going.

Willow identified herself. I couldn't see her from my cell, but her voice carried across the space. "No matter who the fathers are, these children are a part of us. They come from us. We give them as much as we can in the time we have with them. We sing to them, tell them stories of our people, where they come from, and we pray the spark we have inside of us will be in them. The Hunters have bound us so we cannot fight them, but they left our power within us to be passed on."

I closed my eyes and opened myself to their auras and emotions. The more I worked with my Keeper, the more I felt and heard in those moments when I opened myself up to it. I went to the green and violet orb inside me, whispering all the reasons I needed this to work. I needed the intuition and ability to feel what it would bring. Mages rooted in green magic were always more empathetic and emotionally sensitive. When I pulled my fists apart, the power scattered throughout my body and layered with my own. It didn't fight me at all. I wished I understood why sometimes it worked and other times it didn't. The sensations were overwhelming, but I needed to understand. I wasn't a mother. I hadn't had a mother. I needed to feel what they felt.

The protective instinct was everywhere. Hope for the future. Fear of the unknown. Terror over knowing what was to come as the babies left their protection. Anger at the circumstances preventing them from being true mothers. Agony over those they had lost. Love for the tiny heartbeats. More love than I could comprehend. So much so, I could barely breathe, it was so thick in the air. Their gift for giving life had been turned against them, yet they still loved with abandon. It was only those who had recently lost who were weighed down with grief and anger. The darkness spread through them, leaving them on the edge of sanity.

"I swear to you, I will find a way to help you and your children. I don't know how yet, but I will find it." I said the words as loudly as I could. I had been a motherless and basically fatherless child. I knew exactly what that did to a kid. I had an inkling of what it had done to their mothers. And I could only imagine what it had done to the husbands who had no idea their wives were still alive and their children were gone. I struggled to speak, tears swimming in my eyes. The combination of grief and love surrounding me was more than I could take.

"Rynna, please come soon. Please, please be coming soon," I whispered as I slid down to the ground and hugged my knees to my chest.

Chapter 23
Aidan

Elias, Derreck, Nathaniel, Bethany, Will, Rynna, Charlie, and I had been in what we deemed "the war room" for hours. Charlie hadn't left Bethany's side and more than once, I found him looking up at me expectantly. We had been having the same conversation, over and over. The AniMages had been running from the Hunters for years. They had scattered across the globe in small packs, or alone, to evade the Hunters. Lately, the Hunters weren't as focused on them and no one knew why, but they wanted to attack. They wanted their vengeance and they wanted the Queen taken out.

Rynna, Nathaniel, and I had been making the same counterpoints, over and over. "We need to get Amelia out of there. She needs to fully mate with Aidan so she can access her power." Rynna's voice was becoming clipped and I could sense her frustration. I felt the same way, even though it was extremely uncomfortable to have people talking so blatantly about you "mating" with someone. Especially when that someone's father was standing three feet from you, nodding like it was the most normal conversation in the world.

"She is the one who can end Julia's reign," Rynna continued. "It was foretold and that is how it will be. We cannot enter Cresthaven without the purest of intentions. We can only go in to get her out."

Voices raised over each other and the room was suddenly too small and too loud. "Enough." I didn't yell or pound my fist on the table like I wanted to, but I put the alpha power I'd found into it, shutting the AniMages in the room up and allowing the Mages to feel the maddening frustration inside me.

Bethany stood across from me with a quirked brow and a small smile. She crossed her arms and gave me a short nod. At least someone aside from me was impressed that it had worked.

"We're wasting time," I said, looking around the table at each person. "We are leaving tonight and we're going to get Amelia. We are not going after Julia *yet*." I looked at Will and Elias. Will glared while Elias nodded. "I understand what you've told and shown me, but we have to be smart about this. We will go back, but right now, we have one objective and it is to get Amelia out. Now, can someone explain to me the best way to accomplish our objective?"

Derreck stepped up to the table and the large map laid across it. "We're here," he said as he pointed toward our location in Northern California, "and Cresthaven is here, in Washington." Hundreds of miles stretched between our two locations and the distance only served to make me more anxious. "Rynna, Nathaniel, Bethany, and I will leave tonight and drive through the night. We'll take all the supplies we can in my truck and we'll meet you at the rendezvous point."

Charlie started barking low, quick yips until Derreck muttered something about damned dogs and turned to him. "And yes, Charlie, we will stop by my place, pick up Onyx, and the two of you will come with us." Charlie sat back on his hind legs, his ears standing straight up. If Great Danes could smile, I would say he was.

"Rynna?" Derreck gave her the floor and Rynna laid a different map over the first. This one was of a giant home on a huge acreage.

"My sister surrounds herself with only Hunters. Both male and female, though, typically, the Huntresses are inside the home cooking and cleaning. They act as her servants. The men patrol both the building and the grounds. They are all controlled by the collars they wear. The collars only activate when Julia wishes them to, but she has the ability to control their actions and see through their eyes at any time. It's a drain on her to do so, but she can and will.

"We aren't going to have a lot of time to get in and get Amelia out, but as a direct family member, I have the ability to get in the house without it setting off alarms and alerting the Hunters."

I kept leaning down toward the map, squinting as I tried to figure out what exactly I was looking at. "What is this? What's behind the house? Is something wrong with this map?"

"Good gravy, Aidan. Haven't you ever seen *The Labyrinth*?" Bethany had stayed fairly quiet during the discussion, and her voice coming from the corner of the room surprised me. "You know," she continued, "David Bowie? Hoggle? The babe? The babe with the power?"

I just kept staring at her, having no clue what she was talking about. Her eyebrows rose and she threw a hand in the air, saying, "Oh, you are hopeless. It's a maze, Aidan."

I caught Will, of all people, humming. "Is that from the movie?" I asked, clearly judging him.

He shrugged. "I'm an AniMage, not an animal. I've had a TV."

I shook my head. "Let's get back on track. There's a maze. Can we use it?" I turned to Rynna for answers.

She nodded. "We won't just use it. The maze is our lifeline. Julia and the Hunters refuse to enter the maze. The Elders enchanted it and it has the ability to sense the intentions of those inside of it. It will give you what you need, if your intentions are pure. We are on a rescue mission and it will know. But it also means we have to be very selective with who we take." Rynna paused for a moment and looked around the table. "As we just saw, there are AniMages who question Aidan and will likely have more than just the rescue on their minds. Those people cannot come inside with us. The maze will never allow them to leave."

"Cheese and rice, you Immortals like to make things uber-complicated," Bethany muttered from her end of the table and I caught a snort from Charlie, his form of agreement. I nodded in solidarity.

"So, we're going to use the maze to get in, be selective about the people who come with us—maybe Elias can do his 'invade your brain' thing to vet them—and then how are we going to find her? Or figure out whether Cole is there, too? And how in the hell are we going to get them out before the Hunters kill us all?" There were seven or eight more questions rolling around in my head, but those were the most relevant.

It felt overwhelming. There were so many angles to consider and situations that could arise. And while my brain was supposed to be focused on being a leader and making a battle plan, it was bouncing between the conversation at hand and Amelia. I'd had a bad feeling in the pit of my stomach all day. I hadn't had time to shift since the situation with Braxton and I wanted to find her in the dream place I knew existed. I wanted to hold her, reassure her we were on our way, tell her she didn't have to worry. Instead, I stood around a table, wondering if I was about to get myself, and all of the people who were now my responsibility, killed.

"Mikail will help us. He knows we are coming eventually and he will make sure we have a direct path to get to Amelia and, hopefully, Cole. We don't even know that he's there, but right now, we have to go with the assumption. Since we've decided on the plan, I will use Tragar to get him the message and he'll be ready. He's been working with Amelia to help her prepare for what's coming, and I know he's taken care of her." Rynna kept talking, but those last words sent jealousy roaring through me. My wolf howled and the rumbling mix of emotions, frustrations, and fear had me close to shifting.

A hand clamped down on my shoulder and I whipped around, ready to take someone's head off.

"Hey!" Elias put both hands up as he pulled away. "Bring it down a notch, eh? You aren't listening because you're too busy worrying about the Prince hanging out with your girl, and you need to hear what she just said."

"Stay out of my head, Elias." The words were close to a growl as I said them. He laughed and it only shot my rage higher.

"I wasn't in your head. All anyone has to do is look at you to see the green-eyed-monster rearing his ugly head. Well, technically, yours are blue right now, but you get the drift."

I gazed around the room and everyone looked away awkwardly, focusing on anything but me. Charlie let out a snort. Bethany was rolling her eyes, but I also saw the flicker of pain she was trying to suppress as we talked about Micah.

"Oh, don't you look at me like that, Aidan! I don't need your pity. He's not even worth the energy of a kick in the bits, which is exactly what he deserves." She crossed her arms over her chest and glared. Not at me, but I was sure there was a continued rant going on inside her head. I'd had one too many of those lately and could relate.

"It wasn't pity for you, B. It was pity for him. The poor guy probably has more to be worried about when the two of you see each other again than anyone in there." I gave her a smile, trying to diffuse the hostility I could feel growing in the room. I was rewarded with a laugh and her posture relaxing.

"Okay," I said. "Rynna, give us the run down. I want to understand, step by step, how you see us getting in and out. I'd like to know when and how we're contacting Micah, we need to decide who's coming with us, and then I want to get on the road. We're walking into a complete shit show and we all know it." I swallowed down the lump in my throat. "We have no idea where Amelia or Cole could be inside this place, or what kind of condition they are in. We hope we can fend off the Hunters, but we can't be sure. This whole thing is a crap shoot."

"You shouldn't be going with us." I was surprised to hear Amelia's father finally speak. He'd watched and listened, but he had yet to voice an opinion.

"I'm sorry?" I had much less pleasant responses on the tip of my tongue, but this was Amelia's dad.

Nathaniel took a step forward and leaned his hip on the edge of the table. "You shouldn't be going. You're the King of the AniMages and her mate, she is going to need you. You can't die trying to get her out or all of this is for nothing. Without you, she can't fulfill her destiny or the prophecy. And from what I understand, my daughter cares for you. The last thing she needs is to lose another person she cares about."

Not once had I stopped to think about the danger to myself. Even now, as I understood what he was saying to me and knew it made sense, it didn't matter. I straightened and looked Nathaniel in the eyes, trying to make my intentions as clear as possible. "No disrespect, sir, but I'm going in there. She needs me and we have no clue what our connection means or what it can provide her. Me being there could be essential in getting her out alive. There's no prophecy without both of us, so I will either bring your daughter home, or I will die trying."

I was shoving clothes into a bag, my mind in a hundred places at once, when Bethany came into the room we had shared. She leaned against the doorframe, trying to look casual, but she was fidgeting.

"Do you have any idea what you're doing?" She spoke softly, nothing about her question threatening or judgmental.

I stopped what I was doing and laid my palms flat on the bed, my head dropping. "No. I have absolutely no clue what I'm doing." I turned my head and met her eyes. "But I have to. I have to get to her. The feeling that she's in trouble keeps getting stronger. I can't leave her there."

It felt good to say it out loud. To drop the bravado of being a leader and acknowledged that I was scared shitless.

Bethany came over and sat on the bed, patting the blanket beside her. I sat down.

"Did you ever imagine, in the furthest, remote corners of your mind, that this is where we would be today?" She laughed, a dry, brittle laugh, making me wonder whether she was also close to breaking.

"You know you don't have to stay here, or even come with us. You can go home to Mississippi. You can disappear. I'll help you." The last thing I wanted was for her to get hurt. Amelia would never forgive me, and we had become friends.

In true Bethany fashion, she punched me in the shoulder. "Shut your mouth. I'm staying. Amelia is the closest thing I've had to what family is supposed to be in my life."

"I guess I don't know much about you. What's your story?" I asked.

She shrugged, but looked away from me. "Not much to tell really."

I flashed a sarcastic smile. "Not possible. We all have a screwed up story to tell."

"I'm southern. We don't air our dirty laundry." She smiled as she allowed a little more of her accent to show through.

"I'm a guy. You can tell me or not. I'm just saying, if you want to, I'm sitting here." I sat silent and waited, giving her time to decide. I'd never had friends who were girls. Girls wanted to date me, girls wanted to hook up, but I hadn't had girls who were just friends. It was easier to let my charm do the work than building relationships I knew would end as soon as I was relocated to another family in a different city.

"I am the stereotypical southern girl," she said. "I was raised on the pageant circuit with a mom who wanted me to live out the dreams she never got to. When I was finally able to convince her I really wanted to spend my time on a horse instead of a stage, she pushed me into barrel racing, so I could still be the beauty queen in sparkles and rhinestones, while I won bigger trophies and more money. My dad loved coming on rodeo trips with us, but only so he could disappear into the stables and play back room poker games with the cowboys. I can't tell you how many nights I ended up dragging Daddy, drunk and broke, out of a barn and back to the hotel, while Momma got schnaukered with the other moms."

"Is that what you meant when you told me you'd dealt with worse guys than me?" I'd been curious about her comment since she'd made it, but it had never felt like it was the right time to ask.

She snorted an indignant huff of air, telling me memories she likely didn't want were racing around her head.

"Imagine being a pretty seventeen-year-old girl, surrounded by cowboys telling you your daddy owes them money. How exactly do you think they imagined getting their payment?"

Rage spiked through me. I wanted to break their necks. I couldn't ask the follow-up question and thankfully, she didn't make me.

"What they didn't realize was I took Kenpo—a form of martial arts—and the last thing they wanted was a tussle with me. I'm pretty sure one of them may never have kids after the kick he took, and the other one was too busy trying to stop the blood from his nose to keep me there. They weren't the first or the last ones to try crap like that, but I took care of myself."

I had a new respect for the small girl sitting next to me. "Remind me to never piss you off, blondie." I bumped her shoulder with mine and she turned to me, grinning.

"I've given you fair warning. Alrighty, I do believe it's time to go get our girl back," she said, bumping me back and then standing.

"Are you ready for this?" she asked, the humor gone, concern in its place.

"No," I admitted. "But who's ever ready for anything? She needs me and nothing will keep me from her."

Bethany nodded. "I may not have magic powers, but I've got your back, Aidan."

Those words were more reassuring than she could have imagined.

Chapter 24
Amelia

Over the course of the two days, the only visitor to the maternity ward, and my cell, was a female Hunter who refused to speak to me. She brought all of us food three times a day. I waited for the Queen or Rhi to show and prayed for Micah to come through the doors.

I spent hours talking with the women surrounding me. I couldn't see the majority of them, but each one told me about their families, their backgrounds, and what they had been through. We talked of ourselves and our abilities. It was so interesting to learn what each of them had been capable of at full power and strength. Cora was able to project a shield around herself, blocking out every power she'd been exposed to. Others were able to control the elements, to mentally create weapons firing shots no one could see but still feel, and one woman was able to project replications of herself. Micah had only scratched the surface when he said every Immortal had a singular ability outside of those common to their race.

Once we got to the real truths, it became harder to listen. Cora had been pregnant six times. Three of them had been born and taken away. Nadine had miscarried twice. She had to watch as both Hunters and Julia tried to infuse the fetus in her belly with magic, only to kill it in the process. They were filled with alternating fury and grief. The losses they had endured made everything I'd ever complained about seem so small.

When the Hunters came for Cora, she already had one child, a toddler with red hair. Somehow, she was able to get the toddler to run into the forest and hide. The Hunters killed her husband before they took her. Both had shifted, trying to protect their son, and she had not been in her native AniMage form in eight years.

I sat in my cell as tears ran rivers down my face. It wasn't just their stories, it was the emotion

369

permeating the air around me, forcing me to feel it with them as they spoke.

I finally got to the point where I couldn't speak or listen anymore and retreated to the back of my cell. At first, I calmly spoke to the Keeper, but I eventually got angry and tried whatever I could think of to get it to cooperate without removing my cuff. Rynna had told me the cuff should allow me to work with my Keeper for short periods of time. It had worked with Nell and the green power, but I couldn't get it to work again.

Frustrated, I got up and paced the small cell. I intentionally let my mind wander, hoping by giving it space, we would be able to find an answer. Images and scenes flitted in and out. Aidan on the beach the night we met. My father holding me up at eye level as I saw the flash of Hunter power that should have tipped me off to the binds placed on him. Cole pulling me into his chest while I cried and the Keeper power grew. Bethany dragging me from store to store our first weekend together in Brighton, throwing hanger after hanger of clothes over the door as she talked nonstop. The blending of the life I had set out to have and the one I finally had to accept didn't stop. Rynna. Derreck. Charlie. Micah. My head was full of thoughts and emotions.

"You need him." I heard someone speak and it cut into the swirling mess.

I went to the bars of the cell, craning my neck to see who it was. "What? Who is talking?" I asked.

"You need him. Your mate. You won't be able to do what she wants unless you have him. I can feel the power inside you and it is a lock missing its key. He will unlock you." She spoke clearly and surely.

"Well, do you know where to find this mysterious mate? Because everyone keeps talking about him, but he isn't exactly searching me out. I've pretty much had it with people telling me I need some guy I've never met to meet my full potential." I was exhausted, annoyed, and well aware I was taking it out on a faceless voice. The thought that Micah might be my mate was there and gone. I shoved it out as soon as it entered my mind. If he were my mate, then where in the hell was he?

She laughed a light, airy laugh that somehow brought a smile to my own face. "He is yours. He has always been yours. You only have to reach for him and he'll be there."

My smile faded. "What does that even mean?" I asked.

"I cannot give you answers, Keeper. I can only tell you the truth," she responded.

I wanted to argue, but a low yowl interrupted me. I struggled to look toward the cells where Nell and the tiger were being held. I heard it again, and this time, saw the tiger push her paw through the cell bars. She continued to cry as she reached for me and I could feel her hope and desire to get to me. She believed I could help her as I had helped Nell. She was afraid she wouldn't live long enough to birth her babies and they would die together.

I can do this. I don't need some guy, I just need me. I can do this.

I repeated the thoughts in my head as I spoke in low tones. "I'm right here. I'm going to try to help you. I don't know if I can, but I'm going to try." I scooted myself as close to the wall as possible and reached my own arm through the bars. It was awkward, but I was able to twist my arm around until I could grasp her paw. As soon as we connected, her pain and fear slammed into me, taking my breath away.

The most control I'd ever had over my power had been when I was emotional, so I refused to let go of her as her emotions filled me. I dropped my walls and her memories assaulted me next. Like so many of the others, her husband had been murdered before her eyes. She had taken the chance and shifted, hoping to get herself and her unborn child to safety, but she didn't get far before her whole body froze. I had been through Rhi's immobilization trick before and knew how that felt. She was captive in her own body as Rhi taunted her for hours before bringing her back to Cresthaven.

Julia and the Hunters were more brutal in their techniques with the AniMages. They tried infusing power into the unborn kittens and then after they were born. They brought in charms and potions that hadn't been used or tested in hundreds of years in an attempt to give the children power again. The tiger was barely able to sustain another litter, but she loved these children as fiercely as the first she'd borne.

As her emotions fed me, my own anger rose. It was always Rhi standing with Julia, doing her dirty work. He directed the female Hunters, smiling as they tortured these women or their children. Every part of me wanted to kill him. No, death was too nice. I wanted to drain him of his precious magic until he was nothing more than human—the very thing he loathed.

I forced myself to focus and went to my Keeper. This time, the violet cerulean orb was waiting for me. It bounced up and down, hovering in front of my palms, seeming to know it was the only one who could help me. I could feel its need to get to work. The tiger was somehow drawing my power out and I was perfectly fine with it.

"I'm going to try now. Don't pull away," I whispered to her, struggling to form words as I battled our mixed emotions. Within myself, I shoved both of my closed fists into the blue-tinged orb and wrenched them apart while, at the same time, pushing all of my power as hard and as fast as I could out of me and into the tiger. It drained from me and filled her. Her heartbeat was stronger, her breaths less labored. I could feel four tiny heartbeats pitter-pattering at a rapid rate. The blue orb pulled itself back together, retreating into the room it came from, and I dropped the tiger's paw, unable to hold my grasp or even keep myself upright. She was so much bigger than the cheetah had been and it had taken more from me than I expected. I looked forward to the day when the Keeper would simply be a part of me, instead of me acting as a conduit between it and the Immortal we were trying to help or hurt. But, I had no idea whether that day would even come.

My face was cold against the concrete and I didn't have the energy to move to where I had tossed the pillow and blanket when I woke up this morning. I scanned myself and found my tiny violet flame barely burning. It was a tea light candle instead of a fire, but it would rebuild. I just needed sleep. Unable to keep my eyes open any longer, I let it all go.

Chapter 25
Aidan

We left Brighton as soon as possible and the group had been running nonstop. I had entrusted Elias to choose the AniMages who would make the trip to Washington, and there were ten of us. Ten seemed like so few knowing the Queen had an army of Hunters at her disposal, but Rynna kept assuring us we would be able to get in and get out. I wasn't convinced it was going to be so easy, but what did I know?

She, Derreck, Nathaniel, Bethany, and the dogs left yesterday, while the sun was still up. They had food, clothes, and weapons. When I asked Derreck what a gun was going to do against a Hunter, he shrugged and told me a bullet in the head was a bullet in the head. They might heal from it, but it would slow them down. I couldn't argue with his logic. The rest of us would run. There weren't enough vehicles and I needed some space from being continuously surrounded.

Elias had pulled me aside and explained Will couldn't join us. His hatred for Rhi would keep him out of the maze and make him a liability. We had talked to him together, and while nothing had ended up broken outside of a table, Will had resigned to stay with the pack in Brighton and keep them out of trouble. He would bring them to us when we were somewhere safe. Killing Hunters wasn't the purpose of the trip and he understood what was at stake.

Dillon was the hardest for me to walk away from. He begged and pleaded to come with us. A few guys ended up having to take him into the caves and keep him there so he wouldn't shift and follow us anyway. I couldn't bring myself to command him to stay, which had been Will's advice. I knew I had the power and he wouldn't be able to disobey me, but my third foster father kept coming to mind. He would stand over me screaming until I would flinch and then beat me for moving. Just because you had power didn't mean you had to use it.

It had taken me the first few hours to figure out how to block out the thoughts of the other AniMages. As the alpha, their thoughts were directly connected to mine while we were all shifted and I could hear them more clearly than I wanted to. Elias stuck with me, coaching me along until I was able to build a wall, keeping my thoughts private and theirs in the background. I was sure the connection would come in handy at some point, but right now, I needed space.

We were somewhere in Oregon when intense emotions filled me. Fear, hope, and anger I knew weren't mine flooded my system and I almost tripped as I leapt over downed trees and through the forests. The smell of her filled my nostrils. Her hair had always smelled like mint. So many girls often smelled like vanilla or flowers, but as soon as the smell of mint infiltrated my nostrils, I knew it was Amelia. I kept running, pushing myself, and the pack, harder. Her emotions and her power grew bigger and bigger, until I was afraid she would burst. Then slowly, it drained away. I was terrified something was being done to her, until finally the draining stopped. I could barely feel her in my mind. I couldn't do anything, so I tried something Elias had only explained once. I reached out for her.

He had been trying to help me understand how to communicate with the other pack members but the theory seemed sound for Amelia as well. I pushed my own power toward her, following the wavering violet thread. My legs continued to move me forward as my wolf took over our body and I focused on what was in my mind.

She was exhausted. Her breaths were shallow and I struggled to make sure mine didn't try to match hers. I heard her heartbeat slow and felt the moment she slid into sleep, her body forcing itself to shut down in order to conserve energy. All those times she had passed out before, it made so much sense now. Everything about her made so much sense.

I wanted to pull Amelia into my arms and save her from whatever she had gotten herself into this time, but I wasn't there—not yet. So instead, I followed my instincts. I slowly pulled at the ball of power sitting at my core. I likened it to a large ball of string filled with crackling electric shocks. I pulled on one of the strings and brought it to the violet thread leading to Amelia. I wrapped my string around hers, winding it farther and farther from myself, until finally, it snapped, and our two threads merged. The jolt of the combined power and the sensations of her were so much stronger, but she felt so much weaker.

Her anger flared inside me as if it were my own, my blood pressure instantly rising. The insecurity and fear she shoved down and refused to acknowledge was a bitter taste in my mouth. But she had a tiny sliver of hope she held to tightly, wishing Rynna's reinforcements would be there soon. And then there was her strength. Even as her body was weak, a never-ending river of strength connected her mind, body, and soul. It was the reserve she unknowingly tapped into again and again, and it was the reason I could never walk away from her. Strength was not something every person had. Her willingness to put everyone and everything before herself—to actively choose the opposite of what she needed and deserved—was a rare trait. I wanted to be that person for her. I wanted to give her the things she wouldn't give herself.

I poured my own power into her, filling her depleted well enough to bring her back to consciousness. It slowed me down and I was winded for the first time, but I gave her everything she needed. I sat in the back of her mind as she slowly came to. I felt the cold, hard floor under her cheek and saw the bars locking her in wherever she was. It was impossible to keep my own rage in check as I realized she was a prisoner.

Aidan?

Her voice cracked in the same way it always did when she'd wake up after falling asleep during a movie and try to apologize. It was a sucker punch I hadn't expected.

I'm here, doll. Don't worry. I'm coming for you.

She recoiled, fear churning in her mind.

No! You can't come here! You'll never survive them. You can't. She was screaming inside my head.

I can and I will, Amelia. We are meant for each other. I know who I am now. I'm the leader of AniMages. I'm your mate. We are the prophecy. I can get you out. I might be the only one who can.

She was silent for longer than I could handle. *Amelia? Doll, you have to talk to me. You have to help me find you.*

Lies. More lies. I won't let you twist him like this. You won't ruin the only good memory I have left.

And then, she was gone.

Chapter 26
Amelia

I closed the door on whomever was on the other end of my mind. I was so sure it was Aidan at first. I was enveloped in the same warmth and safety he always brought me—like nothing could hurt me or us as long as we were together. I heard him call me "doll" for the first time in what felt like eons and I wanted to lose myself there, wrapped in the cocoon of his voice. But it wasn't real.

Joran had told me it was up to me to find the lies and separate them from the truths. There was no way Aidan was the leader of the AniMages. It made no sense. How could he possibly have gone from a human, to an Immortal, to being the head of the most-hunted race out there? And then, to claim he was my mate? Someone, likely Rhi, was playing on my deepest desires. I could only imagine he and the Queen in her sitting room, laughing. They were playing me and I couldn't allow them to. I had to focus.

I pulled myself up off the floor and then pushed to stand. I felt good. Better than I should have. In fact, better than I had in weeks. I held my hands out in front of me and flicked my fingers. Bright bursts of violet power shot from my hands. I scanned my body and found no weaknesses. My flame was bright, the Keepers were peaceful, and my mind was clear. Apparently, I needed sleep. But now, it was time to figure out how to get out of here.

I called out to the other women. "When will someone come again? What time is it?"

A sleepy voice responded, "You've been out a while, it's almost morning. Are you okay?" It had to be Cora.

"I'm good—really good. Can you see the tiger? Is she okay?" I asked.

"She's great. Honestly, she looks better than she ever has. Her name is Lilith," Cora responded.

"Can you talk to her? And Nell?" A plan was forming in my mind.

"It's gotten harder the longer I've gone without shifting, but on a good day, yes. Why?" I felt Cora's curiosity piquing and I smiled.

"I think I've got a way to get us out of here, but both Lilith and Nell will need to help us. I know they are pregnant, but we need them. Can the rest of you still use your magic?"

Cora sighed. "No, not really. The Hunters have us all bound in one way or another so we can't fight back. It's there—they need us to have it in hopes of being able to pass it on—but we can't use it against them."

"That's it," I whispered to myself. I started pacing, trying to work it all out in my head.

"Hey! You can't just stop. What's the plan?" Cora's voice cut through the space between us and the hushed whispers of the other women grew louder as hope and excitement filled the air. My mind was spinning in multiple directions, trying to vet the plan that was both extremely dangerous but also very possible. There was one more thing I would need, though. I bit my lip, wavering back and forth.

"I can't explain it all just yet, but if I can break the binds on you, can you fight? Can you get the restraints off and work together to get out of here?" I refused to acknowledge I would likely be the one who wouldn't make it out if I succeeded in breaking the binds on them. There were at least twenty women and I barely made it through helping Cole or Lilith before I passed out. Pushing myself that far might kill me, but there was a good chance Julia might kill me anyway, so I had to try. I couldn't allow these women to continue being tortured.

I heard Cora addressing the other women. She was clearly the leader. "Are you willing to fight? Will you work together and help each other? We can make it out. Together, they cannot take us all. And we have what they want. We carry the livelihood of our races inside us. We have the upper hand. Are you ready to get out of here?"

Her words were loud whispers and the chorus of "Yes!" in response gave me goose bumps. I couldn't back out now.

"Okay. Here's what I'm going to do." I laid out the plan, asking Cora to make sure Lilith and Nell were on board and the other women understood what they needed to do. Cora confirmed everyone was in agreement and understood, even Lilith and Nell. Now I had one last task: to get my brother from wherever he was into this cell.

I paced the cell, waiting for the Hunter to arrive with breakfast. My mind kept coming back to whoever had been inside my head. Before this week, I would have taken it at face value. I would have added up the feelings, the emotions, and the sound of his voice bouncing around in my brain, and I would have told you it was Aidan. My Aidan. But now I knew better. With every turn, the Hunters or Julia had been capable of yet another atrocious act I couldn't fathom. I wouldn't put it past them to use Micah for information, and upon realizing what Aidan meant to me, use him to their advantage.

But he had felt so real. I sighed, slowing my steps and resting my back against the wall. I closed my eyes and pictured him—his eyes layers of smoke and ash, either a cocky grin or an intense stare always on his face. I saw him sitting in Esmerelda's, lying in the grass talking to me about growing up in foster homes, and sitting on the beach, looking at me like he held the world in his hands and would give it to me if I only asked. I felt his fingers tangled in my hair and his lips slanted across mine. His hands around my waist, pulling me into the safety of his arms. He told me he loved me and I never had the chance to say it in return. So much had happened so fast, I never got to decide whether or not I really did. I thought I did. When I had to walk away, I poured everything I had for him into my goodbye, but was it really love?

Love was such a strange word. It encompassed so many emotions and assumptions. I knew Aidan made me feel things I had never felt, but I'd also never had another boyfriend. Love implied I would and could share all of myself with him, and I had never been able to do that. Every person who had expressed love for me had made choices that took them away from me. My mother died, my father allowed Rhi's binds, Cole left to find answers, Rynna knew the truth and hid it from me. Did I even know what love was really supposed to look like? Could I love him?

The door slammed as the Hunter pushed in a cart of food, stopping my maddening train of thought and bringing me back to the task at hand. As the nameless Hunter appeared in front of my cell, I pushed my hand through the bars. "I know you don't talk to me, but can you just listen? I have something the Queen will want to know."

Thankfully, she stopped, staring at me. Like the other Hunters I had met, the woman had light brown skin and white hair. Hers was thick and long, pulled back in several small braids feeding into a larger one hanging to her waist. She was wearing all black and her eyes held little emotion. At my plea, they narrowed and she waited. I didn't make her wait long.

"She needs to bring my brother, Cole, to me. He was last with Micah, in his room. I don't know whether he's still here, but if she wants me to attempt to fix these women and their children, he is the only one who can temper my power and keep me from killing them, or myself, in the process. She can ask him. She can bring him here to prove it. I don't care. I just need him. Micah may have taken him somewhere, but she needs to get him back." The Huntress still didn't speak. Her eyebrow rose and then she turned away, tossing a hunk of red meat into the tiger's cage. She was surprised to find her hand coming within millimeters of being bitten off as Lilith snapped at it. She jumped back and I couldn't stop my laugh.

"Make no mistake, Huntress. I am the Keeper." I shouldn't have goaded her, but I couldn't help it. She glared at me and maintained a larger distance as she tossed Nell's breakfast into her cell. The door slammed behind her and my pacing began again. Nervous energy buzzed through me and the Keeper magic bounced back and forth, faster and faster. There was no turning back now.

Chapter 27
Aidan

She had closed me out. She wasn't gone completely, but I couldn't feel her emotions or see through her eyes as I had briefly been able to do. She didn't believe it was me. I wanted to be hurt, but her words made sense. I had explained to Elias what had just happened and he brought me back from the ledge. After thinking about everything she'd been through, it only made sense she wouldn't trust what had just happened. But I had to find a way to get to her again.

We had run all night and arrived at a small cabin a few miles from Cresthaven as the sun was coming over the horizon. We were exhausted, hungry, and dirty. I mentally thanked the genius who had installed a tank-less water heater as one after another of us paraded in and out of the bathroom. The mud caking my fur covered my skin after my shift and it took some solid scrubbing to feel human again.

I got out of the shower and wiped the moisture from the mirror. With both hands on the pedestal sink, I leaned forward and stared at my face. It was the same face I'd been staring at for years, yet it was different. I had spent my life looking into mirrors and wondering who I really was. I would search my features and have silent conversations with myself, asking whose eyes or nose I had. Whether my laugh sounded like one of my parents or if it were my own. Now, I could call upon memories and see them as clearly as I saw myself.

I had my mother's eyes, but the rest of my face was my father's. I had the same collection of freckles over my cheeks and nose and my jaw was cut exactly like his. I had always wondered whether he had the same hassles while shaving. My dark hair matched my mother's but my build my father's. As I stared at myself, an emotion I hadn't expected took hold. I watched the electric blue start from my pupils and work its way out to the edges of my iris. The alpha of my wolf spread through me, my need to show Amelia who I really was becoming paramount. I had to get to her. It was more than how I felt about her. I couldn't help but believe in the prophecy, because an obsessive drive utterly foreign to me pushed and pulled inside of me, screaming at me to get to her.

When I finally emerged from the bathroom, the rest of the pack was in the dining room. I had made them all shower first, wanting to show I wasn't the kind of leader who took first and gave last. As I turned the corner into the kitchen and came face to face with Bethany, I laughed out loud. She was wearing a bright yellow apron, her hands were covered in white powder, and she had pancake batter on her face.

She didn't even break stride as she hip-checked me out of her way and resumed pouring batter into multiple skillets. "Cheese and rice, Aidan. You might have warned me your little horde was going to eat like a bunch of rabid coons." She opened the oven and pulled out a pan of biscuits, turning the pan upside down onto the table. She had no sooner turned her back than hands were snatching them up. I heard a chorus of "Ouch!", "Hot, hot!", and "Ow!" as the table looked to be playing a game of hot potato.

"Where are Elias, Rynna, and the others?" I asked.

"Out back. Elias said they had some catching up to do, so I sent them with plates and let them be," Bethany responded.

Bethany was flipping pancakes when I stepped up and stole the spatula from her hand. "Sit. Eat. I bet you've been at this all morning." She blew a strand of hair that had escaped her ponytail out of her face and for the first time, I noticed how tired she looked. "Sit," I said, more gently. "Thank you, but let me help."

Bethany nodded, but as she sat in the chair at the head of the table, the one I knew had been reserved for me, she threw out, "If you burn my flapjacks, there will be hell to pay."

Some of the younger AniMages I didn't really know stopped eating and looked up, waiting for my reaction. I laughed and shook my head. "Eat, everybody. We're going to need all the fuel and rest we can get. We go tonight."

I took the time to meet the eyes of everyone at the table. I could feel their fear, but also their commitment. "Once you're all finished, get some sleep. We'll go back over the plan again this afternoon."

I finished another round of pancakes and by then, a spot at the table had opened up for me to sit and eat as well. I took the spot to Bethany's left and dug in. We ate in silence as the room emptied until it was just her and I left. I could hear both soft and loud snores coming from various corners of the house. I needed sleep myself, but not just yet.

"She was there—inside my head. I was able to help her and give her some of my power. I saw where they have her, even though I don't know where it is. But she refused to believe I was real. She told me I was lying and just using her." I watched Bethany as I spoke and her expression went from joyous, to questioning, to deflated. I could understand the roller coaster.

"But she's alive and she's okay. And, on some level, she knows we're coming for her, right?" Bethany asked.

"I think so. She was in some kind of cell, so I don't know how okay she is, but I gave her what I could. I'm trying to open the door between us again, I'm just not sure how." I dropped my fork onto the table and my head into my hands. I pulled at the roots of my hair and tried to remind myself I was still figuring all of this out, but I didn't have time to waste.

Bethany's hand covered mine and she pulled it to the table. She squeezed my fingers and I looked over at her. "You're going to get to her, Aidan. As sure as the damn rooster I saw in the backyard is going to crow when the sun rises tomorrow, you will get to her. And what she believes as real is irrelevant right now. She'll believe it when she sees you. She won't have a choice."

Chapter 28
Amelia

It took less time than I thought for the door to the chamber to open again. My annoyance with seeing Rhi was far overshadowed by my joy at seeing my brother. Cole looked good, healthy. I hadn't laid eyes on him since I'd broken Rhi's binds and Micah had brought me back from the brink.

Rhi shoved Cole forward and my brother turned to glare at him, his eyes glowing green. It was good to see, and feel, his power back to normal. The bonus was Rhi's scowl as my brother reminded him his binds had been broken. Cole was wearing the cuffs again, but those would only bind him from using his power to fight, not from having it, just as it did for the women in the room.

The two of them were followed into the room by Queen Julia and then Joran. "The gang's all here," I muttered under my breath. Cole finally locked eyes with me and I was surprised to see his narrow. A strange look came across his face as his brows furrowed and his jaw tensed. I wanted to call out and ask him whether he was okay, but the answer came sooner than I could ask the question. I felt him probing at my mind and opened the door for him, proud that he had figured out how to make the connection.

I'm fine, Ame. Are you okay? What the hell is all this?

Relief coursed through me.

I'm okay. These women are Julia's science experiment. They can't have babies with magic. It's the real reason behind all of this. She's been capturing these women and forcing them to have baby after baby. She has tried everything to give the babies power so they aren't born human and since she's failed, she wants me to do it.

Cole finally made it to my cell door. His eyes widened as he passed Lilith and Nell. They both growled at Rhi, but he ignored them, waved a hand, and my door opened. I stepped back and waited for him to un-cuff Cole. He shoved him harder than necessary and Cole stumbled into me. The door slammed back closed and we were left facing Julia, Joran, and Rhi. I knew exactly why there hadn't been any argument with bringing Cole to me and prayed my instincts about Joran were right.

Julia stepped toward us, her arms crossed and her head tilted to the side, as if she were studying animals at the zoo. "You said you required your brother to temper your power. I have brought him, much to my son's dismay. You've clearly been hard at work while I've been away." Her eyes flicked toward Lilith and she was rewarded with a deep growl and a snap of Lilith's massive jaws.

"Tell me, girl," she said, scowling, "how is it your brother can do what you cannot do for yourself? And don't try to lie to me, dear. You know it won't work." She snapped her fingers and Joran stepped toward me, but his face was a mask of indifference, giving nothing away.

I pretended to be thinking while I explained to Cole what was about to happen.

I'm going to tell her a story, but I'll tell you the truth as I go. Listen carefully.

I kept my gaze directly on the Queen while speaking to Cole through our connection, hoping I could hold two conversations at once.

"Just as I was infused with the power of the Keeper, my mother found a way to give Cole the ability to calm me and my power."

I'm going to take off the cuff and you have to help me stay focused on breaking the binds the Hunters have put on these women so they can fight for themselves.

"I wear the cuff so the Keeper does not overtake me during my day to day, but in the times I need to use her power, I have to have balance. Without balance, she'll overwhelm me and do whatever she wants. Her power is stronger than mine could ever hope to be, but it is very much separate from me." That got exactly the reaction I had hoped from the Queen. She finally looked interested. Rhi, on the other hand, looked suspicious.

You stay with me. Don't leave my side. We have to start with Cora, though. She can create a shield to protect us.

"If you want me to take the risk of removing my cuff and helping these women, then we all need the protection only Cole can give. He has to be able to touch me—skin to skin—or it won't work."

Then we have to free the tiger and the cheetah. They will do the most damage and help keep the Hunters from us. I'm counting on Julia not wanting these women killed. Make sure I get to all of them. Every woman leaves here.

Cole finally interrupted me. *No! You can't help them all, Ame. It's not possible. I won't sacrifice you!*

"It's easier if I can also touch the women. The power exchange is more direct and we will have a better chance of success."

I'm doing this, Cole. She takes their children and likely kills them. This cannot continue. She has to be stopped.

Cole was yelling inside my head and I had to block him out. I focused on Julia, Rhi, and Joran. His face was still blank. Julia turned to him. "Joran, does she speak the truth? Can he do what she says? Do we truly have a chance of succeeding after all of these years?" I hated her excitement. I could feel the truth behind her emotions and it wasn't excitement for these women or their children. It was excitement over her ability to finally rule a people she could control. She could choose who had children and selectively force me to only help those she wanted. As Micah's wife, I would be the ultimate puppet, so long as the full prophecy wasn't fulfilled. If she knew how I controlled the power, she could control me.

I held my breath as I waited for Joran to speak. Cole was finally silent as well.

"Yes, your majesty. She speaks the truth. Of course, we should test her theory, because it is just that, but she wants to help these women."

I had to force myself not to smile. Joran had told the truth and confirmed my words without having to lie himself. Tricky, tricky.

The door to the cell clicked open and swung wide. I turned to Cole and he gave me both a frustrated stare and a short nod. Like it or not, we were doing this.

Chapter 29
Aidan

The sun had set and we were moving as a unit through the forest. A few of the AniMages had shifted into horses and allowed Rynna, Nathaniel, and Derreck to ride so we could make good time to Cresthaven. Rynna and I were in the lead, with her directing. Bethany had stayed back at the cabin with Charlie and Onyx guarding her. She wasn't pleased, but she also understood she was more of a liability than an asset at this point.

As we neared Cresthaven, Rynna hopped down from Eliza's back and waved for the others to do the same. She crept up to me and whispered, "Tell them all to shift into the fastest, most quiet animal they can. As long as we can get to the maze door, we can do this, but the span of distance between here and there is the most dangerous. It looks like the maze top is open, but the enchantment includes a shield. If they try to fly in, they will be repelled and give us away."

I couldn't answer her while shifted, so I simply nodded. I communicated the message and watched the rest of pack shift into various forms of cats. Everything from what looked like a house cat up to Elias's panther. I had yet to shift into anything but a wolf and wasn't sure exactly how to instruct the change.

I pictured a mountain lion and my wolf instantly responded. There was a stretch and snap of expanding and contracting muscles and bones, and when I looked down, I was met with short pale fur and claws more deadly than any I had seen before.

Well done. Elias's compliment was one I shouldn't have needed but was glad to have.

I turned back to Rynna and she nodded. She and Derreck led the way. I was surprised and impressed with their ability to stay quiet, until I remembered they weren't human either. Just like Nathaniel, who brought up the rear, their Mage power was aiding them. While it wasn't a huge distance, it felt like it took hours to cross the three hundred yards from where we started to the edge of the Cresthaven property. We lined ourselves up against the stone wall and followed Rynna's instruction to stay close to each other. As we rounded the last corner, I couldn't help the audible sigh of relief. Rynna was making hand motions in front of an area of the wall she said would contain the door.

She was muttering words as her hands moved in a rhythm of loops and swirls. Finally, she put both hands onto the stone at once and it disappeared. "Hurry, we only have a short window," she called out in a loud whisper and ran through the doorway. We all followed, diving through as quickly as possible. Just after Nathaniel dove in, the stone reappeared. I had given the rest of the pack instruction to stay shifted, thinking they would likely be more effective that way, but I shifted back to human form.

Derreck pulled off the backpack he was wearing and tossed me a pair of jeans and a long-sleeved T-shirt. I pushed my feet into shoes and turned to Rynna. "What now?" I asked.

She was already fumbling around, pushing her hands into various parts of the large hedge wall. "It's got to be here somewhere. Come on, you know you want to help me. We're here to help her!" Rynna clearly wasn't talking to me. I watched, my own anxiety rising as her frustration grew. She moved down a few feet, put both hands into the leaves, and whispered something I couldn't hear. She pulled one hand away and plunged it into the foliage.

"Yes!" she cried, as she pushed and the hedge swung inward. "Come on!" she called over her shoulder.

She didn't have to tell me twice. I took off through the hedge and stopped short when I found Micah on the other side.

He opened his mouth to say something, but before he could, I crossed the few feet between us and had him by the shirt collar, six inches off the ground, and shoved against the leafy wall.

"She's in a cell! They have her locked up like an animal in a cage. That's what you brought her here to be—your prisoner?" I saw the blue smoke enveloping my hands and the thought briefly crossed my mind that I could snap his neck before anyone could stop me. A small hand grasped my shoulder and Rynna appeared in my peripheral vision. Micah still hadn't said a word, his eyes bright red, like two stoplights on a pitch-black night.

"Aidan, you have to let him go. We need Mikail to help us. And he's been helping Amelia. Let him go and he can explain. But we don't have a lot of time."

I gave him one last push against the wall and let him go. He dropped to the ground more gracefully than I would have liked and dusted himself off.

"I had nothing to do with Amelia ending up in a cell. She managed that one all on her own. I told her to stay under the radar, but as we are all aware, she doesn't exactly take to direction well. I've been trying to find her and up until last night, it was as if she had disappeared. My Hunter was gone, she was gone…I was losing my mind looking for them both. I knew she was here and somehow, last night, she did something to break the spell around the room she's in." His words did very little to tamp down the anger coursing through me. I took a half step toward him and he backed up the same distance.

"Aidan, just hold on. I'm on your side. I've always been on your side. I've known what my mother was doing for years. I just didn't have a way to stop it. With you and Amelia here, we can finally put an end to her madness."

I didn't know what he was talking about, but he kept going and I didn't hear a word of it. The door between Amelia and me had been blown wide open and all I heard were screams. All I felt was her life force draining away.

Chapter 30
Amelia

I approached Cora's bedside and she did her best to pull back, even though we both knew she was ready for what was about to happen. The other women did their part—some whimpering while others pulled on their restraints and made a show of not wanting me to come to their beds next. Cole walked in lockstep with me, his presence bringing me strength. Once we were in position, I held out my left hand and Cole took it. His reassurance and calmness was exactly what I needed. He was scared, but as always, he had my back.

I reached my right hand out and took Cora's. I could feel the tiniest flame of power still inside her. The binds had quelled her power down to next to nothing. I could see the orange floating in her system, encapsulating her own brilliant blue power like the candy shell around an M&M.

I looked up at Julia, who stood across the room, as far from me as possible. Apparently, she wanted my results, but didn't want to be collateral damage. That suited me fine as it gave Cole and me more room to work.

"What are you waiting for, Keeper? I'd be happy to give you a reason to move faster." Rhi spoke and it only fueled my commitment. There was only one last thing to do and I was both scared and thrilled. I turned to Cole. "Let's do this, Cole." He looked at me, his hesitation obvious. "We have to. I'm going to be fine. You won't let anything happen to me, right?" I squeezed his hand and waited.

He slowly nodded as his gaze steeled and jaw tensed. I watched him amp up his power, his dark eyes lighting up in a blaze of green. I pulled my right sleeve up and removed the cuff from around my forearm. As soon as it was free of my skin, the cuff was yanked from my grip, stopping just in front of Rhi's outstretched hand. He had learned his lesson from the Queen's mistake and didn't physically touch it. But the Hunter's self-righteous sneer was the last thing I needed to see in the same moment the Keeper power was slamming back together into one dark, dominating force inside me.

Immediately, she wanted to leap for him, but Cole's voice was in my head and his power was helping to keep my mind clear. *Focus, Amelia! Focus on Cora and then get ready to let all hell loose in this place.*

I took a breath and spoke to my Keeper. The dark blot of her power was everywhere inside me. She stoked the fire inside me, my violet flame a bonfire of epic proportions. *You're going to like this,* I told her. *We're going to break this Hunter's bonds, we're going to set those AniMages free, and we're going to let these women take their revenge. But you have to focus. Stay with me!*

Her consciousness invaded my mind. This was going to be a fight, I could already tell. She wanted control. She loved the plan but she wanted to do it her way.

Cole!

He pushed another wave through me and she shrieked in response as her reach shrank. I swayed on my feet with the effort of maintaining control of us.

It all happened in precious seconds and I was finally able to look up at Cora. "Stay calm." I wasn't sure which one of us I was talking to, but I squeezed her hands and sent my power into her, much as I had done for Cole.

The Keeper wasted no time, expanding from me into Cora through the connection. She whipped through her system, blasting away the barriers the Hunters had made. With each broken orange bond, I saw and felt the power inside Cora grow. Her soul sighed as it simultaneously sent power through her in waves. It didn't take long before I knew it was over and she was whole. Cora was one of the few who wasn't currently pregnant, so at least I didn't have to worry about harming a child. I drew the Keeper back to me and pointed her toward the cells. *We have to free them. Whatever it takes!*

It was a dangerous command, but the bolts of violet fire slashed with black lighting were exactly what were needed to pop the two doors from their hinges. At the same moment, Cora enveloped us in her shield and Rhi started to shoot bursts in our direction. He didn't get more than a few off before Julia was shrieking at him, screaming for him to stop.

"They are our lifeline! They are the only ones left, you fool! Don't hurt them!" Her hands enveloped in red flames as Rhi's collar flared red. He ripped at his throat, trying to stop the burn, but she accomplished her mission of keeping him from hurting us.

"Call down reinforcements! We have to stop them from leaving!" She was screaming at Rhi as he pulled himself from the ground, more contempt than I'd ever seen flaring in his eyes.

Cora leapt from the bed as I eviscerated her restraints. We dove toward the next woman in line as both Nell and Lilith took up position near our bed, another layer of protection between us and the Hunters I knew would be here soon.

"This was a mistake! You won't leave here with them! I won't allow this!" I had to block out Julia's threats and focus on the task at hand. The Keeper wanted to take her out now. I could feel her gathering power, her notions clear in my mind.

"More, Cole! I need more control!" He gripped my hand tighter and I redirected the Keeper back to the woman in front of me.

Just as I had instructed, each woman reached out as far as she could and linked her hands with the woman next to her. They were in bundles of four or five women each. I knew there would be no way I could get to each of them individually and we would need them all to fight. We had to have our own reinforcements before more Hunters found their way here. I had hoped most of the Hunters wouldn't even know where to come, but I had no way of knowing what was about to happen. The only thing I knew for certain was there were two entrances into this giant room and we had to expect an attack from both.

It was taking too much effort to speak telepathically, so I yelled over the commotion at Cole, "Don't let her take control, but don't hold me back!"

"I've got you!" he yelled back. I clutched the next woman's hand. She had jet-black hair and bright green eyes. She reached for me with as much determination as I reached for her, but I also saw the child she was carrying.

The Keeper was like a hurricane, a swirling force raging from my heart outward and I couldn't stop her, so I let go and repeated in my mind that there was a child we had to save. Screams ripped from my lungs as it felt like she exploded inside me. Power I'd never felt or known was erupting into my system. A white-hot fire spread through my veins, scalding my insides. For a split second, I felt a tiny heartbeat. I heard the fluttering of hummingbird's wings in my mind and felt the warmth and love his mother held. The Keeper circled the child, over and over, before finally moving on, shooting out of the black-haired woman and into the next woman's hand. Inside my head, she swore this was only the beginning and we would be victorious. She told me I made no mistake in turning to her.

I could barely open my eyes against the pain but I saw Joran fighting on the side of the AniMages as Cora not only held our shield, but sent bursts of her own toward Rhi, who was shoving an irate Queen toward one of the doors. I saw her mouth moving but heard nothing aside from the Keeper in my ears.

My power was flooding the systems of multiple women at once. Binds broke and there were screams of both pain and triumph as their power was restored. Again, I felt the heartbeats of their children and the Keeper spent seconds focused only on them, but she always moved on, never trying to help or harm them. Cole continued to push his power into me and I clutched his hand with more desperation than the woman holding mine. He was the only way I would survive this and I could feel him weakening.

Before the women were completely free, they were shooting blasts toward the Queen and Rhi, sending furniture and medical equipment flying in their direction. I expected the females who acted as guards to come barging through the doors at any moment, but for now, the mothers' motives were their own. I just needed them to keep everyone away from me.

With his collar glowing and the Queen still clearly in control of his power, Rhi couldn't do the damage I was sure he wanted to. He pinned Nell to the wall, but Joran hit him, an unseen fist smacking his head backward before another punch landed in his gut, doubling him over. Rhi tried to fire back at Joran, but Lilith took a chunk of his skin with her massive claws. They continued to trade off while Rhi tried to protect the Queen, physically pushing Julia toward the door.

I pushed harder at the Keeper and pulled more from Cole. We had to free more of the women. I had only gotten to the first five. She had to do *more*.

"You've got to calm down, Amelia. I can't help you if you aren't working with me!" Cole screamed in my ear as he gripped my hand. I could feel him pushing and pulling, trying to keep me in charge instead of her.

I didn't want to hurt him, so I tried to pull my hand from his. "No! There's too many. Let go! Let me go!"

Cole locked his other hand around my wrist, closed his fingers tight around mine, and yelled, "No! She won't take you!"

I pushed harder, glaring at him as I gave her even more of myself. I had to. I had to help them and there were so many left. A hand tugged at mine and I saw the woman next me, as well as the next few, were free and could join the fight. I was also able to recognize Cora becoming drained. These women hadn't used their power in years and here I was, asking them to go all out.

"Cora, stop! We'll be fine. Help the other women get out of their restraints. I'll get to them. Go—fight—find a way out!" I yelled to her as I tried to climb down from the bed I had been sitting on.

I heard pounding and knew it was more Hunters. Julia's reinforcements were finally coming, which meant I had even less time. I took a step toward the next bed and stumbled, falling to my knees.

"Goddamnit, Amelia! I told you not to do this." Cole caught me, lifting me up into his arms. Part of me felt the exhaustion but the rest was exhilarated. The Keeper raged on, wanting the next connection point.

"No, Cole. I can do it. Just take me to them." I pushed the words out as I fought against being pulled under. We had a chance. *They* had a chance.

Cole swore and, with me on his lap, pulled himself onto the bed of the next woman, and placed her hands into mine. His power rushed into me at the same moment I felt something else entirely.

Chapter 31
Aidan

I could feel Amelia fading. There was something else taking her over and it was snuffing out her light. Amelia fought, but she didn't fight the thing inside her. She fought to stay there, to stay present. Determination ripped through me and my wolf howled, the sound filling my ears and quieting the AniMages around me.

"We have to get to her! Something's wrong. Show me—now!" I grabbed Micah and shoved him, needing movement, needing to know I was getting closer to her.

Swearing, Micah took off around a corner. "This way! This should get us to her." I followed him and found an open door. Rynna had said the maze would help us and I thanked whatever Gods existed this one was doing what it was meant to do.

I ran behind Micah as I tried to split my attention between Amelia and what was in front of me. We barreled down hallways and then stairways, a line of Mages and AniMages running toward who knows what. I could feel so much coming from Amelia, power so strong I could barely stand it. Adrenaline, excitement, exhaustion. I heard the *whoosh* of her pounding heart and the small drumbeat of something of else. Unsure of what else to do, I did the only thing I could. I wrapped her thread of power with my own until they merged.

It took longer this time, but the two finally snapped together and I immediately started funneling whatever I could to her. My body slowed. I was giving her a part of myself, but right now, she needed it and I knew I was getting close. The nearness of her set off my wolf once again, but something else built inside me. My chest tightened and I had the urge to rip the door we were approaching off its hinges. Something had popped the top off every ounce of anger I'd ever stored away and I was ready to kill to get to her.

A Hunter came through the door just as we got to it and instead of attacking, as I was about to, Micah stopped and spoke to the man. They both turned to us, finding a pack of AniMages baring teeth and ready to pounce.

"Just hold on! Baleon is a friend. He is different. He isn't controlled by my mother. He will fight for us, won't you, Bale?"

The Hunter nodded and pulled his closed fist to his heart. "I serve Prince Mikail and no other. I fight for our freedom. All of our freedom." The Hunter looked tired. Faded bruises made his brown skin look patched with black and he took shallow breaths, as if fighting broken ribs. I wasn't sure how much good he was actually going to do.

Micah nodded and continued. "We don't have time to argue, we've got to get in there. Don't hurt the women unless they are clearly Hunters! They are our future," Micah yelled back to me and everyone else, but didn't wait for questions as he dove through the door.

I followed, but then stopped abruptly. I had no idea who was fighting or why. The Hunters, mostly female, were grouped in small semi-circles, clearly trying to corral groups of angry pregnant women into small clusters they could contain. A Hunter, who I knew was Rhi, was fighting another Hunter who stood with a cheetah and a tiger.

I heard Elias yell as he also found his way into the insanity. I couldn't understand what he said, but he took off running toward the cheetah, now also fighting off Rhi.

It took me seconds longer than it should have to find Amelia. She was wrapped around Cole and looked close to passing out. He was sweating profusely and shaking as he cradled her. I saw her hand outstretched and clasped around the woman in the bed, who was also holding the hands of the next, and the next. *What the hell was she doing?*

She was so pale and her heartbeat was a faint *thump* in my mind. I could barely find the threads of her power and I knew she was giving everything she had to help those women. I couldn't let her. I couldn't let her kill herself for just a few people. We needed her. We all needed her. *I needed her.*

The burn of a power blast singed my shoulder and I turned to find two female Hunters coming toward me. All I could think was I needed them to be gone and I didn't have time to waste, I had to get to Amelia. The vise grip in my chest tightened until I thought my heart would explode, and then, like a launched rocket, I let out both a screaming roar and threw my hands away from my body. Every Hunter in the room flew backwards, slamming into walls and sliding to the floor. Everyone else looked at me with open mouths and confused stares, but I didn't waste time. I rushed to Amelia.

"What's happening? What is she doing?" I yelled to Cole as I approached. Just as I got to Amelia's bedside, Nathaniel, Rynna, and Derreck surrounded the bed.

"We have you guys covered," Nathaniel declared. He looked down at Amelia, a pained expression transforming his face, before he joined the circle around our bed. I watched the three Mages shield us from the fight as it resumed. The Hunters weren't overtly attacking the women, though it was obvious they wanted to. Their collars glowed red as the Queen sagged against a wall, her eyes closed.

"I-I don't know," Cole said. "I don't know how to help her anymore. I'm doing everything I can." He was struggling to speak and it was clear he couldn't hold on much longer. I could feel his power inside her, struggling to push back the darkness Amelia was feeding instead of fighting.

She looked at me then, her eyes unfocused and glazed over. "Aidan," she whispered, the sound barely audible over the melee around us.

I put my hands on either side of her face. "I'm here, doll. I'm right here. Let me help you."

I closed my eyes and pushed everything I had into her, disregarding everything around us. I pushed at the darkness crowding her system, taking up too much space in her head. I stoked her tiny flame with my own and tried to give her back control of herself, but the darkness did the opposite of what I expected. It didn't fight me as it did her, it pulled at me. It pulled at my power and sucked it from my system in draining gulps. I was terrified to leave Amelia alone, but the rate at which I could feel myself depleting sent a new and deeper fear through me. I couldn't protect her if I couldn't fight for her. I swayed on my feet and struggled to stand. The power inside her sighed and simmered, finally calming, but it was more than I could handle. I snapped our connection apart and the cry erupting from Amelia's lips was like having all the air ripped from my lungs at once. I steeled myself, knowing this was the only way, and turned to Cole.

"Help me, and then help her. You can't leave her alone, but you have to help me." I stumbled a little and fell into Cole.

"I don't know if I can do for you what I do for her, but I'll try." Cole reached out and wrapped his hands around my forearms. I instantly felt more stable and the room stopped spinning around me. I pulled away and directed him back to Amelia. I probably should have taken more, but he had only so much to give and she needed it.

Cole gave me a curious look. I ignored it and pulled Amelia into my arms. "You stay close to me and you stay connected to her. I can get us out of here, but you keep her with us."

Nathaniel, Rynna, and Derreck moved to surround Amelia, Cole, and me. I had Amelia tucked into my chest and it was like carrying a child. She burrowed her head into me and tightened into a small ball. Cole grabbed her ankle, keeping their connection, and stayed just a step behind me. Whatever he had done had at least brought me some balance, but all I could think was I had failed her. How could I be her mate when I couldn't save her? When it was clear I fed the evil inside her?

Chapter 32
Amelia

He was a hazy blur in my mind but I was sure it was really Aidan I saw. He was real. He was here. He told me he would come and he did.

The Keeper had taken hold so tightly, I could barely form a thought of my own. All I knew was there were more women to help, more who were still chained to their beds, bound by the Hunter's power. Someone was holding me and it felt like a safety blanket. *Cole.* Somehow, he was keeping me away from the pain boiling right under the surface. His green energy was surging through me and she hated it. She pushed and shoved at him, agitated he took up space and stopped her from spreading herself everywhere.

And then it changed. A trail of blue fire with single-minded focus wound its way through me. Once it found my core, it churned and whirled around my single flame, pouring itself into me. For a brief moment, I sighed with the relief they brought me. One bringing calm and the other replenishing everything I had given. But she wouldn't let it last. She found him, too, and took hold. She was just as thrilled as I was, but she pulled from him, wrapping herself around him until I couldn't find his light anymore. She stole his gifts to me. He stumbled and I cried out when his presence was gone. They were both gone. They had left me alone to face the demon I had unleashed.

I was ready to give up when suddenly the green energy was back. She wailed in protest as I tried to pull the calm and protection he offered and wrap it around myself, making a cocoon she couldn't find me in, hoping I could make myself smaller and smaller until she just didn't believe I was there anymore.

There were more to help. The thought was there and gone, replaced with quiet retreat. I pulled away from them all and finally let my mind stop. I had to stop. I had to save myself.

Chapter 33
Aidan

We were running as a unit toward the door when Rhi leapt out in front of us. I hadn't expected him, and with Amelia in my arms, I couldn't do anything. The Mages stayed with us, the green and red mixture of their power a shield between him and us. The battle hadn't stopped around us, though the women and the AniMages seemed to have the upper hand.

"Do you honestly think your pathetic little spell will stop me? I will have her, Nathaniel. I told you I would have her and I have had her every day since. Just give her to me and I won't do to your son what I did to you." I wanted to punch him until the smile he held was nothing but teeth scattered across the floor. I didn't want magic power; I wanted ten uninterrupted minutes to smash his head into the concrete.

I could only see the back of Nathaniel's head as he stepped forward, breaking the circle. Rynna and Derreck reestablished the protective barrier but she cried out, "Nathaniel, no! She just got you back!"

"What happened to you, Rhi? We were friends once. We sat around the same fires growing up and we told stories about the world we wanted to live in when we grew older and took the power from our parents. What has my daughter done to you? What did Liana do to you? Why are you bound to terrorize my family?"

I watched the green power building around Nathaniel and the smile I hated form on Rhi's face again. "Do you want my sob story, Nathaniel? Do you want to know what broke me and sent me to this place? You. Your wife. All of you. You did this.

"It was me she was supposed to marry. All those years, I watched you with her and you were nothing. *Nothing.* Just some Mage's son. I would rule our people and Cane would stand by my side. My brother would be my second and we would make the dreams you spoke of come true, but I would have done it with Liana. She was mine. The Elders had blessed it, yet they still let her go! You took her from me and they let you. And then Zendrick took my brother. Murdered him before he was even a man. You took everything from me, Nathaniel. So I have taken everything from you. I will do it again. I will bind you and your son and you can watch while I torture your pretty little girl until she gives us everything we need to restore this world to the proper order."

I had been watching Nathaniel as he inched closer to one of the medical carts, his lips moving quickly, though no audible sounds were coming from him. Rhi was so busy gloating for all of us, he didn't see what Nathaniel was doing. I pulled Amelia closer to me as Rynna and Derreck shared a surprised look. Nathaniel stood in front of the cart, holding a handful of instruments behind his back.

"She never told anyone who it was she was supposed to marry. Not even me," Rynna whispered.

"You will not touch either of my children. Not now. Not ever!" Nathaniel took off for Rhi before any of us could stop him. He ran directly at him, pelting the Hunter with blasts, and knocking him backward as he shouted words I didn't understand.

Cole moved to help Nathaniel and I shouted for him to stop. Derreck grabbed Cole and shoved him back toward Amelia. "No, Cole. She needs you!"

"But so does he!" Cole screamed, fighting against Derreck.

Micah and Baleon came running from behind us as Rhi unleashed his fury on Nathaniel. Soon, it was a combination of red, green, and orange flying back and forth. The Queen was screaming from her knees on the ground, her hands at her temples as she shouted for Rhi to stop and not hurt Mikail. Baleon moved to shove Micah behind him, pushing him toward us. Rhi froze momentarily, the collar around his neck glowing bright red. It finally gave Nathaniel the opening he needed. His lips moved faster and the metal in his hand glowed bright green. But just as he threw the blades, the red of Rhi's collar faded and he was able to move again. At the last moment, Rhi was able to throw out a hand and deflect all but one of the enchanted scalpels. That one sunk deep into his chest, near his heart.

Rhi was flat on his back as Nathaniel ran to him. Nathaniel lifted his arms, power surrounding him and going for what I assumed was the deathblow, when Rhi suddenly yanked the blade from his chest and hurled it at Nathaniel. "You aren't out of the fight until you're dead, Nathaniel. Isn't that what they said when your friend Zendrick killed my brother?"

Cole roared from behind me as Derreck restrained him and Rynna screamed. I pulled Amelia to me, praying she had no idea what had just happened, what her father had done for her.

Nathaniel sputtered, the blade buried in his neck. He started to fall backwards, but Baleon caught him and laid him on the floor as blood poured down his chest and spurted from his mouth and nose. Micah appeared in front of me, yelling and gesturing. My head finally snapped back to the present. I had never watched someone die, but I had to focus on the life I had to save in my arms.

"Let's go! This way, Aidan!" He led us to the only open door and directed us up. "Go until you get to the library. Just keep going up. Once you're there, Tragar will lead you into the maze. We'll do what we can to get the rest out. I'll send as many as I can up in the next ten minutes. After that, get out of here. Run until the maze gives you an exit, just keep thinking about needing to get Amelia to safety and one will appear. Her father's death cannot be in vain."

He was just as beat up as I was and I didn't know how to thank him, so I simply nodded and took off up the stairs. Derreck had somehow gotten through to Cole and by the time we reached the maze, he was back in step with me, his hand around Amelia's ankle as tears streamed down his cheeks.

As we hid in the maze, waiting for the others to emerge, he turned to me. "I never had the chance to tell him I was sorry. To tell him I understood what he had done for us."

The last thing I expected was to see a parade of pregnant women and two large cats following Elias, Derreck, and Rynna into the maze. Micah, Baleon, and the unknown Hunter had fought with us to give the women time to get out. They left Nathaniel's body and we had to restrain Cole from going back down to retrieve it. I sent some of the birds ahead to get vehicles as we ushered the women into the woods. We needed to get out of there and our only hope was that Julia was still incapacitated. Rynna said she was unconscious on the floor with Rhi by her side when they left, giving them the opening to get themselves and the women out. Realizing the women were Julia's only link to the future she hoped for, we knew the Hunters wouldn't come at us full force. They would have to regroup and find a safe way to recover the women. It was our saving grace.

We made it to the cabin and in only a few hours, we were back on the road, headed to California. Micah and Baleon didn't show up. We knew it was no longer safe for them at Cresthaven, but Rynna assured us they knew where we were headed and would find us. We had no idea how to unbind the remaining pregnant women Amelia hadn't gotten to, but Amelia was the only person I could worry about now.

I hadn't left her side. Once we reached Derreck's cabin, I alternated between pacing the room she slept in and lying beside her. She would call out for me while she slept, screaming my name and crying. She never fully awoke, but I could feel the pain inside her. I could only get so far from her before the screaming would start and Cole was still grieving his father, so he couldn't help me calm her down.

I was afraid to connect to her again. Rynna had explained her power and how they called it the Keeper. I could feel the so-called Keeper there, but I could barely find the trace of Amelia's power. It was still deep inside her, but it was a tiny thread that used to be a rope I could connect to. And after what had happened—the way the Keeper had responded to me and taken so much in such a small amount of time—I was afraid if I tried again, I would lose myself to it. That I would be the reason we lost her completely.

A soft knock on the door drew me out. I hadn't allowed anyone in the room with me, not even Bethany, who now stood in front of me. Charlie had stood sentry, not trying to come in, but helping to keep everyone out. He dropped his head as Bethany scratched his ears, clearly welcoming the affection and break from his duties.

"How long are you going to keep this up?" she asked. There was no accusation and I could plainly see the worry on her face. "Don't you think it's time to ask for help?"

Away from the AniMages, the pregnant women I still didn't completely understand, and the Mages, I could finally tell someone the truth. Bethany and I went through this together and she was the only one I'd been able to be completely honest with. With her, I wasn't the King of the AniMages or Amelia's mate. I wasn't half of a prophecy. I was just Aidan.

"They all think I'm her mate, which means I am supposed to be the one who pulls her out of this and brings her back. But Cole is catatonic, Rynna is trying to help the women, and I don't even know what Derreck is doing. Who's supposed to help me, Bethany?"

I sighed and dragged a hand through my hair. I needed a shower. I needed sleep. I needed her to come back to me.

"You need to cut yourself a break, Aidan. Remember, she got herself into this. She chose to put herself out there to try to save those women. I'm proud of her, but she allowed herself to get to this point. You can't be expected to save her from herself. All you can do is give her a reason to come back to us. Maybe you should take a walk. Get some air. Give your mind some time to process. This has been a lot for you, too. I know you can't go far, but I've seen you outside. You don't have to be gone long, just take some space to breathe." Amelia had always talked about Bethany's tendency toward getting right to the heart of things and I appreciated it more than she knew.

Bethany stopped as she walked past me, giving my arm a squeeze.

"She'll come back to us. I know it." She whistled and Charlie scrambled to follow her. It was time for him to eat and spend some time with his brother, Onyx. He deserved it. I turned to go back in the room when I heard Elias call my name.

After much convincing, Elias finally dragged me away from Amelia and forced me to eat. I was staring absently into the eggs he put in front of me as he swore at me, lecturing me again on the need to be planning, not a zombie.

I couldn't take it anymore. I couldn't take the anger, the judgment, or the unanswered questions. The plate in front of me flew across the room and shattered into tiny, jagged pieces.

"What do you want me to do?" I screamed. "I'm giving her everything I can. I'm trying to hear what you're saying but I can't be everything to everyone. You tell me I'm her mate and we need her to survive, so what is it you want me to do?"

"We have to make a plan! We have to figure out our next move. If you think those Hunters aren't out looking for us now, you're insane. We have to figure out how to help these women—my wife, Aidan. How are we going to help *my wife*?" He looked past me and out the window, where Nell lay in the sun. From what I'd learned, she had to stay in her shifted form until the kittens were born.

"We have to prepare for the rest of the pack's arrival and how we're going to house and protect them all. We have to figure out what the Queen having her cuff means. And what about all the women we weren't able to get out? Yes, we need to help Amelia, but if she isn't waking up, then we have to keep going!" I had no idea who this Elias was. The easy-going, calm guy I'd met was nowhere to be found and I was sick of his dictating.

In an uncharacteristic blast of rage, I shoved the heavy kitchen table across the room at Elias. "She will wake up! And you want me to worry about your wife while I worry about Amelia, too?

437

Your wife is fine. Amelia gave her everything she had to make her fine. She'll have her kittens and you'll get her back. You know that. I don't have your same luxury!"

"Stop it." Elias and I both turned to find a red-haired woman standing in the doorway of the kitchen. It was Cora, one of the few we rescued who wasn't pregnant.

"You do have a house full of women. Women who are pregnant, finally at full strength and free from years of imprisonment. Which means you don't have to figure out what to do with us or how to prepare for the arrival of the pack—and what will hopefully be some of our families. We will do it. We want to do it. Derreck has offered us his barn, and we are working to create a space for everyone there.

"The Queen will come for us. She needs us now, more than ever. We have time. Not a lot, but enough for you to focus on your mate. She gave everything to save us and she needs you to find her way back to herself. She cannot do it alone."

I didn't know what to say. "Thank you" didn't feel like enough, but it was all I could muster.

"Thank you, Aidan. Make no mistake, you will save her. You are the only one who can. But your human friend is right, you need a break. And the answers you need are coming. When I know things, I'm sure of them, even when the details aren't clear. I can tell you with certainty that the information you need is coming."

Her words were cryptic, but she said the answers were coming—not here. Right now, being close to Amelia was the only thing I wanted or needed. I walked out of the kitchen without another word to either of them, and quietly slipped into bed next to Amelia. I pulled her onto my chest and reveled in the small sigh she made as she got comfortable. She would wake up. She had to.

Chapter 34
Amelia

He was the thing tethering me to the earth and my body. I could feel him there and I could also feel her need for him. She reached out for him with more strength than I had, and the pain she caused whenever he went away was more than I could bear.

Her darkness sucked the light of my flame into an abyss, like a black hole eating the particles of light and the pieces of stardust from the universe. But when he touched me, she would let go. She flittered through my mind like a child playing hopscotch, waiting for him. We would both wait for him to come back to us. I needed to feel him, needed to know he was really there, that he came for me. Someone had to save me from myself because I could save no one. I'd proven that.

She wanted to drain him. She craved him like an addict and wanted to take everything she could from him. I could feel what she believed. She believed he was the key. He would make us into the thing they prophesied, giving her more power than our world had ever known.

Those same reasons were why I needed him to stay away from me. I knew he had the power. I knew for certain he was the one. I burrowed deeper inside myself, pushing her away, only allowing her to use me to get him when the pain became too much. But she found me no matter where I hid, and she got what she wanted. She always got what she wanted. However, she didn't understand. I wouldn't give him to her. He came for me and I wouldn't sacrifice him again.

Chapter 35
Aidan

Commotion drew me out of Amelia's room. She was restless as soon as I moved away from her and I whispered an apology, but Bethany was right, I needed a break. If whatever was happening was enough to draw me away from Amelia, then it had to be for a reason. Cora had told me answers were coming and someone was clearly here.

Charlie sat on the other side of the door and tried to go inside as I exited. It was the first time he'd tried and it shocked me. I moved to pull him back, but he whined and then growled. I squatted in front of him and he stared at me, whining again.

"Do you want to stay with her? Hey, bud, if you can help her, I'm all for it." He let out a soft *woof* and leapt onto the bed. He lay alongside Amelia and crossed his paws, resting his head on them. As he exhaled, her hair lifted. She was on her side and seemed to calm. I took it as a win and whispered my thanks in his direction before closing the door behind me.

As I got closer to the front door of Derreck's cabin, I heard crying. I wrenched open the front door, fully prepared to face an attack, but found Cora on her knees in the dirt at the bottom of the stairs. Her arms were wrapped around a small redheaded boy and she was sobbing. His hands were fisted in her hair and his small body was shaking uncontrollably.

For the first time, maybe ever, my eyes shone with tears of happiness. Amidst all of this, we never expected one of these women would be Dillon's mother. We had lost Amelia's father, but a family had been brought back together as well. Bethany stepped to my side and spoke softly.

"Can you believe it, Aidan? He got his momma back." She sniffled and I turned, smiling for the first time since we'd left for Cresthaven. "He did, didn't he?"

Suddenly, Bethany stiffened beside me, and the look on her face was a cross between fear and agony.

I turned to see Micah standing in the yard, Baleon supporting him to stand, frozen in place. His expression matched hers and neither of them moved. Baleon looked between them both and then at me, puzzled.

"Beth—" Micah started, at the same time she said, "What are you doing here? You don't belong here."

His mouth snapped closed and she continued. I didn't make a move to stop her, unsure of what the best move was.

"This is your fault, don't you understand? You could have told Amelia. You could have stood up to your mother. You could have helped these women. You could have done something—ANYTHING—and you did NOTHING. THIS IS YOUR FAULT." She didn't give him a chance to respond. She turned on her heel and stomped into the house, slamming the door behind her.

My eyebrows rose and Micah muttered, "Well, that went well."

"I'd say," I responded.

His lips quirked in a half smile and he exhaled deeply. "I pretty much expected something like that from her. There's so much she doesn't understand. So much I need to explain to all of you." He took a step forward and stumbled, the only thing keeping him from face planting were Baleon's reflexes.

Baleon looked up at me. "He needs rest. He wouldn't stop. He fought and he tried to save them, we both did, but we've been running since Tragar helped us escape and he has wounds he hasn't allowed me to tend to."

"Go in the back. Find a room. Do what you need and let us know what we can do to help him," I said. Though Micah shoved at Baleon, he scooped him up as if he weighed nothing and swiftly carried him around the house.

I sat down on the step and dropped my head into my hands. I pulled at the roots of my hair. How was I supposed to manage all of this? I heard voices around me start up again as people went back to whatever they were doing before Bethany's outburst. I picked up Cora and Dillon's voices, but didn't try to hear their words. Because of my self-imposed obliviousness, I was surprised to feel a small poke in my shoulder.

I turned my head to find Dillon standing on the step below me. His blue eyes were red-rimmed and he was still sniffing the remnants of his happy tears away.

"Mr. Aidan?" he asked.

"Yeah, Dillon? What's up, buddy? I see you got your mom back. I'm so happy for you." I tried to smile, but it wasn't there for me.

"Thank you, Mr. Aidan." He looked back at where his mom stood and she nodded, motioning him to keep going. "My...my momma says I should tell you what I know. That my owl is smarter than I am and I shouldn't keep what he says to myself." He turned again and she smiled at both of us. "She says I'm special like her and we have to use our power to help people. So, Mr. Aidan, you have to get her. You have to find her in the place you used to meet with your wolf and you have to make her see. Once you get her to come back, you have to capture the blackness like they captured your wolf. If you can, she can find them and bring them back. Okay?"

He pushed the words out rapid fire and as soon as the "okay" left his mouth, he was jumping off the steps and back into his mother's arms. She was whispering how good of a job he did as she looked up at me, more tears in her eyes. She gave me an encouraging smile that I attempted to return.

I ran Dillon's words over in my mind. They only partially made sense. I had no idea who she was bringing back or from where, but I got part of the message loud and clear. I needed to find her in the woods my wolf had shown me. I could do that. I knew more about helping her now than I had five minutes ago and that was enough for me. I jumped up from the porch and took off through the house. I threw open the door, expecting to have startled Charlie, but he was lying on the bed looking like he was expecting me.

"Let's get her back, boy," I said with a smile.

Chapter 36
Amelia

He was looking for me. I could feel him searching and she realized he was with us again. I took the chance and reached out as quickly as I could to tell him to leave, to stay away from us, but I heard his words before I could speak.

Go to our place, Amelia. I'll meet you at our place. This is almost over, doll.

Just like that, he was gone and she was screaming. But I was smiling. The realization had hit. He knew how to end this.

For the first time, I didn't automatically run from her. She lashed out, wailing echoes in my mind, and the pain was constant, but I was still smiling.

He was coming for me. And together, we could do anything.

Acknowledgments

Abe — I think you'll always be first on this list. You let me spend hours alone, you bring me wine and you listen to me talk about people and places that don't exist, even though every fiber of your being is rooted in logic and fact. It only makes me love you more.

Kristin — You never let me settle for the easy path and I love you for it. Talking storylines over drinks with you is one of my most favorite activities. Let's do it again, soon! We have a third book to write…

The Rebel Writers — Theresa, Caylie, Regan, Kat, Elizabeth and Rachel…I am absolutely certain I wouldn't be here without you. Thank you for being everything I never knew I needed, and some of my closest friends.

My Betas — Theresa, thank you for making me remove over 600 uses of the word "that" and for catching every other writing no-no I'm still learning. Lenore, your passion for my stories is beyond words. I love your rambling explanations of why things do and don't work, don't ever stop being you. And, Mikey, thank you for making sure Aidan sounded like a guy and not a girly version of a guy!

The Rebel Writers Street Team — Ladies, your excitement and your support means the world. I can't wait to start feeding you book three!

The blogger community — I can't name you all, but to each and every blogger I have talked to and worked with over the last two book launches, THANK YOU. I cannot put into words what it means to have you take time from your lives to engage with my world, and then to talk about it continuously to your fans. I wouldn't be able to say I am an Amazon number one best-seller without each of you behind me. I cannot wait to see what's in store for us next!

And, to every person who read Bound by Duty, you are truly the reason I can continue to do this. The fact that you buy my books, review them and share them with your friends is mind-blowing even now. I still cannot fathom that my words have been read across the globe, and I have you to thank for that.

About the Author

Stormy Smith is the author of the Amazon bestseller, Bound by Duty, and Bound by Spells. She calls Iowa's capital home now, but was raised in a tiny town in the Southeast corner of the state. She grew to love books honestly, having a mom that read voraciously and instilled that same love in her. She knew quickly stories of fantasy were her favorite, and even as an adult gravitates toward paranormal stories in any form.

Writing a book had never been an aspiration, but suddenly the story was there and couldn't be stopped. When she isn't working on, or thinking about, her books, Stormy's favorite places include bar patios, live music shows, her yoga mat or anywhere she can relax with her husband or girlfriends.

Other titles by Stormy Smith
Bound by Duty (Book one in the Bound series)

Where you can find me

If you'd like to be alerted when my next book will release, sign up for my mailing list at http://eepurl.com/WLlq1. I promise, you will *only* get new release emails. Pinky swear.

Website: www.stormysmith.com
Facebook: www.facebook.com/authorstormysmith
Twitter: @stormysmith
Instagram: @stormysmith
Goodreads: www.goodreads.com/stormysmith
Email: authorstormysmith@gmail.com

A note about reviews

Whether you loved it, hated it or were completely ambivalent, your review will help others decide if they would like to read my book. Please consider leaving just a few words on the site you purchased from and/or Goodreads. Every review matters and I read them all.

Keep reading for a sneak peek of

FAMILY SECRETS

book one in the Secret Societies Collection

by Kat Nichols

Chapter One

Mrs. Grey was sitting alone at the table, holding a piece of paper in her hand, with what looked like an alcoholic drink in front of her. She didn't drink often, so seeing that glass of amber colored liquid made my stomach drop to my toes. She gestured to the chair across from her, and as I went into the kitchen and slid into the hard-backed chair, my pulse spiked. "Did you know that your father has family in Illinois?"

I shook my head; that wasn't possible. My parents would have told me if I had other relatives. God knows I asked often enough growing up. My mom was killed in a car accident a year ago, and my dad died when I was eight, so I was all alone until the Greys took me in. If I had family, wouldn't they have shown up before now? I started twirling the tips of my long wavy hair in my fingers, a nervous habit I'd had since I was a little girl. My stomach began to churn, and I gripped the table in front of me with my other hand, my head spinning.

"I received a letter from your grandmother. Isn't that wonderful?" She took a gulp of her drink and pursed her lips as she swallowed it down, refusing to look me in the eyes. I just stared at her. "And," she continued when I didn't respond, "they want you to come live with them." She picked up the letter and her voice shook slightly as she read, "'to be raised with the family you deserve to know and who you have been kept from for all these years'."

I pushed back from the table, the chair scraping loudly on the linoleum floor and paced away from her, hands shaking. "You don't expect me to go, do you? Where the hell have they been the last year or all the time before that? My dad died over nine years ago, and they decide to show up now?" I yelled. How could this be happening? I was finally getting settled with the Greys, learning how to be happy again and finding my place in this new world without parents. How dare these people come along now and ruin it for me.

I continued to pace the small room, my shaking hands pressed to my stomach. My breathing accelerated until I was almost gasping for air as Abby came crashing down the stairs. She slid to a stop in the kitchen doorway, a look of apprehension on her face. "Um…what's going on?"

I couldn't talk yet, couldn't put a voice to all of the thoughts racing through my head, so I nodded at Mrs. Grey who gave her the news. When she found out her mom was sending me away, she did all of the things I wanted to do, including begging that I be allowed to stay. She cried, she yelled, she offered to get a job, and, when those didn't work, she threatened to leave with me. That was the final straw for her mom.

Mrs. Grey held up her hands. "Sit down, both of you," she ordered. We sat and Abby grasped my hand, squeezing it tightly, for reassurance or in solidarity, I didn't know. Blood was rushing through my veins and thrumming in my ears, making it hard to hear her when she spoke. "Girls, you know I love having Sophia here, but this is family we're talking about." She looked right at me. "I think you need to get to know them. Now that your parents are gone, they're the only family you have left." Abby's grip on my hand grew tighter as her mom spoke, and my fingers went numb. "Don't you shake your head at me, Abigail Grey. I really think this is the right thing to do. I don't feel I can keep Sophia from her grandmother. Sophia, you'll have your cell phone. We'll keep paying for it so that you can call or text us anytime; and if it doesn't work out, we can revisit it then." She turned back to Abby, who had her mouth open, ready to argue. "This is my final answer."

"So that's it?" Abby asked. "You're just going to ship her off? End of discussion? This is the most ridiculous conversation ever. I can't even talk to you right now." She stormed out of the room, her feet stomping each stair on the way up. Moments later, our bedroom door slammed shut.

I shook out my hand under the table as the feeling came back to my fingers. Mrs. Grey said, "I'm not sure what happened between your parents and your dad's family all those years ago, but I don't want to keep you from them any longer." I tried to speak, but she just continued. "I know you're upset and I'm sorry. I just feel like this is something your mom would've wanted me to do." Her blue eyes filled as she reached across the table to pat my other hand. Then her voice cracked. "I miss her too. Every day. And having you here has made that so much easier, but I have to follow my heart and my heart says you deserve a chance to know your family." Patting my hand once more, she stood up and walked out of the room, taking the paper and the drink with her.

****

After that night we didn't discuss the move, which was fine with me. I wanted to put the whole thing in the back of my mind, and I had, pretty successfully I might add, until Mrs. Grey showed up with boxes. Big, ugly, brown boxes to pack up everything I ever owned and ship it to a place I never planned to go. I wanted to fight. I wanted to kick and scream until I was too hoarse to be heard. I wanted to demand that I stay in California, but how could I? My vision blurred before tears began to fall down my cheeks. I didn't even try to stop them as they rolled off my chin and spilled onto the box I had just filled. Pushing it away, I stood up, dusted my hands off on my jeans, and crawled into bed, letting the tears flow.

The door opened and closed, then the bed dipped as someone sat down. "We can still figure this out," Abby said, rubbing my back.

"There's nothing we can do," I said, my voice muffled by the pillow I clutched to my chest. "It's time to give up."

"Greys never give up," she replied, pulling me away from the pillow.

"Abby, it's over," I said, blowing out a deep breath. "I'm going to Illinois in two weeks and I'm not fighting your mom anymore." Two days after her big announcement, I'd overheard Mrs. Grey on the phone negotiating for more time to pay her bills. Things had been tight ever since Abby's dad had disappeared a few years ago and I was a drain on her resources. With me gone, maybe things wouldn't be so bad for them.

"Sophie, I don't want you to go." Abby grabbed me in a hug, squeezing me tightly.

"I don't want to go either, but I have no choice."

"Yes, you do. Fight back, Sophie. Stand up for yourself for once." Her voice was sharp and she pulled out of the hug, looking directly at me. "Don't let people walk all over you."

"Abby," I snapped, warning clear in my voice, before I heaved a sigh. I didn't want to fight with her, not now, not when we only had two weeks left. "I can't. I just— I can't." She let me go with a sigh of her own before moving to her bed.

"Do you want to leave?" she asked in a tiny voice while staring at the ceiling.

"No, Abby. I already said no, but maybe it will be better if I'm gone."

"What the hell is that supposed to mean?"

"Abby, come on. You know it's hard on your mom, having me here."

"I'm not speaking to that woman right now, so I really don't know what you're talking about." She sniffed.

No matter how I felt being shipped off like a package no one wanted, I didn't want to be the reason they were fighting. "She's doing what she thinks is best for me. If I thought she had anything but my best interests at heart, I would fight - but I don't."

Abby sighed. "You're such a girl scout. I'm leaving before I get mad at you too." She pushed off the bed and stood next to me. "Standing up for yourself doesn't make you a bad person, you know," she said before she strode from the room. We'd had this fight before. I knew she was right, but I hated to rock the boat. I curled back into a ball, wrapping my arms around the pillow, and cried myself to sleep.

Over the next few days, I spoke with my grandmother a few times on the phone. Although the conversations were stilted and a little uncomfortable, she did mention some of the other family I would meet when I got to Illinois. Apparently, I had a second cousin my age who couldn't wait to meet me. Maybe this wouldn't be so bad after all, or at least that's what I told myself as I cried silently into my pillow each night.

****

I managed to get Abby and her mom together on Christmas morning, and we opened presents on the back porch in honor of my last warm winter. It was twelve degrees in Chicago, and I shivered just thinking about it. I was going to miss San Diego, the sunny days, the cooler nights, the smell of the ocean — all salt and seaweed. I'd miss the cute boutiques, even if I couldn't afford to shop in most of them. But most of all, I'd miss Abby. My other friends were more Abby's friends than my own, so it was really only leaving Abby that left a hole in my heart. I knew I had to be strong. I'd been through worse things than this, but then I'd always had Abby at my back. This time I would be on my own. Thank goodness Abby was only a phone call or text away. Besides, there was less than five months until my eighteenth birthday, and then I could do whatever I wanted, including moving back here.

On the last night before I left, Abby and I put on our comfiest pajamas and ate a dinner of raw cookie dough before ending up in the room we shared for the past year. We sprawled on her twin bed and spent the entire night talking, laughing, and crying.

"You better keep in touch," she said fiercely, tears welling up in her eyes.

"I will," I said, my voice thick with emotion. "I pinky promised you like three times already. And stop crying." I made a face, trying to look stern.

"I know, I know," she said, wiping her eyes. "I just hate this."

"I'm gonna miss you too, Abs, and your mom." Abby grumbled at me and I bumped her with my shoulder before continuing. "You don't know how much it meant to me when you both took me in after…"

"We'd do it again in a heartbeat," she replied, throwing her arm around my shoulder. "If things get bad there, your bed will always be here waiting for you."

"Promise?" I asked, holding up my pinky finger, tears forming for what seemed like the hundredth time.

"Promise," she laughed through tears, grabbing my pinky in hers.

The next morning, before leaving for the airport, I did one final check of the bedroom. The only personal item left in the room was a framed photo of my parents from before my dad got sick. I ran my finger over the glass, touching first my mom's face then my dad's, as if I could feel them living and breathing behind the frame. I looked just like my mom, petite with brown hair and light green eyes. My dad was the exact opposite. Six foot plus, with straight blond hair and bright blue eyes. I'm not sure I got anything from him, looks-wise that is, but my mom had always told me that I had his sense of humor. It was unfair that they died so young. I sighed and tucked the frame into the suitcase, carefully wrapping it inside a shirt to keep it from breaking on the flight. I tossed my carry-on over my shoulder and heaved my one large suitcase down the stairs, thumping each one on the way down.

Mrs. Grey heard the racket and met me at the bottom. "Let me take that out to the car for you."

A quick glance at her face revealed puffy, bloodshot eyes and a bright red nose.

Dropping my carry-on, I grabbed her tight around the waist and buried my face in her shoulder, squeezing as hard as I could. She wrapped her arms around me and sniffled into my hair. My eyes filled again. I was so damn tired of crying.

Abby started down the stairs but stopped halfway. I turned my head to peek at her, and she raced the rest of the way down. She slammed into my back, wrapping her arms around us both, and almost knocking us over in the process. We stood there for a moment in one giant amoeba-like hug until Mrs. Grey pulled back. "We need to get you to the airport, Sophia, so you don't miss your flight."

"Or do we?" Abby asked as she looked, hopefully, at her mom.

Mrs. Grey gave a watery laugh. "Yes, we do. Everyone out to the car."

We walked out the door, and I stopped for a final look at the place I called home for the last year. My eyes filled with tears but I blinked them back, walking towards the car with my head high.

Family Secrets is now available!

Made in the USA
Lexington, KY
11 July 2015